THE HILL IN THE DARK GROVE

LIAM HIGGINSON

The Hill in the Dark Grove

PICADOR

First published 2026 by Picador
an imprint of Pan Macmillan
The Smithson, 6 Briset Street, London EC1M 5NR
EU representative: Macmillan Publishers Ireland Ltd, 1st Floor,
The Liffey Trust Centre, 117–126 Sheriff Street Upper,
Dublin 1 D01 YC43
Associated companies throughout the world

ISBN 978-1-0350-6942-2 HB
ISBN 978-1-0350-6943-9 TPB

Copyright © Liam Higginson 2026

The right of Liam Higginson to be identified as the
author of this work has been asserted in accordance
with the Copyright, Designs and Patents Act 1988.

All rights reserved. No part of this publication may be reproduced,
stored in a retrieval system, or transmitted, in any form, or by any means
(including, without limitation, electronic, mechanical, photocopying, recording
or otherwise) without the prior written permission of the publisher.

Pan Macmillan does not have any control over, or any responsibility for,
any author or third-party websites (including, without limitation, URLs,
emails and QR codes) referred to in or on this book.

1 3 5 7 9 8 6 4 2

A CIP catalogue record for this book is available from the British Library.

Typeset in Warnock Pro by Palimpsest Book Production Limited, Falkirk, Stirlingshire
Printed and bound in the UK using 100% Renewable Electricity by CPI Group (UK) Ltd

This book is sold subject to the condition that it shall not, by way of
trade or otherwise, be lent, hired out, or otherwise circulated without
the publisher's prior consent in any form of binding or cover other than
that in which it is published and without a similar condition including
this condition being imposed on the subsequent purchaser. The publisher does
not authorize the use or reproduction of any part of this book in any manner
for the purpose of training artificial intelligence technologies or systems.
The publisher expressly reserves this book from the Text and Data Mining
exception in accordance with Article 4(3) of the European Union
Digital Single Market Directive 2019/790.

Visit **www.picador.com** to read more about all our books
and to buy them.

For Leonie

The inhabitants of rude and mountainous countries are more generally affected with superstition than those who dwell in plains and cultivated regions. That the scenery of a country has a considerable influence on the habits of the natives is indisputable. Hence the manners of mountaineers are more robust and impetuous than those of lowlanders, and their imaginations – darkened by their native scenes – create wild images and phantoms dire, strange as their hills and gloomy as their storms.

The Cambro-Briton, Vol. 1, May 1820

Prologue

March

THE LAMBS IN THE SNOWDRIFT

Uphill he went, in meagre moonlight through the blizzard, a dark speck dwarfed against the monumental land. Each stride he clawed and wrested from the grasping snow, which swallowed him to waist height as he trailed the dog, coursing somewhere far across the buried mountainside. He had bet his life on her ability. On the trust that he had bred her well and trained her better and that she knew, instinctively, why they had come. She would not hear his whistles or commands, nor he her barks, for the wind roared down upon them from the peaks and buffeted his stinging ears, drowned his voice, cracked his lips to uselessness. Nor could they see each other or the flock, for the night was deep and the flurries thick and the moon a patch of pallid filterings through the clouds.

This lofty world was made of shapes and shadows. Here, a drift that blanketed a drystone wall, over which the sheep had fled; there, the branches of a hawthorn, sprouting lonely and begrudging from a blasted crag; high above, the faintest intimations of Crib Goch and Glyder Fawr and Moel Hebog against the falling sky, only there because he knew they were, his memory willing them weakly into being. Yr Wyddfa, too, had vanished in the whiteout. Mightiest of all those mountains and now no more than a vague and looming vastness at the limit of his snowblind eyes.

And he himself a shapeless thing among them – a wanderer adrift of time, as gnarled as the hawthorn and ancient as the mountains and as rugged as the wall. When he paused and stood to catch his breath, one might have guessed him for a scarecrow dressed in many strangers' clothes: an old tweed cap, a hiking coat of oddly modern make, a bright-red scarf the only colour in that deathly scene; chosen, perhaps, so that if he failed he might be found. But when he moved again it was with undiminished purpose, heaving himself upwards on arthritic knees and frost-numbed feet to which he brooked no slowing in his march. Uphill, uphill. The flock was close. He knew it in his bones.

He came to a place where the gusts raced howling between boulders bigger than his house, and here he had to plant his shovel in the frozen pack to keep his footing on the scarp. Around him, tufts of brown grass, holes the dog had marked – too deep or hard for her to dig. And the dog herself, he saw with pride, barely visible in the swirling blizzard, pawing through a snowbank where the sheep lay huddled and entombed. A handful of ewes had struggled free already from the drifts and now stood snow-dagged and forlorn and bleating for their lambs. He knelt beside the little sheepdog on the drifted snow. Packed hard, up here, and polished by the gale; pristine and crunchy and a terrible, lifeless white. She nosed ahead of him into her excavation, and he had to seize her scruff with blockish hands and drag her back so he could dig. Carefully, now, he told himself. The smallest avalanche would swallow one and all, or sweep them off the cliffs into the valley far below. Somewhere down there his wife was waiting, the pinprick of the farmhouse kitchen window all the human light for miles.

The first ewe was buried three feet down. The warmth of her nostrils had melted a cavity around her head, and he laid aside the shovel to clamber down into the hole and wrench her loose, drag her bodily up to the surface. For a moment she stood stunned on her unsteady legs, the way new lambs did, as if this world was one she'd never seen until tonight, before the dog nipped at her hocks and drove her off towards the others. The second was beneath her, deeper still, and the man huffed and grunted as he heaved her out and hefted her into the wailing night. In the hollow where she'd lain, the limp and yellow body of a lamb. Newborn and slick with amniotic fluid – birthed, perhaps, under the drift. In the next hole was another, and another after that, and when the squall abated and the man emerged and sat down shell-shocked, panting with the dog, there stood a flock of near three dozen trembling ewes, and the mountain was a charnel of their dead and frozen lambs.

I

April

OPENING

The funeral procession made its way by lamplight up out of the valley. Four figures in a makeshift hearse drawn by a mule, the horses having all been long since requisitioned for the war. A one-armed man frightful with scars hunched at the reins, his uniform still caked with clinging Flanders mud, and at his side a slack-jawed youth, likewise attired, whose haunted eyes seemed to behold a private carnival of horrors. They would not be going back. In the wagon bed, two women come directly from the lambing: the elder in a gingham pinny; the younger dressed in hasty mourning, sitting upright with bedraggled dignity as the cart jolted up the rutted lane.

She held the dead boy on her lap in an old dynamite box from the quarry. What scraps of him his pals had been able to pick out of the muck. And mingled with the burnt-caramel odour from the residue of nitroglycerine, and their own accustomed smells of lanolin and sweat, and the night air still carrying the scent of melting snow from off the mountains, there were the vulgar top notes of decay. A trickle of dark liquid spilled onto her dress. The journey from the trenches had been long.

The mound, the men had told her. This was his dying wish, and as little as they understood (or told themselves that they did not), they'd promised they would honour it. In his last days of ranting and shell-shocked delirium before the final mercy of the German mortar, he had raved obsessively about the mound in the dark grove.

A steep and rock-strewn field opened before them, and here they left the wagon at a tumbledown stone wall, taking only the lantern and their rolls of picks and shovels and their grisly cargo. The way led out across the slope towards the silhouettes of trees against the crisp night sky. Somewhere to the west, the young woman fancied she could hear the hum of the Marconi station at Waunfawr. An owl called shrilly from the wood. They made their way through an old iron gate into the trees, where the scarred man kept the lamp trained rigidly ahead, and the dark pressed in around them, a colossal, watchful presence. The youth twitched as he walked. The older woman was intoning the Gweddi'r Arglwydd under her breath, although the prayer felt strangely unconvincing so far from a chapel pew.

The mound was in a clearing where the woods gave way to scree. Not one of them had ever set foot in this place before, yet in the lamplight it aroused a deep familiarity. They laid the boy's remains to rest with Easter daffodils. No words were spoken, save the old woman's muttered prayer. They'd come prepared for gruelling work, for on the mountainside the soil was hard and unforgiving, but the digging passed with unexpected ease, like turning fresh-tilled earth. And none of them would ever speak the thought aloud, but all would feel a shudder every time the memory returned to them. It seemed almost as though the stony ground had opened to receive him.

The stream turned up peculiar things with each spring thaw. It was a ribbon of the purest meltwater babbling down a rocky channel from the snow-bound peaks where, just a month before, so many of the year's lambs had been lost to the last winter storm. Unimaginable that this placid brook had fallen to earth as that howling blizzard. Still brilliantly cold, though. Narrow enough a hare could leap across it even at its widest point, and so shallow hawks and buzzards stood in it to bathe. It wandered down across the mountainside: through crags and tussocks on the highest slopes, down upland meadows where it fell in little cataracts between black stones, to run at last along the lower boundary of the Gwynnant farm.

Carwyn had been coming here since he was just a boy, when his old taid had shown him how to pick the perfect stones to mend a wall after the ravages of winter. He had an unerring eye for it. For judging where each piece might slot, so that gravity alone might hold them there a hundred years or more, and there seemed a lesson greater than the practical imparted by his sparing words. A purpose and a place for everything, if one could only see it. How wise and venerable a man his grandfather appeared to him back then – a country patriarch from an unbroken line of wry and humble folk, who left no trace to mark their stewardship of the land. A Taliesin or a Merlin of the modern day, hunkering among the reeds and rushes at the stream-bank, and he would sift through the water's curious offerings like a panner out for gold.

Sometimes there would be chipped and battered hammerstones – fist-sized cobbles smoothed to roundness by the sea that did not belong in an inland mountain stream and might have once lain on the beach at Criccieth or Penmaenmawr. Seashells, too, perhaps from those same coastlines, with holes pierced through to string them on a thread. There were vicious, shiny fragments of knapped flint, still sharp enough to cut with, and less often the whole implements they'd made. Arrowheads both crude and beautiful; chert axes that could still hew wood; the tip of what he thought had been a spear. And bones. There were small bones in great profusion, mostly from fresh victims of the prey-birds, but among them ones immeasurably older, brown with age and bearing marks of butchery or ritual. Two needles made from ribs of hares, and once a fishing hook of similar design. They grew less frequent with the years, but the mountain sent its cryptic treasures every spring as if it wished for him to find them, though if there was a message it was one that he had not yet learned to read.

But most remarkable of all the findings was a figurine of clay. It had been picked out of the stream by Carwyn's greatgrand-uncle, and by all accounts it caused a row at farm shows and at chapel and the local pubs whenever he could be cajoled to show it. The thing was smaller than his thumb, an ugly little object, moss-stained and cracked and missing pieces that might give a clue to what it might depict. It had a head, faceless and bluntly pointed like a crow's beak, and a slouching, armless body with just the nubbins left of legs, and that was all that he could say with any certainty. It might, for all he knew, have been a toy made for a child to occupy them on a rainy afternoon, but it had an eerie artistry about it. No matter how many people looked at it over the years, it seemed none could agree exactly what it was.

To his wife Rhian, it looked like a buxom pregnant woman – a mother goddess or fertility idol in the vein of the Venus of Willendorf. She didn't like to have it in the house because she found its presence sinister. Its sheer antiquity unsettled her; brought thoughts of how one's own small trinkets might be viewed by strangers aeons hence. Old Brynmor Jenkins from up Pen-y-Pass would tap it with his pipe and swear it was a tupping ram, while Dai Bad-English at the Llanrwst farmers' auction saw in it a raven with the body of a toad. He'd shown it once to Mrs Prodgers down the village shop, who said it looked quite like a bull, but she had thought the figurine a foul, ungodly thing and told him not to bring it back. The headteacher, Ianto Pepper, from Beddgelert school – the nearest thing to an expert in those parts – was of the firm view it should go to a museum. And could they not see it clearly was a water deity with a fish's head? Carwyn had attempted, twice, to take it for donation. Had even gone as far as the Amgueddfa Cymru down in Cardiff, but both times he had found himself unwilling to part with it just yet. Try as he might, he could not see the things the others did. To him it remained resolutely unidentifiable.

He kept it with the stream's small treasures in a biscuit tin out in his workshop: a grand name for a tin-roofed former pigsty in the courtyard of the farm, crammed floor to ceiling with all manner of broken things he'd one day mend, and junk with purpose yet to be determined. The sheep came first and left scant time for other tasks. But sometimes, at the end of a long day, when the red sun rested on the treetops down the valley, he would sit out in his fraying armchair with the tin set in his lap, and unwrap the objects from their cotton nests to ponder them. He was not a student of history. The odd-shaped stones were alien to him as letters in an unknown alphabet, but he felt, in some way, their significance. They seemed to him a proof of his belonging to the land – of the Welsh as the last true indigenous inhabitants of Britain. If Wales had been around a day, then the invaders were an eye-blink. Before Edward and his English came, before the Normans and the Vikings came, before the Roman legions came, before even the Beaker folk came with their pottery and their bronze, there had been people like him living in these mountains for a hundred thousand years.

This evening, though, would leave no time for idle wonderings. It was a season of fast-fading dusk, the sky still bright above the bands of cloud but the sun already dipped below the high horizon and the valley dark with pooling shadows from the peaks, as if the night was spilling from its depths. Spring warmth turned back to winter chill. Drops from rain that afternoon hung glistening on the bars of gates and the budding boughs of trees. The grass was still patchy with snow, and the air so damp he could almost have wrung the water from it like a washcloth. The little collie, Eira, cut low-backed among the daffodils in the bottom field, casting in a pear shape out around the grieving flock and carving off a ewe her master singled out. He had recognized its stiff-legged gait and knew that time was short if it was to be helped.

The best of dogs she was, his Eira. The finest sheepdog in the dozen generations he had raised, bred from a pair his great-grandfather won at cards the day Prince Edward was invested at Caernarfon Castle. There was something of a dice-roll when it came to working dogs. He had been mostly blessed with good ones (and he knew that there was good in every dog in a way he didn't think was true of people), but he'd had his share of bad ones too: plain-eyed ones who'd lost their hunting traits and walked upright approaching sheep; high-strung ones that flanked too close or stressed the ewes or bit the lambs. One dog that disregarded his commands entirely and left one day to seek its fortune by itself. He was kind to all of them, and those that could not work became house dogs for other families. But if the bad were few, the truly great ones were as rare as rooster teeth.

He put two calloused fingers to his mouth and whistled sharply, twice, and Eira came about and faced the now-lone ewe. She had a powerful gaze that seemed to freeze the sheep there to the spot, long enough for him to quietly approach and flop the unprotesting animal onto its side, where he knelt himself in the wet grass. He knew from the smell as soon as he got close, mingled with the usual sheepy reek of lanolin and dung. A sour, sickly odour. The poor thing's udders were swollen taut, shiny as balloons, the teats hard cones of dark and angry red from which seeped foetid strings of bloody pus. Mastitis. Not the worst case he had seen, but another day and it would be a different matter. He probed for abscesses and found with some relief that there were none. The rest of the flock watched nervously – forlorn and purposeless with just their handful of surviving lambs – as he dug in his pockets and came up first with a spray can of bright-blue salve to soothe the inflamed udders, and then with a needle which he pricked under a fold of skin. When that was done, he patted the ewe's woolly flank and scratched the dog behind her ear and told her, 'Da iawn, bach. That'll do.' At least, he hoped it would.

For a long time afterwards he knelt there with the stricken sheep and the contented, panting collie and the cold damp soaking through his overalls and found himself incapable of summoning the will to move. The lambs, it was. Their loss had been a bitter blow, the crossing of a line that would not be felt fully until market day. Another in what seemed like an unending uphill battle just to make ends meet, and in whose fallout even these small setbacks like one ailing ewe began to stack up into insurmountable catastrophes. He looked west across the valley bottom where the stream danced down into the woods and hollows, following the set sun out towards the sea; east, uphill past drystone walls first laid by hands that had built castles, to where the farmhouse nestled in its peaceful nook; north and south nothing but mountains, sharp and unforgiving, steeped in myth – the abode of witches and giants and gods. All of it his and Rhian's, horizon to horizon. Bought and bartered by his ancestors for centuries, a parcel at a time, and clung to doggedly through all the cruel universe could throw, only to be lost, at last, on his poor lookout. The debt collectors would be on their way. Even were the prospects good, the wolves kept from the door, they had no children to inherit it, and so the long, unbroken chain would finally break with him. Today was his sixty-fifth birthday.

He pictured some rich landowner from England, or perhaps a ruthless businessman grown tired of the city – who would snap the place up as a bargain at an auction sale. Gut the house to make a second home (or third, or fourth) and use the uplands for a shooting estate they'd visit maybe once or twice a year. Super Ruperts, he and his friends used to call them. That was the way of things. The Gwynnant farm would be far from the first round here to meet that fate, and neither would it be the last. Maybe Rhian's father had been right.

It was a shout that snapped him from his wallowing. At first what sounded like a woman's anguished cry, and then some moments later a voice calling out for help. He could not pin down a distance, for its source seemed neither very close nor far away and changed direction with the breeze. The valley contours here could play all kinds of odd acoustic tricks. But Eira must have heard it too. She sat stock-still with ears erect and clever little head cocked so to better catch the sound. Even the sheep were skittish and alert. It came, he thought, from the old lower pasture, down beyond the wood and stream – an unkempt, disused place grown thick with ferns, where no paths led and nobody had any business being after dark. He called, 'Hello?' and waited for an answer.

In the intervening quiet, his mind fetched up old fireside stories from his nain. He thought about the gwyllion – the fairy hags that used to haunt these lonely mountain fastnesses and lure unwary shepherds to their doom. In the morning, his grandmother said, someone would find the poor wretch dead from cold or broken at the bottom of a cliff from which he must have tumbled in the dark, and wonder how he had so badly lost his way. One bedtime she had told him of a man who spied a frail old woman climbing Tryfan on a stormy night, and how he'd called to offer shelter at his cottage, for if she stayed out in the awful weather she would surely die. When the old crone did not respond, at first he thought her deaf, and so he followed her in hopes of catching up, running ever faster in pursuit while she remained a distant figure half glimpsed through the teeming rain. The man had known these mountains all his life, but the old woman led him on and on until he reached a place he'd never seen before. A place of looming stones. Of leaning, fallen megaliths. There at last she stood unmoving in the storm and waited, lank and dripping, for him to approach. Hesitantly now, mistrustful on that lonely, barren summit. And finally – and this was what had given Carwyn nightmares as a boy – she turned to him with hanging skin and drooling maw and eyes as white and dead as pickled eggs, and he had realized too late she was a gwyll. His grandmother's imitation of her cold, inhuman cackle still lay curdled somewhere in his decades-later dreams.

'Hello?' He wiped his sheep-soiled hands across his trouser fronts and set off down towards the trees, in the direction where he thought he'd heard the voices, the little collie trotting at his heels. The gate to that part of the farm was shut with chains that dated from before his father's time, and grass and thorns and nettles had grown twisting through its rusted bars like climbing plants. He had to hoist himself up over it with Eira tucked beneath his arm and shivering. In both directions, rafts of briar and deadfall girded the wood tight. What kind of silly buggers could have lost themselves down here, in this tangled and unusable corner of the farm where even he himself had never been?

All was quiet in the wood. Faded wheel ruts left by horse carts traced the way towards the lower field. He reached to feel the folding knife in his coat pocket – carried for unknotting dags and prising stones from hooves – in a superstitious reflex, remembering his old nain's tales of banishing the night folk by the drawing of a blade. It brought him little comfort in the mossy-smelling, watchful dark.

The sense of not-aloneness swelled until it made his hackles rise. He was about to turn and head up to the house, cursing himself for a credulous fool frightened by old wives' tales in his own back yard, when the voice cried out again. 'Help us! Please!' It was followed by another, closer to. 'Is anybody there?'

It was, then, with mixed feelings that he realized the beings on his land were of the flesh-and-blood kind, and he shouted answers as he picked his careful way in their direction. At first, he felt a spluttering, almost comical annoyance and frustration at these trespassers intruding on his peaceful life. Next there came relief that he had not gone mad or senile yet, imagining the dark alive with disembodied cries and every tree and shadow occupied by unseen presences that wished him harm. Just people, obviously. Ordinary folk.

He caught sight of the man first, just beyond the tree-line with a torch strapped to his head. A reedy, youngish fellow, by the look, whose silhouette was rendered quadrupedal by a pair of trekking poles, and hunchbacked by the shape of an enormous rucksack which he carried with the grace of someone being ridden by a horse. The woman was much further down the field behind him. Similarly accoutred and submerged beyond the waist among the rampant ferns. It seemed to Carwyn she was sitting at the base of a small hillock rising squatly from the undergrowth. There was a look of tired panic and dishevelment about them both that eased his apprehension.

'Lost then, are you?' he called out.

At this, the man jolted and spun and nearly overbalanced with the weight of his pack. 'Oh, thank God,' he panted, and when he turned to look at Carwyn he was hidden by the glare of the head torch, but his incredulous relief was nonetheless apparent. Eira was already bounding at the interloper's feet.

'For a start,' the man replied, grasping Carwyn's proffered hand with all the desperation of a drowning sailor clinging to debris. He wore expensive hiking gear that looked brand new save for fresh rents where he'd been snagged by gorse and bracken. 'Lost, frozen, hungry, exhausted. And to top it off, my wife's just turned her ankle coming down your mountain. She thinks it might be broken.' He spoke an unaccented English-English that revealed no clue as to how far they had come.

The wife waved, wincing, and Carwyn hobbled over to squat where she nursed her injured leg. She shook his hand, too, gratefully. 'Katie,' she offered. 'And that's Ben. We've just come up over Snowdon from Lanber-Riss – is that how you say it? The snow on the summit's beautiful, but we must have dithered and we can't believe how quickly it's got dark. Is this the Miners' Path?' She held her ankle and drew a sharp intake of breath.

He gave a sympathetic smile, revealing his ramshackle teeth. 'Not quite – you've come down the wrong side of the mountain, see. The snow, it is, it throws you.'

'Then I don't suppose you could point us back towards the road?' the man asked with a note of worry in his voice. 'Or at least a proper path. These ferns are vicious. Are they always so bloody *sharp*?'

'To Llanberis? That's a good five-hour walk in daylight, even if you aim to leave the missus here. At night you're liable to end up even more off-track.' The man and woman's faces both broke out in matching looks of dismay. 'How've you managed that?' he asked her, gesturing to her foot.

She laughed and winced again. 'I stepped in a big hole, just there. What is it, a badger sett?'

The husband turned his head to shine the torch where she had pointed, but in the growing dark it was not clear what it might be. A foot-sized hole of bottomless black with tufted grass and bracken growing from its lips, right at the base of the knoll, but whether animal or geological or something else entirely, he could not discern. While they were speaking, Eira had begun to dig at its periphery. She smelled, perhaps, a rabbit or a fox.

'Can you stand?' he asked. 'Or hop? I think you'd both best come with me up to the house. It isn't far, and we can get you warm and fed and on your way. How's that?'

Carwyn and Eira led the way back through the woods and up the pitch-black fields, the man and woman following with cautious gratitude: she, with an arm slung around his shoulders, limping. Stopping frequently to rest. They struggled over wooden stiles and steps cut in stone walls, with the ghostly shapes of sheep awake and watching out of the enormous, ice-edged dark. He carried both their bags in penance, for he felt a fool now for his trepidation. For giving in so easily to fears of nursery bwgans when it was just these poor hikers, wet behind the ears and needing help. He wondered if they might have similar misgivings about him, this rough old backwoods hermit come, for all they knew, to lure them off with murderous intent. They might think *him* the gwyll-like figure, leading them astray. How could he blame them if they did? What a curse hindsight was, he thought – revealing all with perfect clarity only once the need to know had passed, so one was left to dread things which would ultimately turn out well, or stroll complacently into disaster.

They had stopped, and when he turned to see why, they were gazing up beyond the dark bulk of the mountain. 'Is that –' the Englishwoman gasped in disbelief – 'are those the Northern Lights?' A faint ribbon of green shimmered, undulating in the sky, growing brighter, then dimming and brightening again with a mysterious pulsation. It shifted through a cold and vivid spectrum streaked with arctic blues. The colours were reflected in the couple's eyes. They stood bathed for a moment in its glow until it sank below the ridgeline and left them again in darkness.

'I doubt it, this far south,' he said apologetically. 'It's been happening the past few weeks.' Then, seeing their looks of disappointment, added hastily, 'It might be, though, you never know.' He didn't have the heart to tell them it was probably the neon lights of a new nightclub up in Bangor or Llandudno.

The smell announced the house before it came in sight: a tang on the cold air of chimney smoke and red diesel. Closer still, there were aromas of cooking. The farmhouse squatted in a recess of the valley that was sheltered from the harshest weather. It was an unpretentious stone-and-slate construction no showier than the barn beside it – stout walls and squinting windows and a swaybacked roof that sagged so there was barely a straight edge in sight – and where it was not cradled by the craggy land it sat beneath a towering ancient oak. A relic of a house. It had stood when Cromwell and King Charles had marched their armies into war, and besides the few clues to modernity it might still have belonged to that belligerent time. An electric bulb buzzed in an aluminium dish above the door, bathing the courtyard in erratic light. A pickup truck and the wheelless husk of a tractor were parked beside the well. The old tŷ bach where, as a boy, he'd had to make a nightly barefoot dash was home now to a pair of geese that spent their days in fragile ceasefire with the rangy farmyard hens. And not a scrap of ornament nor ostentation, nor a single thing in all the place that did not have a use. It was the only house for miles.

When Carwyn came into the courtyard, Rhian was sitting on the doorstep, lacing up her boots. She looked greatly relieved to see him. 'Where've you been, you daft sod? I was about to come and look for you.'

He cocked a thumb behind him and said, 'Guests.'

The couple limped apologetically out of the dark and introduced themselves, and Rhian greeted them with brusque, unpractised hospitality. 'Come in then, and we'll get the kettle on and see about this ankle. There's a pot of cawl there that'll stretch, and a piece of birthday cake as well.'

She led them through a hallway packed with boots and wellingtons and coats, into the cottage kitchen where the hikers had to duck between the ceiling beams. Carwyn brought through extra chairs and squeezed them in with difficulty at the cluttered table by the great range stove. Eira was already curled up in her bed beside the ash-pan. The woman's ankle was not broken, Rhian told her after probing it and moving it about (though she admitted that her expertise lay more with sheep), but it might be badly sprained. A space was cleared amid the mess of red-stamped paperwork, and with the barest minimum of conversation Carwyn served up steaming bowls of mutton cawl with crusty bread, and tea in varied mugs. The English couple seemed bemused, like witnesses to some arcane religious rite, but accepted all the offerings with tired appreciation.

'It's a lovely place you've got here. Have you lived here long?'

Carwyn and Rhian looked at one another's hands, the calluses and wrinkles and the ingrained dirt a testimony to their many years. 'Quite a while.'

'It must get awfully lonely up here in the winters, though,' the wife continued, and the husband added, 'Have you ever been snowed in? I bet it's like *The Shining*, is it?' He laughed and patted Carwyn's arm to show that was a joke.

A smile, a shrug. A swig of tea. 'It's all we've known.'

'Still, it beats the rat race, that's for sure,' the man went on. 'And you've got each other, I suppose. And all the animals to keep you company as well.'

'Sometimes I can't tell which is which,' sighed Rhian with a put-upon affect, and for a moment it began to seem she might recall the pleasantries of conversation that had withered from disuse. But the impression was short-lived. 'If there's foxes digging holes down there, we'll have to see them off,' she said to Carwyn suddenly. 'We've lost enough lambs as it is.' To this he only nodded, looking off out of the darkened window as if tallies of their loss were written in the condensation on the glass.

The husband cleared his throat. 'Alpacas,' he said, and then, met with looks of blank incomprehension, 'our neighbour down in Surrey has alpacas with her sheep. They're big and brash enough to run the foxes off, apparently, and they don't bother the sheep at all.'

A moment's silence followed, in which Carwyn appeared to chew the thought as he might the suggestion that he try to shear the geese for wool, but eventually Rhian broke the awkwardness by saying simply, 'Fancy that.'

The hikers were relieved when Carwyn got up and announced that he would drive them to their car. If he'd insisted that they stay the night, they would have been in no position to refuse, and though they thanked their hosts sincerely, they were glad at last to get out of the house. There was a sense there of unspoken wrongness that they could not put a finger on; the oppressive, heavy dread of some looming calamity that hung like hearth-smoke in the cosy nooks and crannies of the cottage. In the light and comfort of tomorrow, when they were safely back across the border and a friendly doctor was assessing Katie's ankle at a pleasant, airy surgery, they would tell each other it was surely a mundane affair: an illness or financial worries or a bad divorce on the horizon. Not things to be discussed with strangers, but which could sour an atmosphere like curdled milk. But in that farmhouse kitchen, they had both been struck with fearful but inchoate premonitions, and a feeling of a host of unseen eyes that peered in at them from the outer dark.

'How were the girls?' asked Rhian when the guests had gone.

'All right,' he said. 'They'll be all right.' Then thought to add, but did not say aloud, 'And so will we.'

She curled up on his lap in the big armchair by the fire with Eira at their feet and he felt her weight settle against him, the lights off and the television muted so it bathed the room in flickering bluish light.

As if reading the run of his thoughts, she tucked her head into the cradle of his collarbone and asked, 'Do you think our two adventurers will get home safely?'

'Oh, I expect they will. They'll have a story to tell now about the pair of country bumpkins they ran into. "Outside toilet and a tin bath in the kitchen. Never heard of electricity or running water. Him, a gurning simpleton, and her, a toothless crone."'

'A crone!' she laughed and swatted him.

He nodded. '"And neither of them spoke a *word* of English."'

Her smile was the smile he'd loved since he had been a little boy, and it filled him with a fragile hope. This was not the first time they had been through hardships. As long as they had each other, they would manage somehow – something always turned up in the end, in often unexpected ways. He was not a believer in God, nor in a fair or just world, nor in fate. But he did believe in Rhian. In the two of them. In their proven aptitude to try and fail and try again until they muddled through. They would manage because they had to, that was the truth of it. There could be no other way.

The next day he rose, as always, long before the dawn. It had been another night of roiling, shifting dreams from which he could unpick no thread of meaning in the aftermath, no logic that might tie them to the day. What he remembered came in flashes. A tree ablaze, a crown upon a desolate peak, the entrails of a ewe. He woke up tired and shivering. There was a skin of frost inside the windowpanes, and the yard was covered by a pall of icy fog through which the cockerels had not ventured out to crow. He dressed in silence by the bed and gave the hikers of the night before no thought except to hope they made it safely home, and he did not wake his wife nor stop to eat a bite of last night's dinner at the stove, for there were pressing matters to attend.

Two springs ago, a fox had dug into the chicken coop and killed all but a couple of the hens. He'd found the place a grisly slaughterhouse of feathers, blood, and mutilated birds. It had carried only one away to eat, though, and at the time it seemed a senseless and malicious waste, but later he supposed the vixen meant to take them all to feed her cubs, and was disturbed before she could return for more, or else had been bewildered by the panic of the hens. Wild instincts were not made for crowded coops. He bore the foxes no ill will, and had especially little patience for the ludicrous displays of pompous cruelty hiding in the guise of tradition – the huntsmen gathered with their bugles and their breeches and their blood-red coats to tear a frightened little animal to death and call it sport. And though the practice had been banned for many years, it went on still in rural parts without concealment. It pained him even to think of it, sentimental codger that he was. He saw in them, he thought, too much of Eira, or perhaps of Rhian and himself: another humble creature of the mountains doing what was needed to survive.

So after that he'd built a trap – a cage he modified with wires and springs to catch them as humanely as he could. He'd even added pads of foam around the door so that it would not hurt them if it snapped shut on a leg or tail, and Rhian made a woollen cover so he would not scare them when he lifted it. For bait, he used a tin of Eira's food (or half a tin, he wasn't made of money). Then he'd leave it overnight close to the den, and in the morning he would drive the captured fox a few miles down towards the coast and shoo it off into the woods to be somebody else's problem.

He found the trap in a corner of his workshop and set it in a wheelbarrow while Eira watched him patiently. He spoke to her with absentminded fondness. Nonsense phrases. Questions all rhetorical about who was a good dog, and whether it was indeed she who was the best of all. When he backed out into the yard, the hens and geese were standing in the little doorways of their runs, an eerie, quiet congregation in the mist. They waited like this every day for Rhian with their feed, but in the damp, undawning twilight their sheer stillness was unsettling. If he died one day within their reach he had no doubt they'd pick him to the bones. The sky hung low and leaden as he bumped his way down through the fields, the rainclouds draped around the peaks like veils over the mountains' faces. It was the kind of weather that felt to him most truly isolating. More than snow, more than floods, when each small valley was contained beneath its roof of hanging overcast so that the world beyond was purely speculation. Nothing left but this poor, rocky Eden with its man and woman and its beasts and surely its forbidden fruit.

The bottom woods took on a different aspect in the breaking dawn. Less menacing, and full of birdsong that announced his coming as he oldmanhandled first the cage and then the dog over the disused gate. It was a tranquil place, he now thought – a strip of true Celtic rainforest unaltered and unbended to the whims of men. A place unchanged from what it would have been a hundred or ten thousand years before. How silly that his parents and grandparents had forbidden him to come down here, and sillier still that he had heeded them for the frightening vagueness of the prohibition. No reason why – just don't. Careful going, though, down among the rough and lichened stones with beards of brilliant green, down through the dripping, twisted trees that spread their roots to drink out of the stream, among the moss and fungi where it would not be unthinkable to catch just fleeting glimpses of the Tylwyth Teg, or little wizened goblins hid in every hollow log. Along the path a squirrel broke and fled, and Eira seemed to weigh up giving chase and then thought better of it. There was a long day's work ahead.

The old field, too, seemed altered from the night before. It was a sea of frost-tipped ferns in shades of emerald and bronze, from which the fog had not yet lifted, and rising out of it the tufted grassy hummock with the foxhole at its base. Different, somehow, in its layout from what Carwyn had expected – the ferns a little taller; the woods a little thicker; the slopes of scree on all three sides a little steeper than he'd seen them in the dark, so that he could not fathom where the hikers had come down. And the mound curiously central to it all, as though not natural but made in strict adherence to a deep logic or structure he was not quite able to discern. No time, though, to waste on wondering. He set the trap and baited it and stepped back to inspect the spot when something in the burrow caught his eye.

Staring out at him from deep within the hole, there was a face. Not a fox face, but a human one, as clear as day, the visage of a bearded man. He stumbled back and almost sat down in the ferns, his gaze fixed on this mirror image of himself that glowered out at him from underground. It was a few feet down, lit just so by the rising sun. As he edged closer, he could see that the hole was not in fact a burrow at all, but a small cavity where soil had given way. A narrow horizontal perforation in the bottom of the mound, a foot across and maybe four deep, and at its furthest point, the face: a crudely carved stone face about the size of an orange, worn roughly smooth but still clearly recognizable for what it was.

He remembered one of Rhian's stories of the sons of Helig – local chieftains who had fled their flooded kingdom in the days of the first saints – and how three times they tried to build a chapel somewhere hereabouts, and all three times it had collapsed. A family curse, some legends said. In other tales, the ground they built it on was bad, corrupted by some older thing beneath the earth. Eventually they chose a new site at Llanaber by the sea, and that church was still standing to this day. Was this, perhaps, a vestige of those failed attempts? A Celtic Christ abandoned in this godforsaken mountain cove by monks afraid of native superstitions?

He eased down to all fours to squint into the hole, his eyes adjusting slowly to the dark, and for a long, uncanny span of seconds it felt as though the face was scrutinizing him as well. Taking measure of him disapprovingly, as if he were himself the unexpected visitor, found where he did not belong. The hole looked deeper closer up, exhaling damp and earth and age. Something not unlike a churchyard smell – a grave-scent that betokened sanctity and death entwined. There was a kind of hypnotism to the hole as well, a beckoning, a pull akin to looking down a cliff-edge or a waterfall, and staring in between the tufted grass around the opening and then the fern-roots hanging from the tunnel roof, he had the sense of gazing out across a dizzying abyss of time. Both nauseous and exhilarating. It was Eira who began at first to dig. She pawed the loose earth from the edges of the cavity, and though the morning was now well advanced and there were other duties to attend to, Carwyn went and fetched a trowel from the barrow and knelt to join the excavation.

II

May

GROWTH

The doctor's day had been demanding, but routine. One suspected case of scarlet fever, to be treated with a course of Epsom salts and nitre. A month of total bed rest recommended for a lady stricken with hysteria. Laudanum for a dental abscess; opium and turpentine for a particularly nasty bout of constipation; a lancing of two boils, removal of an ingrown toenail, and the calming of a superstitious panic at a baby born with teeth. It was a time and place where one could be a doctor largely without need for formal training or qualification, by virtue of possessing an authoritative manner, an anatomy textbook, and a good supply of pills and tinctures that produced, if not necessarily a cure, then at least the appearance of results. An uncharitable observer might have deemed him a con man, a confidence trickster preying on the ignorant. He saw his role as more that of a travelling minister. The bearer of a soothing fiction whose propensity to heal or harm depended greatly on the attitude of the recipient.

His final house call of the evening was the Gwynnant farm – a place he very seldom ventured, for the shepherd families of *those valleys were a stubborn, independent breed who scorned his modern science in favour of old wives' remedies and other dubious practices. It was in recent memory that Mary Jones had walked barefoot for six-and-twenty miles across the mountains for her Bible, but traces of other faiths still lingered here, pagan in all but name. He knew that he would not be summoned until absolutely necessary, when the affliction had grown dire indeed. On the rare occasions when the farmers called for him, death was always close upon his heels.*

It was with apprehension, then, that he drove his trap up the steep lane between hedgerows that bloomed with may and buzzed with butterflies and bumblebees. The pony must have sensed his nervousness, because she shied at every movement, though the evening was a pleasant one. It was a peaceful place, a world away from the uprisings down in Newport and Merthyr that made front-page news in every paper. And yet the vagueness of the Gwynnants' plea unsettled him – one of the younger sons come down on foot to fetch him (running all the way, by his appearance), and unwilling to say anything except to beg that he attend them urgently. He had seen many dreadful things in his career. They cost him sleep: a quarryman crushed flat by a wagon wheel and still alive; a young girl with an ulcerated stomach caused by eating her own hair; the cholera outbreak of '32, when he had helped to throw the dead into a deep trench in the churchyard. There was a terror in this boy's eyes that foretokened something of that order of abhorrence.

He tried to quiz the lad on the drive back, as gently as he could. And all that he could glean from him was that the family had begun to sprout – there was no other word for it – to sprout with growths. A grim, almost visible miasma seemed to hang over the farmhouse, as it often did in places stricken with a sickness. It appeared the animals had not been fed, but neither did they clamour for their fodder. They hid away. The occupants did not come out to greet him either, but as he pulled into the courtyard, he imagined he could glimpse their hideous, disfigured faces watching from the windows.

Carwyn spoke about his boyhood seldom, and sparingly, and gave little conscious thought as to the ways its contours shaped his later life. When asked, he would say he spent it in two looming shadows: of the mountains and of his own familial line. In a land where kin and cousins seemed the second most abundant thing besides the rain, he had been an only child – a rarity that might, to village wives who gossiped over garden walls, have been a symptom of a family in withering decline. As such, he had been spared the wrangle for inheritance which meant that other, bigger farms were carved up piecemeal, generations at a time, until the last were left to head for pastures new or stay to fight for patchwork scraps of steep and bottom.

From birth, there was no doubt that he would grow to be a farmer. It was the natural, inevitable roadmap for his life. He would learn the ways his father and his grandfather would teach him. Any education beyond that was deemed superfluous and suspect. After all, what use were sums and Shakespeare to a man whose workplace was a windswept mountainside, whose calculator was his knuckle-joints, and whose poetry was written in cloud shadows, hawthorn berries, shapes of flanks and fetlocks? When the time was right, he'd marry a prospectless farm-girl with no claim upon her brothers' land, and their relationship would be mostly transactional. They would breed sons of their own and pass the farm and all the knowledge that came with it down to them. A link in the chain was what he was. It felt to him a kind of rustic royalty.

THE HILL IN THE DARK GROVE

For his first years, that was very much the way he'd lived. He looked back on his youngest self as something of a grubby highland prince, a figure in the image of the mighty kings of Gwynedd (in spirit, if not stature) who had held these lofty lands from England's grasp. A pocket-sized Llywelyn Fawr whose realm encompassed all the eye could see, who had no jealous siblings to dispute his crown. He had only the most rudimentary of schooling, making the long trek to the classroom at Beddgelert only when he felt inclined. His education came in other guises. Each morning he was turfed out in the yard to play among the dogs and chickens, or left free to rove over the hillsides and return before full dark. Some days he'd perch high on a ridge and watch his father or his taid working the flock, or scrabble with his mother through the hay and bushes, hunting eggs, or listen to his nain tell stories of the dangers that awaited little boys who strayed too far or failed to heed their parents. She made no distinction between perils earthly and otherwise, but of the former there were plenty.

Alongside every memory of catching tadpoles with a jam jar in the lake, or being sent out with a slice of wimberry pie and coming home blue-lipped, or hurtling down the top fields in a feedcrate go-kart, there was a dire counterpart. A near-daily brush with tragedy. Almost drowning in the swollen stream in search of treasures in a downpour; being pelted by a sudden fall of hail and seeking shelter in a hollow tree which housed a nest of adders; most of a night spent small and lost and freezing on an unfamiliar bit of jagged landscape, sensing awful, hungry presences around him in the dark. His parents saw these misadventures not as warning signs to keep him on a shorter leash, but rather as formative and necessary tests of character. They viewed the mountains as a crucible in which resilient souls essential for this unforgiving life were smelted from the ore of curious, foolhardy children. He could go where he pleased, so long as he stayed out of the lower field.

There was an implicit vein of Cymreictod – of Welshness – running through his childhood, too. Not one defined by such base things as nationality or race, but by living in stoic opposition to all English influence. He was taught it was a humble thing to be – a thing to take pride in, fiercely, but only quietly, and not at the expense of others. His mother said it was particularly *Sais* to think oneself superior based on accidents of birth. To be Cymraeg meant carrying the embers of a dying torch. A remnant, unnoticed, perhaps soon to be gone. There was no pretence of old imperial glory like there was with being English; no rebellious, stubborn bravery like the Scots; none of the whimsical, lyrical melancholy of the Irish – only songs and stories and the tongue. Dragon flags and sheep jokes and self-deprecation. 'How does a Welshman find his sheep in the dark? Irresistible.' In the house they spoke a mongrel language mostly made of Welsh with English scattered in and sprinklings of invented words that were a mixture of the two: plîs, helo, pwdin. He could smile at the absurdity of these things and thoughts in hindsight, but growing up they had been all he knew.

He first saw Rhian Nevett in the late spring of his thirteenth year, and something in him even then had sensed that she would be a wrench in all his family's best-laid plans. In those days he was a knotty little twig of a boy, consisting of grazed knees and uncombed hair and dirty fingernails, and he spent the long days tearing out across the soaring land like youth and liberty incarnate. He had walked the few miles to Beddgelert with a mind, that afternoon, to go to school. The pair of harried teachers seldom paid much notice to his habitual truancy. They'd had enough of butting heads with farmers who were loath to see their offspring educated well enough to leave.

The lane that linked the farmhouse to the road sloped down at such a cant that it was utterly impassable in winter, but that spring it was a verdant trench of rutted grass and dandelions and stinging nettles shoulder-high. He passed along the shoreline of a black and shining lake. Great rocks and boulders sprouted in the shade of trees, where bluebells grew in wild abundance and the mountains either side lowered their heads as if to drink, and the sky above was pristine as at first creation. A lime-green Standard Vanguard Sportsman overtook him, piled with suitcases and picnic hampers, and he could picture still its chromework gleaming as it faded down the road. Children in the back seat bound for summer holidays. Stone walls soft with moss, just wide enough for it to pass. He left the road and took a path that crossed a thin slate footbridge where the lake became a stream which fed into the Glaslyn River, and here the valley widened to a sweep of flatland between slopes attired in heather and gorse where people's washing dried. Past tumbledown stone cottages, and the spoil-heaps of the disused Sygun copper mine, and on along the river to the town.

It was a glorious day of nascent summer that sapped all his desire to go to school. Instead he stopped in Mrs Owen's shop to buy a dozen penny chews, and crossed the humpbacked medieval bridge outside the Prince Hotel (where not too many years before a meteorite had crashed down through the roof and landed on a bed). His way led out into an open green where cows grazed. Moel Hebog loomed above the stone-and-ivy cottages; white steam rose from a narrow-gauge locomotive at the station; bumblebees flew lazy sorties to the flowers at his feet. He came to a spot beneath a sycamore tree, where a rusted iron fence enclosed three stubby standing stones marked with a plaque he could not read, and he hopped the railing and sat down in the shade to eat his spoils.

Before he had begun to chew, a voice above him almost made him choke. 'D'you know the story?' When he looked up, there was a girl about his own age sat astride a limb, though in the leafy dapple of the tree she seemed not like a girl at all but rather a kind of nymph or dryad manifested in the glade. Every feature of her implied otherworldliness. She had hair the iridescent ink-black of a jackdaw's feather, which fell in loose and lustrous ringlets down her back, with broom and meadowsweet woven into the curls as if they grew there. Fair Blodeuwedd from Nain's stories born again. She went barefoot in a home-sewn gingham dress, and her skin was pale and freckled, and her knees all scabbed and grazed like his, but graceful where his own were clumsy. Her nose was upturned in a way that gave her something of an impish air, but it was her eyes that held him dumbstruck, for they were a piercing golden green that seemed to lay him bare and root him to the spot. The words she'd spoken stumped him like a riddle. He sat in foolish silence for a long time looking up at her, and his young mind thought her without contest the most perfect being that ever there could be.

She asked again, 'Well, do you know it?' and he spent a

THE HILL IN THE DARK GROVE

further moment slowly sounding out the writing on the plaque, lips moving with the effort, before he shook his head. 'I'll tell it you for one of those.' She gestured to the white paper bag in his hand, which he offered up without discussion. He would have given every one to have her speak to him and still feel he had come off better in the trade. She came deftly down the far side of the tree and perched atop one of the stones, where she took the bag and scrutinized its meagre contents at great length before she picked out something and returned it. 'Diolch,' he said. 'Thanks.'

'It was long ago,' she began, chewing, 'in the days when there were dragons still, and Prince Llywelyn used to come here hunting with his dogs. Old Gelert was his favourite – the bravest and most faithful hound that ever was – he'd been at the prince's side since both were pups.' Carwyn could imagine that – he, too, had been around dogs all his life. He nodded for her to go on. 'Anyway, on this one trip Llywelyn brought along his baby son. He couldn't take the baban out to hunt, of course, and so he left old Gelert with him in the tent to keep him safe. But that night after a long day chasing deer he comes back to the tent and what do you think he finds?' She spoke this question like it was rhetorical, and he sat silent and enrapt. 'The place in chaos and the crib upturned and the baban nowhere to be found. Just Gelert with his mouth and fur all smeared with blood. And blood all round the tent as well, as if some dreadful murder's happened there. Nefoedd wen, he's ate the baby whole! So Prince Llywelyn grabs his spear and stabs it through old Gelert's heart, and at that very moment there's a cry. A baby crying sharp and loud. And the prince, he lifts a flap of tent that's fallen down and underneath he finds his son

37

there, safe, and next to him the body of a great big wolf. They say he never smiled from that day on.'

'Is there a moral to it?' Carwyn asked. 'Nain says there's usually a moral.'

She shrugged. 'Don't kill your dog?'

'And this is where he buried Gelert?' He looked about them at the quiet graveside where they sat.

The girl smiled knowingly. 'That's what they say. These stones were put up by the landlord from the Royal Goat, hardly a hundred years ago. He thought it would bring tourists. There's other stories where old Gelert was a hunting dog that chased a stag for miles and miles until they both fell dead right on this spot. Or he might not have been a dog at all, but a saint whose bedd – whose grave – is somewhere round about. My dad says you should take these stories with a pinch of salt. There might be truth in all of them, but you've got to find it for yourself.'

'I like the one about the prince the best.'

'Me too, but that's three I've told you, so you owe me two more fferins.'

He gave the bag to her, and for a long time they both sat and ate without another word passing between them, until after the last few sweets were gone she asked, 'Why aren't you at school?'

'It's too nice out. Why aren't you?'

A cow had come to crop the longer grass around the fence, and they both watched it while the girl seemed to measure out her reply. 'I'm running away. Not just for attention, mind, but properly. For good.' She spoke with carefree nonchalance as if this was something she had done a hundred times before.

It did not occur to him to question her sincerity or her motives, and so he only asked where she would go. She waved a

THE HILL IN THE DARK GROVE

hand in the direction of the Aberglaslyn Pass. South-east. Out beyond it nothing but a stretch of moors and mountains running unbroken the full length of the country. Beyond that, Cardiff? Paris? Timbuktu? 'It's dangerous,' he said. 'You shouldn't go alone.' At this she rolled her strange, unsettling eyes.

He spent the better part of the next hour telling her about the terrible things his grandmother warned were in the pass: a dreadful, birdlike creature living high up in the pines on the steep slopes, whose wailing foretold death; a narrow cutting where once highwaymen had preyed and now nightly was infested with ysbrydion – spirits – impossibly tall and thin ones, and limbless ones, and ones with broken, malformed heads, and ones which crawled along the ground like snakes; and the degenerate remains of clans of giants, and corpse candles, and a wheel of fire that rolled quietly along the river road at night. 'You might think it's stupid,' he said, 'but my nain says it's all true, and she knows lots of things.' Frustration had joined his growing alarm. He wasn't sure she was even listening.

'Come with me then.'

He laughed.

And she repeated, 'Come with me.'

In other circumstances he might have made excuses. His mam and dad would worry, he had a long walk home and couldn't stay past dark. Perhaps after all he would be struck with sudden urgency to go to school, or remember some imperative and crucial chore back at the farm that wouldn't wait another minute. If all else failed, he could have told her truthfully that he'd already stretched the slack constraints that ruled his life as far as they permitted, and venturing beyond their safety felt like stepping out into a void. An uncharted

39

blank, where may be dragons. The hitherto unsuffered punishments that might await him there were all the worse for their unknowability – not only the chastisements of his parents, the threats of whippings never thus far carried out, but other fates beyond their power: deaths and accidents of every type his superstitious little mind could yet conceive. He might recall a film they had been shown at school, a cautionary psychedelic nightmare in which klaxons blared and strange men leered and leched and lured trusting children to their cars. Danger comes in unexpected guises, was its message. 'No,' his answer should have been. 'Let's both go home.'

Instead he stood and pulled a tuft of grass and fed it flat-palmed to the cow, who stretched to reach it through the railings. He went to the tree and found a likely-looking bit of branch and hung on it with all his scrawny weight until it broke away, and then he snapped off the remaining leaves and twigs so that the piece that he was left with was between a club or spear-shaft and a walking stick. This he swung in fluid arcs to test its heft, and finding it not quite satisfactory, trod on it to break it shorter still. The girl watched this with patient curiosity. When he was done, she said, 'I want one, too.'

While he obliged, she went and fetched a leather satchel writ over in wild penmanship with names he did not recognize. The Kinks, the Hollies, the Tremeloes; Mary Hopkin, Tom Jones, Amen Corner. She emptied out the satchel's contents with evident pride at her preparedness. 'I've brought a radio for emergencies,' she said: a bright-red pocket-sized transistor that might at best pick up a Liverpool music station; 'and provisions,' which consisted of a can opener and a tin of pear halves and a tin of Ideal milk. 'Wet-weather gear, of course,' she went on, taking out a tartan plastic raincoat rolled into a ball. Lastly, and uncommented upon, was a copy of *Under Milk Wood* worn as threadbare as a Bible, and a total absence of any practical necessity whatsoever. No torch, map, matches, compass, toothbrush, fish hook, change of clothes.

He could think of no response that would not give away his horror at her packing. Instead, he made what he hoped would sound like an approving affirmative noise, tried a grin that felt lopsided but mostly convincing, and promised himself silently that this would be the first and last time he would let a strange girl talk him into running off with her.

She led him over a rotting girder bridge where once the railway line had crossed the Glaslyn, over sponge-soft sleepers that sagged beneath their steps, with weeds and wildflowers sprouting from the putrefying wood. They dropped scraps of paper down through gaps between the transoms and then watched to see whose would emerge the fastest. On the far bank, the path pressed close along the river, which grew white and clamorous and wild as it tumbled over rocks into the gorge, and they could feel the misting of it on their faces. Tiny rainbows shimmered in the spray. The way ahead was no more than a narrow, undulating course of stepping stones, worn smooth by centuries of footfalls, and in places makeshift boards were laid to span the breaches where the land had slipped away. Carwyn crossed these wobbling planks with trepidation, but the girl took them entirely in her stride, barefoot and as graceful as a high-wire acrobat. Further on, the footpath grew so narrow at a bend they had to press themselves against the rockface to continue, and midway round he felt that he might have to cling there for the rest of time above the raging water, for the way both forward and back seemed equally precarious. He pictured himself as a weathered skeleton fused limpetlike onto the cliff. But the girl called to him that he hadn't far to go, and at her impatient urging he completed the traversal. On the far side he stood panting while she slapped his back as if to knock the breath back into him.

When they walked on, he asked, 'Where are we running to?' and she answered, 'Just away.' He sensed in her a tautness underneath the poise. Here in the beauty of the glade, she remained the fay, ephemeral creature that accosted him from in the tree, but there was a high-strung need to go that seemed to harry her. They climbed up to a gravel railway bed and through a dripping tunnel cut for trains, and in the dark she reached out wordlessly to take his hand and let it go as soon as they saw light again. Then back down along the river when that way became too overgrown. Some of her nonchalance returned as they increased their distance from the village, but she cast frequent nervous glances back along the path as though the Cŵn Annwn – red-eared devil dogs – were loosed upon her trail. The pass might have been part of it. If someone was to come their way the possibilities for hiding would be sorely limited, nowhere to go but back along the ledge or leap into the torrent, but the woods were resonant with birdsong and the only footfalls were their own, and for an hour they did not see a soul.

They came upon a fisherman angling for spring sewin from a tree limb arching high across the gorge. He cast his line into a pool of perfect, vivid blue, where veins of copper from the mountains leached into the water. The colour was like something from a dream. The man's catch was laid out on the rocky bank like bars of solid silver in the dappled light.

He called out, 'No school heddiw?' as they came along the path.

'No, mister. See, we're on the run,' said Carwyn. The girl gave him an elbow to the ribs.

To this the fisherman nodded with indulgent gravity. 'That sounds very serious, very serious indeed. Well then, you'd better take a fish to feed you on your travels.' A dubious look passed between the children, only fleetingly, but the man pressed, 'Go on, it's more than I can eat. There's more where they came from.'

'And you'll not tell anyone we came this way?'

He seemed to ponder this a moment, and said, 'So long as you don't tell my wife I'm here, then it's a deal. She'll have my guts for garters.' He pinched a thumb and forefinger along his lips.

They thanked the man and went on with a trout as long as Carwyn's arm slung over his shoulder like a sack, soaking through the back of his shirt and making a meaty slapping sound with every step. Loose scales stuck to his arm and glittered there. Beneath their feet the stones grew mossy and the trees pressed closer overhead, and off through tangled thickets either side. The path climbed steeply upwards and the river fell away into a sharp ravine, and looking down from such a height into its black and boiling depths, it was hard not to imagine very different fish might live down there. Sightless, slimy, slithering things eructed out of fissures in the earth. Old things grown foul and hateful in a cavity that sunlight never touched. He shuddered, thinking of his grandma's stories of ysbrydion in the highwaymen's old hunting ground, and wondered if this might have been the place. But while he held tight to the fish and to his fighting-stick, the girl marched on ahead completely unperturbed. Had they not come so far, he might have thought of turning back, but he could see the sun was setting and was loath to go back lonely in the dark.

High in the woods they came to a road, and the road crossed over an ancient stone bridge, and the bridge was wedged between the two sheer banks of the ravine, far above the roaring water. They stopped to look across it, and the girl said, 'Do you know this place? There's a story to it.'

He turned out his pockets. 'I don't have any Black Jacks left.'

'This one's on the house, for coming with me.' They sat down on a fallen log, and the girl picked up a stone and cast it over the cliff and waited for a splash. 'My dad says the Devil built it, or whatever stood in for the Devil in those days, and his payment was supposed to be the first soul out of every few that crossed it. But the locals brought the wise man Robin Ddu up to inspect the work. Robin took one look and told the Devil it was the worst bridge he'd ever seen – he bet it wouldn't even hold the weight of a loaf of bread.' Carwyn furrowed his brow at that unusual measure of architectural integrity, but she held up a hand for him to wait and see. 'I know, I know. So, as you'd expect, the Devil's pretty miffed at this, and he makes Robin fetch a heavy loaf and throw it on the bridge.' She seemed to revel in the telling of it; saw the old tales not, as Carwyn's nain had brought him up to do, as grim and frightening cautionary lessons, but rather as a thing to be enjoyed.

'Did the bridge fall down?'

'Of course not – there it is. But, see, Robin brought a dog as well, and the dog ran out and snatched the loaf and took off with it over to the other side, and so the Devil had to leave with just a dog's soul as his pay.'

The bridge stood old and still and silent in the baleful evening light, with tendrils twining through its ancient stones, and the branches of dead trees all gaunt and reaching from the chasm underneath. An ordinary bridge in every sense. '*Then*,' he said.

'What?' Neither noticed that the birdsong had all stopped. Even the river sounded dulled.

'That time it was a dog's soul. How many souls since then though, do you think, if the Devil gets the first of every few?'

'It's just a story. Look.' She got up and started out across the bridge, but he stopped her there and took her by the shoulders and for a time they stood fixated on each other's faces with an intensity that not too many years hence might only have dissipated with a kiss.

He thought for a time and then said, 'Should I throw the fish across?'

'It has to be alive.'

'Let me go first then, just in case,' and she scoffed at his unnecessary gallant posturing but let him go.

Cautiously, he stepped onto the span, feeling the way with his walking stick as though unsure of its solidity – as though afraid that if he strode with too much certainty the structure would reveal itself to be just an illusion, and he would tumble through it down into rocks and races far below. Or he might find, on setting foot on the far bank, that he would turn and see the world behind him changed, or gone, and that night a near-identical boy would show up at his house to take his place. He wondered if his parents would remark the little oddities: an appetite for unusual foods; a sudden aversion to metal cutlery; a certain coldness in the eyes. But by the halfway point his confidence had grown. He crossed the last few paces almost with a dancing step, and waited, feeling proud and breathless and relieved, for the girl to follow after him.

'Well?' she asked. 'Still got your soul?'

He patted his shirtfront and his pockets. Shrugged. 'I wasn't really using it anyway.'

They went on together hand in hand, downhill towards the far side of the pass. Down where the trees and brambles pressed so close about them they could see each other and the track and little else. The sun, perched on the mountaintop, was only a suggestion through the overgrowth. After a time there came a distant droning in the air, more a sensation than a sound, like a note slightly beyond the edge of hearing, but felt still in the fine hairs and the back teeth. An aeroplane, thought Carwyn, or a distant lorry on the Traeth. But steadily it rose above the muted rushing of the river and stopped them both there in their tracks. To the verdant, resinous perfume of the pinewoods there appended other smells: old moss and slate and something deep and musky and organic that reminded him of fox dens. There was a sudden cawing and a flight of crows and blackbirds passed together overhead, and the drone grew to a slow and mighty rumble moving somewhere up the slope. They could hear what sounded like the rending of uprooted trees, branches snapping. A mighty crashing like a landslip or a boulder of colossal size come loose and rolling. An ocean liner steaming through the woods. They could not see what it was that came towards them, but it darkened the already fading sun, and as it neared they both stood frozen while the world around them shook. There was a sense of terrible enormity about it – a presence larger than the mountain. Older than the stones. More awful by some considerable margin than the puny Devil of the bridge.

For what seemed like an hour but could only have been minutes they stood still and felt it pass. When he turned back to the girl's face, he could see his own look of incomprehension mirrored there. 'What is it?' he mouthed as pine cones rained around them. She did not answer but gripped tightly to his hand, and he to hers, and there was little they could do but impotently raise their sticks and hope to go unnoticed. Clods and pebbles bounced across the path. Trees shook. But eventually it moved off to the south, its deafening crashes shrinking first back to a rumble and then shortly to a drone and then not there at all, so that the birdsong gradually returned, and when the children came out pale and trembling from the woods and gazed across the open vista to the distant sea there was not a sign that anything had ever passed that way.

The lane led down from cliff and forest into sparser woods, and then to fields and hedgerows as it dropped into the bottomland. A swath of estuary polder reclaimed from the sea – a silted fen as broad and flat as a lagoon and entirely alien to Carwyn's mountain eyes. The marshy ground was woven through with serpentine salt creeks and causewayed tracks that led to lights of fishermen's houses at the river mouth. Porthmadog harbour like a clustering of fireflies. They passed along a hillside that still caught the last rays of the sun while the night grew like the rising tide to swallow up the plain, keeping to the higher ground as though mistrustful of the not-quite-land below. She told him of the Cantre'r Gwaelod – a great kingdom lost beneath the waters of the bay. How one day, long ago, the oceans rose and waves crashed through the floodgates and the dykes and drowned that prideful country stolen from the sea. How some days, when the tides were right and weather clear, you could see roads and walls and ruins on the seabed, and in times of danger distant church bells might be faintly heard above the surf.

At last she led him to a cottage partly buried by a landslide. It was an ugly, crooked little dwelling made entirely of stone and hardly different from the cairns of boulders strewn around it, save that it had token nods to windows and a roof of steeply canted slabs. Mosses covered it. A stunted alder tree had spread its roots throughout one knobby wall as though to keep it from collapsing, and it seemed in all that nature had conspired to both uphold and hide it. A shock of thistles sprouted from the chimney, and grasses grew out of the roof like unkempt hair. Carwyn said it had about it something of the witch's hut from fairy tales – a deceitful house of gingerbread – but the girl told him it was a tŷ unnos: a one-night house, where if the builder could construct it in a single night and have a fire going in the hearth by morning, they could claim the land on which it stood. She told him if they lit a fire tonight, it would belong to them. He found the thought enchanting.

'Ladies first,' he offered, but she insisted he go on ahead.

'It's safe,' she said. 'Don't be afraid.' He did not think to ask her how she knew.

The door was rotten and it gave with little need for forcing, sending centipedes and beetles skittering into cracks. It exhaled a puff of stagnant, dusty air. Small though they both were, they had to duck to pass under the lintel, but once inside they could stand comfortably. The floor was pounded earth, crisscrossed with trackways of small creatures, and leaves lay in drifts against the bare rock walls. A single room. It looked to have been plundered wholesale for anything that might have been of use, for it was utterly devoid of any scrap of furniture or decoration right down to the windowpanes, leaving nothing but the fragments of a porcelain plate, a huddle of mouse-eaten blankets where a tramp might once have spent the winter, and a spinning wheel that was of no use now except perhaps to spin the gossamer of spiders into silk.

The girl gave it a look of disappointed consternation, with her lips pursed and her knuckles screwed into her hips, but then declared with sudden cheerfulness, 'It's perfect, don't you think?'

There was a deep, lopsided fireplace where Carwyn swept the leaves together with his feet while the girl used her stick to brush away the thickest of the cobwebs, and within an hour of trial and error they had struck a spark with flints and moss and had a modest fire burning. The smoke backed up in the clogged chimney, gathering between the ceiling beams, but they were both immensely proud of their proficiency and sat a long time wordless in the glow. They cooked the fish on skewers and picked it to the skin with greasy fingers, and afterwards they ate the pears with milk straight from the cans while the girl told stories like none he had ever heard.

When it grew late they bedded down on the bare floor and

talked on like old fishwives with a lifetime's worth of gossip to relay, until it began to seem that things could stay like this for evermore. He had no thoughts of home. Was too young, yet, to think of the concern his family must be feeling. Paid no mind to the practicalities of finding food and water and new clothing as they grew. He saw instead an unending succession of days just like this: they would fix the house up any way they wanted; they would gather berries, they would hunt with spears and arrows, they would fish for sewin in the Glaslyn; the girl would tell him stories, and they would not be dour or dark or frightening, but something more akin to an initiation in a club. They sketched out their plans together with a certainty that only children could, where nobody and nothing could stand in their way.

They woke at the first seagull cries of morning, with the red sun blazing horizontal through the windows, thick with floating motes of dust that smelled of salt and steam and summer. Dew dripped from the eaves and from the branches of the alder. Ochre-coloured cattle grazed down on the islets in the marsh, and wading flocks of grebes and godwits picked over the sands. The bay was a shining sheet of polished metal, a mirror for the brightening sky, with tiny fishing boats and slate ships to-and-froing to the harbour at Porthmadog. The Ffestiniog steam train moved across the Cob. The girl brought out her radio and tuned through different notes of static interspersed with only fleeting voices or the snatches of a song, and with no music more than this she set it on the lumpy windowsill and danced out in the dooryard. She sang 'Calon Lân' with verses Carwyn hadn't heard before.

THE HILL IN THE DARK GROVE

'Shall we go down into town?' he asked her, shaking scraps of last night's fish into the bushes for the crows. The day seemed poised to be another fine one.

'What for?'

He felt suddenly uncertain, afraid that if he could not furnish a sufficiently exciting plan she might call their adventure to a close. 'Well, we could try to beg an ice cream or a newspaper of chips to eat out on the harbour wall. There's bound to be a chip shop.'

But before he even finished speaking, a thunderous voice came booming from along the hillside, and the girl was suddenly wide-eyed. 'It's him,' she whispered. 'Hide.' There was no time to ask who 'he' might be, because the girl pulled Carwyn to the fireplace and pressed him back into its darkest corner as a fist began to pound on the low roof. She held a finger to her lips. The door was thrown open with such force it fell apart upon its hinges, and a red-faced, ogrish man in oil-stained overalls came bursting like a bull into the cottage.

He did not hesitate nor look about, but strode straight to the inglenook where he dragged the girl out by her slender wrist while she beat at him and bit him and her blows fell on him as ineffectual as rain. 'If I come out here to fetch you one more time, I'll smash this shitheap to the ground, you mark me, geneth.' For a breathless moment, as he leaned into the fireplace, Carwyn saw his face in frightful detail – his hair as crow-black as the girl's, his young eyes dark and bloodshot, his fury painted lividly in all his features – and it seemed the visage of a giant or a cawr come down from off the highest peaks to eat their bones. He smelled of cigarettes and motor oil. 'I've told you these boys are no good,' he raged. 'I've *told* you.' Time grew sick and viscous. On foolish reflex Carwyn lunged and seized his stick and interposed himself between the doorway and the man. The man came on, the girl in tow.

'Stop!' his boy-voice bellowed. 'Let her go!' He gripped the rough branch like a bat and swung with all the small might he could muster, breaking it across the man's stout knee. It stung his hands and he could not remember if he yelped. The man did not react at all, but brushed Carwyn aside and hauled the squirming girl through the low door and out into the red sky of the morning. Her protests faded off into the distance and were gone.

III

June

MIDSUMMER

They grew to dread the setting of the sun. When darkness fell, the children of the village were tormented by most fearful nightmares, though by daylight they could not recall, or would not speak of them. Tapers burned in every window, parents sitting wakeful, restless, waiting for the shrill screams to begin again. They had forgotten what it was to sleep. For near a week the crops had gone untended. Weeds straggled among them, and in the dusk and dawn a great sounder of boars came boldly from the forest to root up the unkempt fields. Blame, as is its tendency, fell quickly on the outsider. The minister, preaching that Sunday morning to his dark-eyed, listless congregation, asked for half a dozen volunteers. A deputation would be sent up to the mountainside to talk with her.

Mam Elias, they called the crone. Nobody knew how old she was, precisely, but all agreed she must have been a great age, for she'd been elderly already when the village grandmothers were girls, and none remembered any tale of how she had arrived, nor a time before she had been there. They talked of her as though she were a feature of the landscape.

She lived in a rough hut of branches perched atop an ancient earthen mound. The barrow, they would whisper out of earshot of the church, of a chieftain or a giant or a primordial god. On Midsummer's Night she'd venture down into the valley gathering herbs, perhaps believing as the Druids did that they would be made potent by the sun at its zenith. People came from far and wide to seek her wisdom, and even the devoutest followers of Howell Harris's Methodist revival would leave offerings in her glade: a brace of hares, a honeypot, a leg of mutton.

That night the villagers could see the glow of fire up on the mountainside, and in the morning when the deputation straggled back into the church, they could not settle on a single version of events. They only meant to question her, the miller said ashamedly; she was already fled, the tailor claimed. The clerk said she had hid herself inside; the wainwright swore that he had heard her cackling in the nearby woods. The innkeeper refused to speak, and only grumbled vague dissent, but there were livid scratches on his face and arms. Whatever was the truth of it, they put her hovel to the torch, and as the fire took hold the tanner said he saw the Devil dancing in the flames. (A fortnight later he ran mad and drowned a little girl down at the riverbank.) The ashes were still smouldering when they left the desecrated place at daybreak.

Few dared go up there after that. On times a poacher or a roving tinker new arrived from other parts would tell a strange tale of a ruined cottage they had stumbled on by moonlight, only to find it gone when they awoke. On Gathering Day, the revellers and herb collectors scorned that mountain, claiming that a wicked stench pervaded it. Parents took to frightening their unruly offspring with stories of unearthly shrieks and laughter that would echo from the crags at night. And by the time the children so afflicted by the nightmares had themselves grown old and died, even those recollections were already folklore, swiftly lost among the melting pots of nascent industry.

It took Carwyn the best part of a month to excavate the carved stone head. He had to go about it inch by inch, painstakingly, because the patch of ferns was dense and hardy and voracious, the fronds razor-sharp and seeming to encroach upon the cleared spots overnight almost as fast as he could shear them back. Each evening Rhian would rebuke him gently for the cuts that etched his face and arms like bloody Ogham script. The earth around the hole, too, was inconstant – not only thick with roots but absolutely riddled with the burrows of small creatures, as well as larger voids, so that the layout of it shifted and it felt prone at every moment to collapse. He had no desire to sprain an ankle like the Englishwoman had, and then be left to drag himself back to the house. A few weeks of injury was something they could ill afford. Nor did he wish to damage any fragile artefacts that might yet lie concealed, or overlook them in his haste.

Most of all, the farm would not allow him real time to fritter on such idle curiosities. There were walls in need of mending. Grazing groups to be rotated between pastures so the summer grass had time to grow back plentiful. Ewes to be treated for worms and flukes and scald and scab mites. Livestock sheds to be deep cleaned. He and Rhian felt the flock was strangely fragile this season, more so than the spring's disaster with the lambs could take sole blame for. It was as though the usually stout and hardy mountain sheep were plagued by some lingering malady that left them stunned and blighted. There was a raft of further cases of mastitis throughout May, twice as many as the worst years he had known. Then came lameness – footrot that advanced with frightening speed despite the dryness of the spring, and left the sheep with hooves abscessed and stinking. At dipping time, they shied and bit and one of the ewes drowned in the mobile dipper. Their fleeces became lank and shabby, infested with legions of scuttling flies. They grew skittish and uncooperative with Eira's herding. They looked harried and haggard and thin.

And so, much of May and early June was occupied with Carwyn taking care of them as he knew best: moving them on daily to wherever the grass was lushest; supplementing them with silage long after the need for it had passed; watching for the slightest signs of limping or discomfort. Some evenings he and Eira sat out on a stile while he spoke softly to the flock. Old jokes Rhian had told him, and comforting platitudes, and disjointed musings that had little meaning or merit but were good enough for sheep.

'A tourist from London walks into an antique shop down in Harlech,' he was telling them, while Eira listened patiently with one ear cocked, 'and on the counter there he sees a skull. "Whose skull is that?" he asks the antiquarian, I can't do the accent, and the antiquarian says proudly, "That, sir, is the skull of Owain Glyndŵr. I can let you have it for a bargain – just a hundred pounds."' The sheep grazed on in no great hurry for the punchline, but seemed reassured, he thought, by the sound of his voice. '"Incredible!" the tourist says, "I'll take it!" and he hands over the cash. Anyway, the week goes by and that same tourist wanders in looking for another deal, and this time there's a smaller skull for sale. "Whose skull is this one?" asks the man, and sure enough the antiquarian says proudly, "That, sir, is the skull of Owain Glyndŵr. I can let you have it for a bargain – just a hundred pounds." An owl came gliding low across the field. "'You must take me for a fool," the tourist scoffs. "You sold me Glendower's skull last Saturday." "Oh yes," the antiquarian replies, and he holds the little skull up with a knowing look. "But this is when he was a boy."'

Each night he rolled into bed long past the late midsummer sunset, and he rose again each morning while the dawn was only watercolour paint-strokes on the canvas of the sky. And even through the night, the ewes and lambs were wakeful, their uneasy bleating making for a restless, haunted sleep. Rhian warned him he would work himself into an early grave – the one that he was digging in the bottom field – but he pleaded vigour, mollified her with excuses. In any case, she woke and worked and slept according to the sun herself. And without the flock they were as good as dead or destitute.

There was precious little time, then, for the buried head. A quick half-hour after breakfast when the water troughs were filled, the valley sides already like a suntrap. Another few inches deeper over lunch, with a trowel in one hand and a strawberry jam and cheddar sandwich in the other, while the blowflies and bluebottles went humming through the ferns, and Eira dug holes of her own around him, and soldier beetles crawled out of the hogweed to inspect their handiwork. Perhaps a surreptitious torchlight foray when he'd made his nightly recitations for the sheep. Every moment he could spare was spent on excavation.

'Why *now*, though?' Rhian asked him one day as he dressed. 'It's not like you to get het up on something so impractical. Whatever it is will still be there in a few months' time and we can both go digging to our hearts' content. We can dig our way to Patagonia if you want to.'

But he could only smile and shrug and say he didn't know. Only that he felt compelled to get at it. To hold it in the sunlight and examine it. To understand exactly what it was and how it came to rest beneath his field, as if the very act of knowing might reveal some thread of urgent truth that would in turn provide a deeper context for his life. A sense whose lack he felt increasingly. He would have laughed if anyone had said the head was speaking to him – it was nothing quite so grandly metaphysical – but rather something in him speaking to himself. 'Just curious,' he told her. 'It'll keep me up at night if I don't know.'

'Take Eira with you, then. I'm waiting for a call from the insurance and the fallen stock people, and I don't want her underfoot. Where is she?'

He gestured out into the yard, where Eira had corralled the hens and now was herding them, low-shouldered, back towards their coop. 'Out there, smelling.' Indeed, Carwyn too thought there might be a changed smell in the air these days. He caught it sometimes, faintly. He put it down as some pollution of the lowlanders or far-off city folk and their inscrutable infatuations. Not modernity, that is, for he was used to that. He had known the hum of the high-voltage pylons in the valley where rain hissed and sizzled on the wires, giving off a scent of ozone like a coming storm. This smell was not modern. Only new. An earthy sweetness, vaguely unpleasant in a way that made him think of compost, rotting vegetables, liquid at the bottom of a bin. Some days it was strong but brief – a whiff, a whisper – others, hardly there at all. He smelled it now as he watched Eira herd the chickens, but when he turned back to Rhian it was gone.

Shearing week came late in June, after a tense few days spent watching for a reasonable spell of fickle north Wales summer. Dry enough that the fleece would not be damp and difficult to work. Not so warm the ewes in wool would overheat while gathered in the pens. Carwyn had a sense for it from years of patient observation. Or rather, the sheep themselves did, and their predictions were more accurate than those of any weatherman. Their wool grew long and thicker in the prelude to the harshest winters. They butted heads before strong winds. If rain was on the way, they stayed near walls and huddled tight together long before the heavens clouded and the first drops fell. He and Rhian spent a week constructing pens and chutes and sorting gates behind the long barn; laying down a plywood shearing floor inside; buying extra antiseptic, hoof-shears, maggot oil. The night before they sat together on the farmyard wall with Eira at their feet and watched the blood drain from the sky, the moon rise and the stars emerge, and felt like runners waiting for the starting gun. Old comrades on the eve of one more battle.

'Red sky at night,' Rhian said, and he nodded slowly but did not complete the phrase.

He dreamed of oversleeping. Of being late for urgent things, forgetting something vital. Pacing on a platform where displays announced his train was more and more delayed as precious time ebbed out of reach like sand-grains in an hourglass; pacing outside the headmaster's office, destined for a caning; pacing in the lime-green, disinfectant-smelling hallway of a hospital. He dreamed of waiting under floodlights on the shearing floor, armed with a brutal pair of hand-shears like his grandfather had used, while an audience of stern stone faces watched him from the dark. He dreamed of shearing lambs, and when the wool was peeled away in one piece like a coat, he found instead the dead and wasted body of a child. He dreamed of walking out along a ridge beneath a sky of unfamiliar stars and looking down to see the farm ablaze. The mountains all wore crowns of jagged stones. The next morning Rhian told him he'd been talking in his sleep, but she could not make out what he said, if they were words at all.

It took an hour of practised chaos to herd the flock into the sorting pens, Carwyn and Eira guiding the great bleating, surging, wild-eyed mass into an alley made of scrap and twine where Rhian deftly swung the shedding gate to split them into groups – ewes to one side, lambs the other. Their discordant bellows filled the valley like the lamentations of the damned. As loud in unison as trumpet blasts. The hot, manurey reek of them drew swarms of vicious, biting flies that plagued the sheep and dog and humans as they laboured in the sun. Inside the barn, Carwyn unhooked the smooth-worn handpiece from its socket and then donned a pair of sackcloth moccasins to better feel the movements of the ewes, the act of shearing like a dance made half of lifelong learning, half of instinct. His father used to shear with clippers driven by a hanging two-stroke motor. His taid had used a pair of hand-shears like two knife blades on a spring.

And back in one unbroken line to herders clothed in furs and skins who shaved the coarse wool off their half-wild breeds with bronze combs or with sharpened flints. One of the earliest trade commodities known to man.

Rhian released the first ewe to him, and he caught it up and rolled it with a twist onto its back and held it gently with his knees. When its feet were off the floor, it ceased its flailing. A state of calm came over both of them. He began with the crutch of filthy wool around its tail, beshat and stuck together in a mass, where flies might find a tempting spot to lay their eggs. Then onto the brisket and the belly, reaching one hand deep into the fleece to pull the skin taut so the clipper would not nick the folds. The handpiece kicked and jolted like a thing alive. He rolled the ewe onto its side, opening out the fleece round to the backbone with long sweeping blows, and while he worked he sang to it and soothed it and blew softly in its nostrils, and he felt its breathing and the tension of its muscles like a healer laying hands upon the sore afflicted. It felt thinner than he would have hoped. 'Easy, now,' he said. 'You're safe.' The sheep had bled a little from a snag of skin, so Rhian took a cobweb from the window and applied it to the wound to help it clot. 'Sorry, cariad.'

Swallows darted in and out the glaring square of open door. He sheared off the remainder of the wool in one neat piece which Rhian rolled and bagged, and let the skinny, shell-shocked ewe into the indoor pen, where it stood trembling, bleating for its lamb. His mother told him once that they smelled different to each other after shearing, and the herd had to establish all its hierarchies afresh. That seemed a hopeful concept to him. He wondered how much kinder all humanity would be if any day the rich and powerful might find themselves the lowest of the low, and those they used to trample suddenly in charge.

Not long ago, the sale of wool from summer shearing would have paid the farm expenses for a year. There was a time in living memory when wool had been like Jason's golden fleece. It was flame-retardant, insulating, biodegradable and breathable, and when you sheared it off be buggered if it didn't grow right back again in time to meet next year's demand. These days, each fleece might fetch them thirty pence – less than the cost, all told, of their equipment and supplies. Some years they simply burned the bales. He and Rhian stood at those pyres scorched by agony and anger, and afterwards they would trudge to the house in silence, reeking still of oily smoke, with all the guilt they had once felt at seeing fire, but none of the vindication. The act of shearing, now, was mostly for the flock, to keep them cool and clean and comfortable throughout the warmest months, and it had taken on the quality of ritual. A purification. A rebirth. The ewes were funnelled through a passage all befouled and burdened, and emerged into the pristine sunlight made anew.

They had sheared perhaps two dozen ewes when Rhian gasped and muttered, 'Iesu Grist'.

She had let the next young gimmer ewe into the barn, and the wretched creature came onto the shearing floor with hesitant, hobbling steps. Its eyes were clouded, and flies lighted in them and around the nostrils. Its wool was lank and fell away across the hindquarters in a brownish, foetid mass the colour of a rotten apple, which crawled with terrible, ravenous life. A sickening odour emanated from the animal in waves. Carwyn spat into the hay and took hold of the stricken ewe and stroked its ears. 'There, bach,' he said softly. 'There's a good sheep, aren't you?' The flystruck wool sloughed away in his hands in foul, moist clumps. Beneath, the sheep's skin was raw and bloody, black to livid, angry red and covered every inch in wounds and lesions. Flies and maggots swarmed upon it. There were bitter tears in Carwyn's eyes, and he could not be certain if they were from pity for the ewe or for himself or for the sheer godawful stench. What a failure this was. Unforgivable.

Rhian said, 'How has it got this bad? You've checked them every day.' Her face was deathly pale. Carwyn supposed his own was, too. He could not tell if there was a note of accusation in her question.

'We've not long dipped them either.' He brushed away as many of the larvae as he could, and she passed him over a tin of Battles maggot oil, which he poured with grim abandon all over the ewe. There was a stomach-churning moment of nauseous anticipation. Time seemed to hang. And then a great uncountable multitude of maggots came boiling out of the sheep's skin, squirming forth in dying throes from every hole and wound and orifice where they had burrowed in their awful gluttony. Erupting out of little clustered cavities resembling the texture of a sea sponge. So many that it seemed the poor sheep's body could not have contained them all, and would collapse without them like an emptied sack. A hollow shell. The ewe endured this all with dead-eyed resignation. 'Impossible,' he said under his breath. The dead and dying maggots lay in drifts like profane snow upon the shearing floor. 'There, del, it'll all be over soon.'

He knotted up a makeshift halter out of rope and led the ewe out to the yard. It followed him on trembling legs across the sun-baked open ground to where he hitched it in a patch of shade beneath the trees. Then he went into the house and brought it out a bowl of water and another bowl of oats and grapes and celery, though the animal just lay breathing rapid, shallow breaths and showed not the slightest interest in the water or the food. Rhian came out with the maggots swept into a plastic bag and laid it in the sun to kill any survivors, and Eira trotted after her to sniff the bag disdainfully. He sat down in the dirt and tried to fathom out the kindest course of action. Iodine might help with the infection. Flystrike ointment would be soothing on the wounds. With time and care the ewe might make a full recovery. But in his heart of hearts he knew that was not true – to wait would only delay the inevitable and prolong the poor thing's misery.

With heavy steps he went into the tool-shed and unlocked his shotgun. It was a plain and purely functional piece of his equipment – not a weapon, but a tool no different in his eyes to all the picks and forks and shovels that he kept it with – and he took no pride or satisfaction in the having of it. He loaded it with birdshot. Took it out to where the dying ewe lay panting in the shade. He held the muzzle at about a hand's length from its forehead, aiming through the skull and down the length of its gaunt body. 'I'm awful sorry, bach,' he said.

The rest of the day's shearing passed without incident, but it was nervous work. Carwyn felt suddenly tentative, his hands timid and uncertain with the clippers so each blow did not take off quite enough wool and he had to go over some parts a second time. The fleeces came off choppy or in ragged strips. And what was more, it seemed the sheep had heard the shot or sensed his hesitation, and grew restless and skittish. They squirmed and bit. He leaned in close and parted the wool with his fingers, and he probed the skin for any sign of greenbottles or maggots, but there were few. Certainly nothing even close to the one flystruck ewe. But still, he could not miss another; it would be the final deathblow for the farm. Untreated maggot infestations could devour a sheep alive and leave only the skeleton. He had seen it when he was a younger man – a carcass picked to just a seething mass of bones and wool down in the basin of a silted pond, vaguely sheep-shaped, moving with the animation of decay. The image of it lingered in his mind. It began to feel like he had lost his rhythm, lost his instinct, and after several slow and untidy attempts, Rhian told him, 'Give it here,' and they changed places for the remainder of the day. Their forearms were anointed with lanolin like the holy balm of Gilead.

That evening Eira took to limping, seeming languid and morose and out of sorts, and when he and Rhian checked her closely, they found there was a tiny flake of flint embedded in the soft pad of her forepaw, and the paw itself felt hot and swollen. He stroked her and soothed her and used a pair of tweezers to extract the splinter, and afterwards he made himself a bed of cushions so that he could spend the night beside her on the kitchen floor. First thing tomorrow, if she was no better, he would take her to the vet. They could ill afford to lose her. Without a dog, Carwyn was just an old, slow man pursuing quick and nimble sheep around a mountainside. He worked with Eira, or he did not work at all.

He had held her proudly in one hand the day she came into the world, the last one of the litter, born inside an intact amniotic sac. When she was just a few months old, she herded half a dozen baffled ewes into the kitchen during dinner, and he had known then that they had been blessed with a truly gifted sheepdog. Rhian had gone out the following day and come back with a collar with an engraved silver tag. Their working dogs never wore them – that seemed to him a thing for pets – but they awarded one to Eira like a medal. She had unfailing instinct. Not only for the sheep, but for him, too: whenever he was feeling ill or down, she'd nose her way onto his lap, or lick his face, or just sit quietly beside him. For near ten years the little collie had been his faithful companion, and he loved her every bit as fiercely as he would have loved the son or daughter that he never had.

It was a great relief, then, when he woke up the next morning to the sound of Eira lapping at her water bowl. The heat and swelling in her paw had gone, and she seemed back to her old self again. He, on the other hand, felt bruised and brutalized by the night on the flagstone floor, as though he had absorbed her pain by a kind of osmosis. A fair and necessary trade, he judged. Discomfort passed, and was the currency for which the greatest things in life were bought.

But the next night he dreamed again of awful things. He was sitting at the kitchen table plagued by the buzzing of a great multitude of blowflies, but he could find no source that might explain the noise, and the dream-Rhian swore she could hear nothing at all. One moment it seemed small and distant. The next, almost inside his ear. At length, he was able to deduce, with the calm acceptance of a nightmare, that it was coming from within himself, and with that understanding it subsided. He itched all over. When he looked down at his hands, he saw his palms were pitted with a nest of deep and close-packed holes, like honeycombs, and in their depths he could see many carved stone faces peering up at him. It was getting late, and Eira had not come inside, so he went out into the yard to call her in and after an interminable time she came around the far end of the long barn in the moonlight. There was something strange about the way she walked, as though her limbs could not be willed into cooperation. She tottered one way then the other like a drunk. Her fur seemed to hang loosely. Her head lolled almost to the dirt. Something was dropping from her mouth. And then as she came close, he realized with dawning horror what was wrong. It was not Eira, but her skin, imbued with putrid, boiling life and steered blindly, puppetwise, by a host of wriggling maggots. The Eira puppet raised its head and regarded Carwyn with a motion that was horribly boneless and hydraulic, and the last thing he remembered when he woke up sweating was the look of pained betrayal in its empty, sightless eyes.

In light of these strange dreamings, his desire to unearth the head took on a sharper urgency across the coming days. He had long since disabused himself of his grandmother's notion that dreams were veiled communications from the gods, which might predict the future or impart life-changing revelations or grim auguries of doom. For his nain, dreams might foretell ill health, a season of good hay, a wedding or a windfall. He viewed them now with a more corporeal regard. As clues, perhaps, to the preoccupations of the under-mind. A sort of nightly filing of the day's events into the recesses of memory, a storing and consuming and discarding. Mostly they were little curiosities that he and Rhian might share for amusement over breakfast. He dreamed once that he was in a heated argument with a goose who was ungrateful for the scarf and wellingtons he had bought for it. Rhian dreamed she had to play host to a boisterous deputation of white mice. He dreamed of lying paralysed while the malformed silhouettes of faun-legged, antlered things went capering past the windows in the dark, and they laughed about them in the morning and made jokes about what they might signal. Too much cheese, or too much isolation.

And so he and Rhian both concluded that the head's appearance in his dream must be a symptom of something subconscious. A need that would subside once he had dug it up and set it on the kitchen table and examined it, and then consigned it to a dusty corner of the workshop with the idol and the arrowheads and all the other oddities the fields disgorged the way a healing wound might expel foreign objects. The remaining days of shearing passed in feverish anticipation, as slow and restless as schooldays in the wait for summer. He thought of little else.

'Do you think I've lost the plot?' he asked one evening as he kicked his boots off at the kitchen door. Tufts of wool clung to his trouser cuffs.

She looked up from the teabag she was fishing from the sink to use again and shook her head. 'You've got me curious, too, with all your carrying on. If it means that much to you, get it dug. Just don't kill yourself doing it, it's going to be a hot one.'

And it was, already notching up another in a series of summers that crept ever warmer, winters ever slightly more severe, bringing plants that flowered in just slightly the wrong season, birds and insects unseen in these parts, like tiny omens of a future in upheaval. 'Too hot for June. Too dry.' There was a note of worry in his voice – the weather not just small talk, but the keystone to the whole precarious construction of their lives. There could be no other place in all the world, he thought, where one could feel the seasons quite as sharply as here in the mountains.

'At least we'll have good hay.' Her smile was small and brave and endearing, and he kissed her beardily on the cheek as he and Eira went out of the door.

It was the day after the solstice when he finally resumed his digging. He spent the morning hacking out a clearing in the ferns, which had grown back in his absence to conceal his prior works. There seemed to be more holes than he remembered having dug. He had opened up a tapering trench, about waist-deep, in front of where the head lay buried, working outwards from the mound. It had taken near two months of careful excavation, chipping away with pick and trowel at the hard-baked, stony soil, inch by inch, and finding no more for his efforts than a rusty horseshoe. But today, despite the heat, the earth was loose and yielding, and the work felt light.

He came upon a layer of stones that bore the marks of tools, and when he had uncovered them more fully, he could see what looked to be a line of crude foundations. For a long time, he sat down on the edge of the trench and scratched the scruff of Eira's neck, and wondered when those stones might last have seen the light of day. And why they had been left in situ rather than dug out to serve some other function in a country where good building stone was worth its weight in gold; where even mighty castle walls were scavenged down to nubs to build the cottages and cattle sheds of peasants; where the carven slabs of Celtic tombs and capstones out of ancient cairns were rooted out to bridge a stream for sheep to cross, or stand as gateposts at a drovers' inn. In their relation to the head, he guessed them to be part of the ill-fated church from Rhian's story, built back when the cult of Christ was yet a new and suspect thing in this high-pagan wilderness. A bastard upstart clothed in scraps of older faiths.

The head itself came grudgingly into the light of day. It sat perfectly upright amid the randomness of earth and stone around it, and it was difficult to imagine it had come to rest so neatly there by chance alone. It seemed it had been placed with some deliberateness and care, and buried. A pregnant silence seemed to overhang the thing. Some silly, superstitious part of him refused to look about for fear he might glimpse fleeting figures watching from the trees or ridges or among the tangled ferns. He pulled it gently up out of the clinging dirt and free of the thin roots that stretched and snapped in turn like strands of hair, then brushed the damp soil from its contours and lifted it to better cradle its uncanny weight, and he was struck by an uncomfortable sense of birthing. Not vastly different from the countless ewes he'd helped to lamb, or the cows, back in the day, that he had helped to calve, or a time about which he now mostly managed not to think.

He laid the head face up in a nest of rags and blankets in his wheelbarrow and bent to examine it more closely. Eira gave it no more than a cursory sniff before returning to her digging.

It was a crude suggestion of a man. A lump of pitted, rough, light-coloured stone about the size of a grapefruit – a little larger than he had first estimated now he saw it in the light. Its features had been heavily eroded by the weather, and Carwyn guessed it must have stood exposed for a great many years before it went into the ground. The nose and ears had worn away entirely; the eyes were featureless and almond-shaped; the mouth a thin, chiselled line. There were the very faintest hints of carvings meant to represent thick hair and a beard, and a rugged, broken portion at the neck where it might have once possessed a body or a column. To look upon it stirred a sense of hazy recognition, and it felt to him like stumbling upon the likeness of some long-lost relative or ancestor. A proof that men like him had walked these mountains in the distant past and left their legacy in stone, and that ages hence someone might chance across some relic of his own, and recognize themselves in him. If it could speak, it would have whispered reassurances that he was not the fading remnant of a family line, but part of a much greater continuity.

When he had gathered up his tools, he covered the head over with a blanket and barrowed it back up the hill towards the house. At the gate beyond the woods, still locked with chains and overgrown despite his many visits, he had to tuck it under his arm as he had done with Eira, and then set it carefully on the grass while he went back for the wheelbarrow and the dog. The effort left him breathless and sweating. The heat of the day was catching up to him, and he was beset at once by all the tiredness and soreness he had lain aside to dig – an aching in his joints, a stiffening of his lower back, an unaccustomed numbness in his arm that prickled down to pins and needles in his fingertips. His mouth tasted faintly metallic. But he was buoyed, too, by a newfound energy and optimism. An intuition deep within his bones that this discovery, as unassuming as it seemed, might mean the end of their ill fortune.

IV

Holly

CLAIM

After the disastrous attempt to rescue Sir John Owen from imprisonment at Denbigh Castle, they had ridden hard over the moors. There was a troop of Roundheads hot upon their trail, and their hope was that they might yet lose them in the mists that cloaked these heathlands even at the height of summer. Their mounts were of poor stock – a pair of stolen nags fit only for the knacker. The long-haired Cavalier's white mare had been shot out from under him at Naseby by a cannonball, and he still keenly grieved the loss of that fine animal. The other man, a mercenary Frenchman who spoke scarce a word in any tongue, was more accustomed to fighting afoot. The others were all gone. Symkyns dead, felled by a mighty sabre stroke that broke the blade in two and cleft his head apart from nose to nape. The Cavalier had seen Gerard and Pettitt cast down from a ladder in the rout, and he presumed the rest of their companions likewise scattered and pursued, made prisoners, or slain.

He rode with the mute Frenchman high into a bank of cloud, where their hat brims grew heavy in the damp. The long pistols at their saddles useless, now, except as clubs. A pale sun rose at their backs and outpaced them across the high and barren country, where their way led down into a swale and climbed again through villages of backwoods simpletons into the mountains. On the low slopes of a great peak that they took to be Snewedon, they passed a farmhouse where a thatcher and his boy were at work on the cockscomb of the roof, with further sheaves of batting laid out ready in the yard. Dusk came.

As they descended from the brow of the next hill, the clouds no more than wisps now, and their wet coats steaming, they beheld a maiden of uncanny fairness bathing in a brook. A farmer's daughter from the nearby cottage, both supposed. Dark of hair and countenance, as these mountainfolk so often were. The Cavalier declared that he would claim her as his spoils and ravish her somewhere discreet while the mercenary should keep watch for any kin who might come searching. The Frenchman seemed to understand that he was being asked to wait his turn and signalled his displeasure by the brandishing of his ferocious hanger sword. When the long-haired man yielded, they looked back to see the girl had gone – withdrawn, perhaps, into a nearby wood to dress, or to await them.

Without a word, the mercenary spurred his horse, and a moment later he, too, disappeared among the thickets. Left thus alone, the rider felt a strange misgiving. He looked about, but could see no one watching him, and yet he sensed he was observed. As his nag crossed the stream, he happened to glance down, and for a moment fancied that he glimpsed a great and terrible leviathan in the depths, though this must surely have been imagination, for looking back he saw that it was no more than a shallow trickle that a man could stride across without wetting his spurs. Soon after that the trees enveloped him, and he passed into emerald twilight. No sign of his companion, nor the maiden, nor even a bird. He dared not call to them for fear of what might answer in their stead. It would be worth it yet, he told himself, when he could have his turn with her, and on the morrow he'd be clear across the strait to Anglesey.

Ahead, down in a glade, he spied a hovel of rough branches perched atop a knoll. The Frenchman's clothes lay in a heap below. Must not have even waited to undress inside, the knave, the Cavalier thought with a smirk. But as he ventured close, his scorn turned to a foetid bolus in his throat. The heap of clothes was only one of many – several fresh, and others grown so mossy and decayed that he could scarcely tell what they had been. He swallowed drily. All about the clearing there were strewn the mouldering coats and boots of countless men.

They watched the white van coming from a long way off, labouring up the valley lanes like a conspicuous intruder in that place of hay trailers and livestock trucks. It was a sweltering July morning, towering skies the colour of a glacier hanging high above the peaks, the mountains crawling with the tents and caravans of day trippers and picnickers and ramblers. Carwyn knew that there were some down in the tourist towns for whom these visitors brought a transient modernity. Novelties to tempt the locals into parting with their ways, until with time they vanished altogether, defeated not by foreign occupation nor by force of arms, but by the lure of shiny gadgets promising convenience and ease. He and Rhian had remained unmoved. Not so much out of principle as practicality. What use was a computer or a smartphone in a place where good reception was like gold dust on the wind? These things, for them, were curiosities at best. They thought of them (when they spared them any thought at all) with anthropological suspicion, as one might the peculiar trappings of a distant people.

He stood with Rhian in the yard, where still the stain of the unfortunate ewe remained indelible upon the earth, and the air held the faintest ghost of pyre smoke from three more they'd had to burn since then, and sipped strong tea in silence as the van advanced below them. These last weeks they had waited grimly for the day of its arrival. A letter had foretold it. Between their tasks they would survey the busy summer traffic on the lanes and watch with ominous anticipation the approach of any likely-looking vehicles, the way lookouts on these very peaks had waited for the coming of King Edward's armies long ago.

Sleep, those past few nights, had come fitfully. He would wake sweating at odd hours in the boiling stillness of the house, with the clinging vestiges of nightmares foggy at the corners of his mind. He would wake with a sudden, powerful thirst, or with a desperate need to urinate, or to find the room so stifling that he had to open all the upstairs windows for a breath of air, and padding across the dark, familiar landing he would find himself afraid in ways he had not felt since boyhood. Child-fears plagued him. He checked in empty corners and behind the doors. He turned on more lights than were necessary. He kept his gaze averted from the bathroom mirror, and from the teeming shadows at the bottom of the stairs.

One night he had started out of sleep with the moon high on the mountaintops and the red lines on the bedside clock announcing some inhuman hour, and gone down to the kitchen for a glass of water. The house seemed altered somehow, like a misremembered dream – the creaks of floorboards playing slightly different notes, the ticking of the wall-clock just a fraction of a second slow, the accustomed home-smells ever so subtly tainted by a hint of foulness, like a clogged drain or a gob of dropped food underneath the fridge. He found himself mis-stepping on a stair, as though their spacing was a fraction off. The stone head stood on a sideboard in the downstairs hall. An eerie realism to it in the instant before the light came on, so that he imagined it possessed more life and detail than it truly did. A bushy, bristling beard; a thick head of auburn hair; the nose pounded almost flat; the neck a grisly wound. And the eyes – those almond eyes were worst of all – alive and watchful. He filled his glass and pulled a chair up to the kitchen table, where Eira woke and nosed her way into his lap, and there he sat surrounded by the mess of sternly worded paperwork and told himself that it was worry that was keeping him from rest. The van. The van would come, and after it had gone things would resume normality.

There had been several false alarms. One ominous white shape along the road turned out to be a minibus of kayakers bound for the rapids. A couple crossed the end of their lane without turning and wound on towards Beddgelert. A siren went by blaring feebly in the distance.

'Reminds me of back then,' he said, and saw without her saying so that she knew what he meant. It had been almost fifty years ago that the police had come for Carwyn and his family, hunting anyone who might have information about a string of arsons on the Llŷn and Môn and Ceredigion coasts. Anyone who might be harbouring nationalist extremists. Any Welsh person they wanted to, it seemed.

'It was the week before Christmas, wasn't it?'

It was. He remembered his frail old nain, not long a widow, shivering in handcuffs and a dressing gown where they now stood; his dad in quiet tears, his mother trying to remonstrate with a stone-faced detective; himself nineteen and mute and numb and seething as they scoured the house for evidence that wasn't there. Afterwards there had been coffee from a Styrofoam cup in a cold interrogation room. A man who mispronounced his name. Questions that he hadn't known the answers to. He could not think of a time when he had felt more

THE HILL IN THE DARK GROVE

violated. And the next day, when they were released, Rhian had visited and burned with all the righteous fury that the Gwynnants were too shell-shocked still to feel, and gone home swearing vengeance.

'It won't be like that,' she said now, reaching up to lay a hand on his shoulder – he placed his own on top of hers and squeezed it gently. 'These bailiffs aren't like the police.'

He smiled. 'They might be worse.'

'They might be. Or they might not come at all.'

But today the van came on, growing from a distant speck meandering up from Capel Curig, passing Matchbox-sized along the far side of the lake among the hiking groups and camper-vans, then lost among the trees and boulders and emerging larger still, grown to quarter scale. It paused down at the junction of the lane, as if to check its bearings, and then turned laboriously up towards the farm. Carwyn downed his dregs of tea.

'You'd best go,' she told him.

'Are you sure? You don't want me to talk to them?'

'I'm sure. We'll do it like we planned. Debts in your name, assets in mine. Now go on with you.' She shooed him playfully, but he could sense her nerves. He squeezed her hand again and went.

He found a spot up in the hayloft of the long barn where a knot-hole gave a tunnel-vision view across the yard. The van pulled through the gateway and sat idling there while Rhian went to meet it, and he saw her speaking briefly with the driver before motioning for him to park. Two men emerged – bullish, hulking fellows dressed in short-sleeved uniforms that lent them the appearance of a pair of schoolboys sprouted into giants. Their manner was conciliatory in spite of their intimidating size, and they seemed to Carwyn like the bearers of bad news, men about some unpleasant but necessary errand. He felt the prickling in his hand again, and flexed it and examined it until the feeling passed. They strolled to where Rhian awaited them, rocking back on their heels, their thumbs hooked in their padded vests, and she greeted them with polite standoffishness.

'I'm Mr Ritchie,' the first man announced. 'This is my partner Mr Mears. We're High Court enforcement agents. Is Mr Gwynnant home?' Carwyn could not see from where he watched, but felt her bristling at how they mistered through their overtures, the way a visitor might ask a child if she could fetch her parents to the door. The man spoke with a soft Glaswegian burr, and it touched a raw historical nerve, the idea of a Scotsman sent out here on English pay to hound and hassle fellow Celts. There was a tragic fellowship to it, and a sense of mercenary treachery, and centuries of long injustice all thrown in together. 'We're bought and sold for English gold,' he muttered to himself, but did not know where he had learned that snatch of poetry.

Rhian said, 'He's somewhere, but I'd not know how we'd get a hold of him. He'll be out with the sheep till dinnertime, you see.'

The two men paused to take in the enormity of the landscape and seemed daunted by the prospect. 'Does he have a mobile phone?' the second man asked.

She smiled and shrugged apologetically. 'Wouldn't be much use up here even if he did. The landline's bad enough. You'd best come in, I'll put the kettle on. We might be waiting quite a while.'

They balked at this. The drive into the mountains must have been a long one, and it was clear they did not relish the thought of wasting the entire afternoon, so for a moment it began to look as though they'd give up and return another day. Then the first man knelt and patted Eira's head and asked, 'He's gone herding sheep without his sheepdog, has he?' He raised an eyebrow as though hoping he had caught her in a lie.

'This one's retired.'

Next, he jerked a thumb towards the pickup and the trailer. 'And the vehicle? He's left that, too?'

'That's mine, I've got the paperwork. He goes on foot. He has since he was young.'

'Anything else belonging to the partnership? Anything the two of you own jointly?'

She shook her head. It had been her idea to structure their ownership shrewdly with just such an eventuality in mind – some things in his name, some in hers, until the trail became too convoluted for all but the most dogged of debt collectors to untangle. 'The house?' she said with a shrug. 'The sheep, the land.'

The conversation shifted back and forth this way for quite some time, until it became clear a stalemate had been reached. Eventually the bailiffs were content to take stock of the meagre goods that they might seize, promising they would be back to speak to Carwyn, and they thanked Rhian and returned the way they'd come.

Carwyn descended shamefaced from his hiding place to watch them go, the van diminishing to a smaller replica and then a Matchbox toy and then a speck until it vanished back into the east. 'What would people think of me?' he asked. 'Cowering in the hayloft while I leave my wife alone to face the debt collectors. My nain and taid are rolling in their graves.' And they really would have been, he thought. They had been the kind of people who had lived their whole lives owing nothing more than the price of a sheep or two one market day, to be repaid in kind the next. Their liabilities were not writ on any balance sheets, but kept in tallies inside fellow farmers' heads, their word as good as gold for it was secured against their very reputation. How messy the world had become.

She told him, 'Don't be daft, it's what we planned. We do this as a team. If you'd been here, they'd have stripped us bare. Let's just get the money before they come back. The BPS payment is coming at the start of next month – if we're careful, that should last us till the lambs are big enough to go to market.' She gestured vaguely to the flock. 'We're going to get this sorted, Carwyn. We can manage it. You've never failed me yet.'

He took her hand and for a long time they both stood in silence at the wall, watching the tiny shapes of picnickers down in the valley. August felt a long way off. 'Well, at least you've married the man with all the best debts in the world,' he said eventually.

'How's that?'

'Every one of them's outstanding.'

Her solemnity broke into a grin and she swatted at him, and for the briefest moment they reverted to their younger selves, when woe had been a far-off cloud on the horizon.

He dreamed, that night, of faceless bailiffs emptying the house. A great, unending throng of them pushing and jostling at the door, stripping the place down to the skirting boards, the lightbulbs, the picture hooks. He watched them cart away the big oak dresser, the love-spoons he had carved, Nain's china plates and lustre jugs. Even Eira and the flock. Rhian remonstrated with them fruitlessly while he hid trembling in the hayloft, but they were deaf to all her protestations, until eventually they carried her off too. When they had gone, he climbed down to survey the damage, and it was worse than he had feared. Every last bit of the farm was gone: every piece of hay, every blade of grass, every scrap of evidence that they had ever been, save for the bare shell of the house and outbuildings. He wandered dazed among the lifeless ruins, the night sky blank so that it seemed even the stars were forfeit, and when he came into the hall he found the only thing untouched was the stone head.

The bedside clock read 2.16 when he awoke. The room was sticky and airless, but when he looked over to the window he could see that he or Rhian had already propped it open wide. The curtains hung there limp and motionless, and outside a lidded eye of moon peered in from between Lliwedd Bach and Gallt y Wenallt. Otherwise the dark was absolute. Rhian was saying, 'Carwyn,' as she gently nudged his shoulder with a sweat-damp palm, and as he swam back into consciousness his first thought was that there must be a fire. He could smell, just for an instant, an odour of burning.

'What's wrong?'

She passed him her glass of water from the bedside, for his own was empty, and said, 'I think you were having a nightmare. You've been talking in your sleep.'

'I'm sorry, bach. What did I say?'

'Nonsense, most of it. I couldn't make it out. But you kept

saying, "Y pen wedi ei gerfio o garreg." The head carved from stone.' He looked suddenly bashful at this, as though he'd spoken some great foolishness, but she regarded him with mild concern. 'I want it out of the house.'

He nodded. 'In the morning.'

'Now.'

And thinking of it, he began to see that she was right. What if the head was not a stroke of luck, but rather a bringer of misfortune? Indeed, the head seemed more and more an uninvited presence in the house. He could feel it as he lay there, as one can feel the company of visitors in other rooms; not like a ghost, but something tangible. It crept into the background of his dreams and waking thoughts.

He stood groggily and stepped out to the landing. As he went, he turned on all the lights: the corridor, the stairs, the downstairs hall. Even the outside bulb above the porch. The head was where it always was, of course, inanimate and harmless. It looked, there on the sideboard in the cluttered hallway, both at home and utterly out of place, but there was not the slightest hint of ill intent about it. A lump of stone, no more than that.

Eira had woken and waited, sleepy, in the doorway of the kitchen, her tail half-wagging. She did not follow when her master went out to the yard in only boots and underpants. Carwyn took the head into his workshop, where he set it on a shelf and pondered for a moment how he might be rid of it most advantageously, and it occurred to him it might be sold instead of cast away. As he tramped back towards the house, he fancied that he saw a stag down in the closest pasture. The moonlight was not bright enough to make it out for certain, and he had the porch light at his back which cast the outer night in deeper darkness, but he believed he saw the shape of antlers picked out in the moonbeams at the wall. It was completely still. So much so that he began to think it might have been a fallen branch or unfamiliar sapling, and after a time he left it standing there and went back to his bed and sank into a deep and dreamless sleep.

The next day was the hottest of the year. Hotter than any July he had known in all his long life on the mountain. By breakfast time the sun was already a searing ulcer on the blistered sky, and the thermometer on the wall of the long barn seemed fit to crack or melt. Carwyn made his rounds to check the flock, with Eira panting at his heels. The pastures were sere and parched to yellow and the sheep themselves packed cheek by jowl in every scrap of shade, the flies thick and lethargic on their faces. The stream was dry. No treasures, now, among its bed of stones. He found a gnarled old holly limb propped up against the pasture wall – the stag, you silly sod, he thought, from in the night – but there was not a tree nearby, nor so much as a breath of wind that might have blown it there. The logical, ridiculous conclusion was that the sheep had somehow brought it.

'You had me going there,' he said to Rhian with a wink when their paths crossed. 'Very funny.' She was a devil for these little tricks: a pickled onion in his tea, a Halloween mask on the dog, a breadcrumb trail of tantalizing notes around the house that led eventually to the washing-up. The look she gave him of confused incomprehension was convincing, he could give her that. He took her in his arms and squeezed her playfully. 'I'm going down to Rhod's this afternoon if you fancy a ride out. Have an ice cream on the prom.'

When she spoke, he could hear the edge of tiredness in her voice. 'Rhod Jones? You're taking him the head?' His nod seemed to relieve her. 'That sounds lovely, but I'd better not.' She laid her ear against his chest as if to listen for his heartbeat. 'I mustn't have slept last night – I'm shattered.'

'Oh?' he asked, concerned. Eira was sitting close at Rhian's feet, pressed up against her as she did when one of them was ill. 'Go and put your feet up then. I'll finish off out here and bring you in a paned. How many sugars was it again? Twelve?'

'Twelve sugars,' she confirmed.

When the morning's work was done and Rhian's cup of tea made (with her customary single sugar cube), he put the stone head in the pickup and set off towards the coast. After a moment's hesitation, he had brought the biscuit tin of sundry artefacts along as well, not knowing if he was prepared to part with them but curious to learn their value if he got a chance to ask. Three times, he'd gone into the shed for them and come out empty-handed. Once he'd even got as far as starting the ignition before going back. Forgetfulness was part of it – 'What did I come in here for, now?' he asked himself aloud, but there was also a reluctance, something in between embarrassment and jealousy. It couldn't hurt to ask, at least, he thought as he drove through the gate.

He passed the way the van had gone the day before. Down the long farm track to the proper road. Along the lakeshore where the shiny cars of visitors were crowded on the verges while their owners swam and frolicked in the glassy water. Past ancient walls and hedgerows where the tourists' litter gathered in great rafts like flotsam at the tidemark: fast-food bags and coffee cups and crumpled foil from sandwiches, and almost everything that people might conceivably discard, so that one with a mind to pick through it might discern the details of the jettisoners' lives. A record scrawled across the countryside in rubbish.

He drove the narrow, winding lanes out of the peaks and valleys of Eryri. Up passes where the road edged flush along each precipice and unpeopled immensities of landscape fell away as far as sight. Down into low dells beneath the jagged spoil tips of the quarries. Over rolling yellow moorland like high desert in the sweltering sun, and finally out into the valley of the River Conwy that flowed northward to the sea. Gentler country, here. A broad alluvial plain between soft, wooded hills, and villages raised in old stone. A place of pleasure boats and caravans and country shows. Rural still, but on the fringes of modernity.

His grandmother had told him once the story of the Afanc – a foul, slithering leviathan down in the muddy riverbed, whose rages caused almighty floods. It was the death of many heroes who were sent to slay it, their spears no more than pinpricks in its ancient hide, and it would not devour them but leave their drowned and bloated bodies as a warning for the next. His nain had left the story there, but some years later Rhian told him how it ended. The daughter of a local farmer went down to the riverbank one day and sang the beast a lullaby. A crowd had gathered at the sound of her enchanting voice, sure that the monster would emerge to claw the foolish child into the depths, but to their bafflement it slid onto the bank and fell asleep. An allegory, Rhian said, for when the river had been tamed. Or a threat for children tempted to swim in its lazy but deceitful currents. A memory, perhaps, of some grotesque primordial deity that lingered still in the local imagination. Carwyn wondered what it would think of its river now – the lowest he had ever seen it, scarce more than a viscous trickle in the drought.

The auction house was down a backstreet in Llandudno. It squatted in an underbelly secreted away behind the faded, threadbare splendour of Victorian hotels that faced the beach across the sunny promenade – a red-brick hangar at the far end of an alleyway where bold and rangy seagulls picked through bags of refuse and the key-cutters and junk shops all had rusting metal mesh across their windows. Protection more from vandalism, Carwyn thought, than theft, for there was nothing in any to warrant the effort of breaking in. Traffic noise drowned out the crashing of the surf. The back door of a cafe filled the air with greasy frying smells. A painted sign read, *Rhodri Jones & Son: Antiques and Salvage Auction. Established 1985.*

A bell tinkled above the door as he entered a squalid room piled full of such a quantity of dusty, cobwebbed sundry objects that he had to pick a careful path between them. He came face to face with a life-sized porcelain doll in Welsh traditional dress. The husks of spiders hung like crewmen in the rigging of a model sailing ship. Ranks of glass eyes in taxidermized heads regarded him. At the far end of the room there was a desk near buried under all the clutter, upon which stood a varnished yew-wood box bearing the inlaid gold inscription, *Cofiwch genhadaeth Clawdd Offa* – Remember the mission of Offa's Dyke.

He liked the sentiment of that. As he was looking for a price, a shabby man came in from deep within the warren of the place, and after a moment of unrecognition exclaimed, 'Carwyn! Where've you been hiding all this time? I thought you'd bloody died! I've not seen you since—' He tried to calculate and looked embarrassed by the answer. 'How's Rhian?'

'It's been a while, let's leave it there,' he laughed. 'She's well. We've all grown old. How are you, Rhod?' They clasped each other warmly and a flood of reminiscences and polite trivialities ensued. Health and families and old acquaintances enquired about; drinks and dinner invitations offered and declined. In the dim back room of the auction house, the two men could have been brothers whose lives had followed opposite trajectories. But it was clear that Carwyn had some pressing matter on his mind, and inexorably the tenor of the friendly visit shifted towards business. He bent to lift the stone head out of his duffel bag and laid it on the desk with something of an air of ceremony. 'What'll you give me for this?'

The man examined it at arm's length, turning it over in his hands and feeling its contours like a phrenologist, before he asked, 'What is it?'

'You tell me. It was in my bottom field.' It occurred to him, as he was saying it, it must have lain there undiscovered all his life, and he found the thought discomfiting in an amorphous way. Like looking back through childhood photographs and noticing a stranger in the background of them all. 'I just want rid of it, to be honest with you, but what do you think it is?'

A long, pursed inhalation of the kind a car mechanic might give to a tricky diagnostic case. 'Shrine or chapel decoration, looks like. Early Christian effigy. Any context?' Rhod fished in his shirt pocket for a pair of half-moon spectacles while Carwyn brought his rusted biscuit tin out of the bag and spread its contents on the desktop. Everything except for the clay figurine. 'Iesu mawr, that's a hell of a collection. Some of these arrowheads are seriously old – see the leaf shape? That teardrop, that's classic Neolithic. You could be looking at six thousand years there, minimum. The later ones have barbs and tangs – there you go, like that one – could be three, four thousand. And all these found in the same place?' Rhod raised his eyebrows. 'From the quantity it looks like somewhere that's been occupied over a massive period. Mind you, I'm not saying the head's anywhere near contemporaneous with those. Anywhere *near*. Early medieval, I'd say. Nothing else close to where you found it?'

Carwyn did not explain his bone-deep sureness that there was – that the head was just the glint of ice above the water. Instead he said, 'I haven't looked, to tell the truth. The flints and things are from the stream. We've been finding them since I was small. The head more or less dug itself out of the ground last month.' He wondered how much of the tale of its discovery he should share. There was much he still did not completely understand himself, and something deeper than the fear of looking foolish that convinced him he should hold his tongue. 'There were some slabs and fragments round that might have been the foundations of something, but I've barely scratched the surface.'

His old friend only nodded. 'Hard to say, then. Early Christian, definitely – I've seen something like it at St Cadfan's Church in Tywyn. They found the carvings there being used as a gatepost for a pigsty. It's not my area of expertise. Some kind of saint or Christ figure, if I had to guess, but obviously it's a long time later than these other bits. Sixth or seventh century, at the earliest.'

Carwyn rubbed his chin. He wondered how the locals must have looked upon those early missionaries – strange wandering paupers with a hint of madness hanging over them, come to peddle their new upstart god to people who had deities aplenty. Harmless eccentrics they had likely seemed. But what they planted grew unchecked and rampant from the sowing of such humble seeds, while the old world was weeded out or withered, and the head had been a mute observer from the very outset. 'What's it worth then? Would a museum take it? It feels,' he searched for a word and failed to find a fitting one, 'important.'

'Local one might do, if you wanted to donate it, but I doubt they'd pay.' He had deduced the thrust of Carwyn's questioning. 'Collector's what you want. Flints are ten a penny, unfortunately, even ones as nice as these. People have been using flint for half a million years, you know? Metal only for about five thousand. Metal's a flash in the pan by comparison.' Enthusiasm radiated from him. Carwyn's hopes rose that there might indeed be money to be made from his discoveries, but the thought was joined by a sour taste of jealousy. 'I'll be lucky to get a fiver each for arrowheads. Might get fifty apiece for the two stone axes. The head itself? Few hundred, maybe, if I can find the right collector. Say five hundred for the lot?'

'A thousand.'

He shook his head. 'Seven-fifty's as high as I can go. Seeing as we're mates.'

'Up front? Like I said, Khian wants it gone, but we really need the money, Rhod. Things are tight.' It pained him to say that aloud. 'You wouldn't try to cheat me?'

His friend looked genuinely hurt at the suggestion. 'Coc y gath, Carwyn, you know me better than that. Seven-fifty I'd be lucky to fetch for them at sale. If anything, it's me who's going to end up out of pocket. I'd keep looking, though, if I were you. If there's this much, there's likely more, and more would give us context, and context means value. You might even have a major find on your hands.'

'I found them all in different places though,' Carwyn said guardedly. 'These are all from the stream. The head's out of—' He paused. 'Out of another field.'

'All on the farm though, no? All up and down the same hillside a matter of, what, a mile apart? A religious site's my guess, with several thousand years of use, or one that's been abandoned and resettled over generations.' While he was speaking, he began to count out banknotes from a roll.

Carwyn wandered. Without a thought for destination, he meandered through a haze of fish and chips and car exhausts, the pavement baking in the sun. He made his way towards the seafront like a dreamer, a lone stranger in the bustling throngs of tourists, until he fetched up on the pebble beach beside the crusted iron footings of the pier, beneath the looming headland of the Orme. There he picked his way along the shore, where children raced across his path to splash into the surf, and aged couples strolled with ice creams on the promenade, and gulls wheeled vulturelike and cried and fought over their scraps. He felt adrift. A foreigner in his own country, an anachronism in his native time. He sensed a menace in the vacationers' gaiety. A seed of change akin to that the early Christian monks had planted, hid carefully beneath a front of harmless innocence, whose damaging effects would not be felt for generations. The town itself was evidence of that – a hardscrabble village of fishermen and miners not much past a century before, and then suddenly a gleaming jewel of Victorian resorts, where rich Englanders flocked by train and boat to take the air, and now something else entirely. An already-faded shadow of its reinvented self. The crescent of the bay curved off into the distance, lined with dilapidated edifices haunted by the ghost of grandeur from a heyday that had come and gone.

The loss of the head weighed upon him in a way he knew was utterly irrational. Its absence soured the beauty of the summer day, and he mourned it like the passing of a friend, as keenly as he'd felt the aftermath of his grandparents' and parents' deaths. 'And why not?' a voice inside him chided – he might well have spoken it aloud – for it had been a presence all his life and all of theirs as well, and it had perhaps always exerted influence in ways he could not fathom. It was betrayal to sell it. The money was a burden in his pocket, thirty pieces of silver for a treasure whose true worth might be beyond his estimation. He picked a pebble off the beach and cast it with a cry into the sea, and the people at their picnics watched him side-eyed and kept their children back. With the force of sudden revelation he felt that the head was an ambassador to something vital, something bigger. Rhod had surely seen it for what it was. He had been a fool to part with it for lack of patience, like slaughtering a ribbon-winning ram lamb just to have chops for dinner. The glinting ocean and the sun and all the soaring mountains seemed to cast their judgement on him, and at the urging of some inner gravity he found himself drawn back towards the auction house. There seemed no other choice. He would lay the money right back in that greedy conman's hand and brook no protestations to the contrary. The only thing that mattered was the head.

'Rhod wasn't interested in the slightest,' he told Rhian when he got back to the farm. 'Said it wasn't worth a sheep's fart and I might as well hang on to it.' She looked away from him and answered this with just an 'Oh,' and in that sound he thought he read a multitude of things. Her turned back seemed an accusation.

That night the flock was restless. Their bleating carried on long into the small hours, the way it sometimes did when something had disturbed or frightened them. The unaccustomed heat, perhaps, which had remained syrupy and cloying even at this altitude, even long after the sun had set. He wondered if a fox had got among them, but the lambs had grown enough now that they could fend for themselves, and whatever spooked them seemed to linger rather than pass through. They were sensitive to things invisible: the pressure of the air, rumblings deep underground, the magnetism of the earth. Carwyn lay wakeful, listening. He fretted for the sheep, of course – readied himself to throw his ageing body out into the dark to drive off any threat that came for them. And he worried for Rhian, for the bitter wedge of tension that his lie had driven in between them. But in the deepest undercurrents at the farthest corners of his mind, he thought about the mound. There might be more, Rhodri had told him, and with every iteration of the thought he grew more certain it was right – the head was like a capstone, or a stopper in a jar, and its discovery would lead him to the rest. What other treasures might be out there right that moment, lying just beneath the topsoil of his mountain? Gold and silver, possibly. Trinkets for which collectors with more money than sense might pay a fortune – windfalls that might save the farm. But also priceless things that never could be sold. Things that belonged to the land, and woe on anyone who tried to take them.

He remembered patchy details of another story from his childhood – of a hill that had for many centuries been known as Bryn yr Ellyllon. It seemed that locals treated it with superstitious terror, for they would tell each other tales about a giant spectre clad in golden armour that the old wives called the Brenin yr Allt, the King of the Hillside. They spoke about it as a cursed, unholy place. Only the very brave or very stupid ventured near it after dark. But in the middle of the nineteenth century, when such stories had themselves grown old, a group of quarrymen was working on the hill. Odd objects turned up in their digging: amber beads and urns and shards of bone. They came upon a buried cairn, and at its heart they found a wondrous cape of beaten gold – the mantle of a mighty Bronze Age chieftain. Carwyn did not believe the stories of the ghost. He had not even as a boy. But he rather thought the folk-tales must have had their roots in something real, the locals passing on the stories of the royal grave-mound year by year until they faded out of human recollection but persisted in their legends. The trace of memory of a king, and sacred heathen ground, and golden treasure in the hillside.

Rhian rolled over against his back and whispered, 'Are you still awake?'

He first thought to answer but did not. There was concern in her question that he did not need, that would bring only worry, nagging, disapproval. She was fussing over him more and more. Instead, he deepened his breathing to better feign sleep and felt a frisson of childlike excitement. Tomorrow, when the morning's work was done, he would resume his excavations.

V

Hazel

ASSEMBLY

The midwife did not grumble at the lateness of the hour. Though her rheumatic knees protested at the steep climb up the well-worn path, she was glad of the coolness of the night. In any case, it was expected of her trade to be fetched out any moment, and to any place, and such variety had once been pleasing to her. She had birthed babes in fields of wheat, and in church naves; in a fishwife's shanty on the pebbled shore of Llyn Padarn, and in the keep of Dolwyddelan Castle in a mighty storm; last winter in the camp of Owain Glyndŵr's tattered army on the snow-bound slopes of Moel yr Ogof. But what she craved now was routine. A bowl of rabbit stew, a chair to sit and watch the sun set in the cradle of the peaks, a stock of firewood for the coming cold. With all the new lives she had ushered in, she felt that she had earned a peaceful, solitary death.

They waited in the clearing in the moonlight, solemn as a parliament of owls. She did not know why they assembled here for matters such as these, and neither, she supposed, did they. Tradition, its roots lost to time, continuing to draw them here the way that ghosts might haunt a house long fallen into ruin.

The baby and its mother sat atop the mound, apart a little from the others. As the midwife approached, she was surrounded by a press of people keen to tell their version of the tale. The father was off fighting under Glyndŵr, and the timing of the birth was suspect. There had been rumours of unhappiness and immorality about the household even when the man was home, and it was clear his fealty to the Mab Darogan had not silenced them. The mother, they said, was a dreamer – one whose watch over the infant had been known to lapse, and as a consequence the child was fairy-struck – perhaps already spirited away and substituted with this plentyn cael, this changeling, in its place.

Stiffly, she squatted beside the mother, who told her flatly that the baby bore no love for her, nor anyone. It had a ravenous appetite, she said, and tried to bite her when she nursed it, and she had salved her breasts with lanolin but they were chapped and sore. She was weary. She handed the child to the midwife without affection, almost at arm's length. A dangerous, ill-tempered thing. But when the midwife moved aside the swaddling clothes, she found only a smiling baby girl. Her face was broad and flat, her eyes unusually angled, her ears small, her tongue protruding slightly, but no more a monster than the men and women gathered here to judge her.

Behind her, a debate had broken out. They should place a horseshoe in the cradle, said the priest, for it was well known that the Tylwyth Teg could not stand metal. More than one voice advocated for the baby to be left here on an iron shovel overnight, and come cockcrow the real child would have been returned. Others counselled mercy – best treat the plentyn cael with gentleness, lest the Fair Folk answer cruelty in kind. A grizzled veteran girded with a sword believed the best course was to slay *the creature forthwith, before it could cause untold misfortune. In the commotion, no one saw the midwife slip away into the night, the babe still bundled in her arms. Only the mother watched her go.*

By the summer Carwyn turned eighteen, he'd grown into a strapping lad. The image of a mountain chieftain's son, belonging to a bygone Wales when Rome was still a rumour on the breeze. Farm work had made him strong-backed as a longbowman; unkempt as a hedgerow Druid; hard and rugged as a Celt rhyfelwr. He might have fought with Caradog against Scapula's legions, or driven back the Norsemen at Enegyd, or crossed the Severn with Glyndŵr, and he would not have looked a stranger in those armies. He was an altogether fierce-looking feral youth.

But for all his warlike presence, the abiding sense for those he knew was one of awkward softness, as if he was embarrassed by his strength. He would have made a truly awful battle chief, for he would sooner pick wild berries than a fight, and when his sometime classmates waged their schoolyard skirmishes he mostly tasked himself with dragging them apart. His father had entrusted him with his own starter flock, and young Carwyn tended them with a religious dedication. At lambing time, he slept out in the pasture to watch over them, and one night a year or so before, a badger came across him in his sleeping bag, almost nose to nose, and he could still picture its look of confused startlement as it tried to puzzle out what this creature was. He gave names to the flock and learned to recognize each ewe. Last winter, he had lugged a rusty stove out to the barn and spent the snowy evenings cowled in sheepskin like an impostor among them, feeding logs into the fire while his parents watched from the warm house and called him mad. His mother said he was a method shepherd, like those actors she had heard about. He had to know what it was like to be a sheep, he reasoned, so that he could know exactly what they needed.

He had adhered to his agnostic attitude to formal education, attending school when the urge moved him, or when it was raining, or when he came across an interesting object in the stream-bed and wanted to ask a teacher what it was: 'How old is this?' 'Five thousand years or so.' 'What about this?' 'Could be ten thousand. Back to work.' Mr Morgan in particular was an authority on all things prehistoric – the kind of fledgling teacher who seemed utterly unsuited to the job, but whose enthusiasm was infectious, not yet dulled by the drudgery of a tiny rural comprehensive. He told the class one day about a cave in Cefn Meriadog, where that very year a team of archaeologists had found a fragment of a human jaw. It had not seemed to Carwyn the most monumental of discoveries, until Mr Morgan added that it was Neanderthal and had been dated to 230,000 years ago. He wrote it out in words across the blackboard. Two hundred and thirty thousand. The sheer number floored Carwyn, even as a restless schoolboy on the cusp of adulthood. A little fragment of a fellow person separated from him by a dizzying immensity of time – twenty times older than his oldest flint-shard arrowheads, fifty times older than the Pyramids, a hundred times older than Christ – the relic of a boy not vastly different from himself who lived and died along the River Elwy. And still just yesterday compared to the age of the mountains, themselves only an eye-blink in the unfathomable time span of the cosmos. His own life felt minute against such vastnesses. Everything he had was fleeting. He was going to die, and be reduced to bones, and then to fragments, and then finally to dust, until even the very thought of him was inconceivable, and all the while the universe would march ahead relentlessly into the alien, abyssal future.

The only other thing that could reliably coax him to those final years of school was rugby. It was as close as many of the mountain farm-boys came to a religion, and they were not lacking, at that time, in muddy, red-jerseyed messiahs to emulate, for this was the heyday of Gareth Edwards, Barry John, JPR Williams, and others whose names would echo through the annals of the sport. A glorious golden age perhaps never to be repeated. The school could cobble together only a poor imitation of a team: a mob of clumsy, spotty boys outfitted in mismatched and mended strips, some playing in their work boots, fresh from mowing hay with strands of it still poking from their hair, practising their tackles on a burlap sack of soil and scrummaging in schoolyard dirt until they looked like ochre-painted cavemen straight from Mr Morgan's class. But what they lacked in style, they made up for in spirit. They were outclassed at nearly every game by bigger, richer schools from towns along the coast, but they were never made a laughing stock, because they played with wild and reckless fervour, like a tribe of highland savages. Carwyn was selected mostly for the fact that he turned up reliably to practices. Their sports teacher was very much a beggar, not a chooser.

He next saw Rhian Nevett on the day of the match-winning try. His memories of it came in snatches of sensation – the smells of grass and talc and Deep Heat in the changing rooms behind the village hall; the scratchiness of his old jersey; the clatter of studded boots along a lino corridor into the sudden brightness of a summer afternoon. Something gladiatorial in that emergence. She had been standing out beyond the uprights on the far side of the pitch, a somehow singular figure in the press of farmers come grudgingly from their flocks, and local children shouting after older siblings, and the well-dressed parents brought by bus from some expensive public school. Even five years on, he knew her at a glance. Blodeuwedd in the summer, grown up flower-wise – taller and thornier and more beautiful, with water mint and harebell in her curls. He recalled a young man in the blue-and-white stripes of the other team, a pristine fifteen printed on his back, returning to her with an ice cream from the van, and that this blond-haired stranger had lifted her and kissed her before jogging out to take his place. She had whistled after him with fingers at the corners of her lips, and the noise had shrilled and then been lost among the rising murmur of the crowd.

The match was a chaotic, grinding slog, both teams afire in the heat and unwilling to cede an inch – flying viciously into the tackles so that as the clock ticked down into its final minutes, the score was close and every boy was bruised and bloodied and bone-tired. But something in the sneering attitude of their opponents lit a fire under Carwyn's team. What happened next seemed to take place in short, surreal vignettes. Slow underwater motion. The visiting supporters on the touchline had struck up a mocking chant: *Does your livestock know you're here?* The pitchside clock showed two more minutes left to remedy a three-point deficit. There was a messy clearance, the opposition driving deep into Carwyn's team's twenty-two, the ball coming loose out of a misthrown line-out, almost to his feet. He remembered seizing it, and looking up surprised to see a glimmer of an opening, and launching his last weary strength into a desperate charge. Hands grasped at him as he burst free from the scramble, he felt the faintest brush of reaching fingertips against his sleeve, and then he was away. He tore up the wing as though his boots might set the grass aflame. Like shit through a goose, was how his father would describe it afterwards. There was a sense of several people closing on him very fast, but only the opposing full back standing in his way. He could still picture the look of surprised realization dawning too late on his rival's face as Carwyn chipped the ball over his head – the tall boy stretching, leaping, falling short. He remembered chasing, chasing the ball with all his might as it dinked and bounced towards the goal line, and last of all the crowd erupting as he dived headlong to score. Even at the time, it felt like he was living moments out of someone else's life.

The aftermath had faded into the low-definition reaches of his memory reserved for less momentous things, reduced to mostly static images. A blur of the pursuing players crashing down on top of him a sliver of a second late; of standing stupefied among his teammates as they rushed up to congratulate him; of being hoisted up onto the shoulders of the crowd and bobbing there above them like a coracle in a cascade. He felt like the recipient of a thorough beating. Half blind with sweat. Dizzied by a potent cocktail of emotions: pride and exhaustion and euphoric disbelief, and if he thought about it hard enough, he could still summon up the ghosts of those sensations, the way the scent of whisky lingers in long-empty bottles. The way he sometimes caught a trace of his grandmother's perfume on the landing. But what came back to him most clearly was the sudden tug of disappointment when he looked across the thinning scatter of spectators and discovered that the girl was nowhere to be seen.

He spent the evening in the crowded, smoky barroom of the Tanronen Hotel, being bought endless pints of bitter by well-wishers from the match, until the stout oak ceiling beams grew bendy and the patterns in the threadbare carpet roiled and shifted and pulsated like the markings on a cuttlefish. It was his first real foray into quantitative drinking. No sooner had he swilled the dregs of one glass than some teammate or old toothless village patriarch would set the next one down before him, and it would have been the height of impoliteness to refuse. 'You did well, boy,' they all told him. Their faces blended with those in the sepia photographs of quarrymen and washerwomen on the walls.

At some late hour after normal closing time, he became aware that he was going to vomit. The impenetrable mass of people at the bar had shaken him by the hand and trickled out, so that only the most dedicated drunks remained, and Carwyn found himself alone behind a raft of beer mats and empty pint mugs at the little polished table as if pondering how to build himself a means of getting home. He had sobered somewhat, but he had been reluctant to get up when all his friends began to leave, for he feared his legs might yet betray him if he tried to navigate the perilous terrain of stools and chairs that stretched between him and the door. His stomach sloshed with every movement. Ridiculous, he thought, to have consumed so large a quantity of anything, like drinking gallon after gallon of tomato soup. He resolved to stay and try to keep it down, tried not to think of it.

Instead, his thoughts were drawn towards a print of Vosper's *Salem* like the one that hung in Nain and Taid's room – an old woman standing in a chapel in a stovepipe hat and shawl – and the more he looked the more convinced he was that he could see a multitude of hidden figures. Not just the famous Devil in the frills and folds and paisley pattern of the cloak (which Vosper, to his dying day, denied was ever there), but translucent, ghostly faces pressed against the chapel window; monstrous forms among the congregation; writhing horrors in the grain of wooden pews. He felt his head spin and his gorge rise, and he stood and lurched across the canted floor and out into the night.

He burst into the fragrant darkness, loose from the last clinging scent of sweat and smoke and stale beer from the barroom. The pavement seemed to tilt and roll beneath his feet. Across the road he staggered, seeking purchase in a world grown volatile and wavering, until he fetched up at the humpbacked bridge across the Afon Colwyn, the river just a babble in its rocky bed. There he stood, draped on the parapet, retching empty mouthfuls of bitter, beery air into the glistening shadows like a speaker of some foul primordial tongue, and even the river stones seemed to surge up before his eyes and fall away again in nauseating repetition.

He had enough sense to know it would be unwise to try to make the journey home. The moon was full and bright, and the clear sky awash with stars, and the familiar looming shapes of mountains would have funnelled him along the valley so he could not lose his way; but he had premonitions of stumbling into the lake or stepping off a precipice or meeting something lurking in the dark.

It occurred to him that he might just sleep where he was, suspended by his armpits the way Victorian poorhouse inmates used to nap hung over lengths of rope. Or curl up beneath one of the arches of the bridge, a troll in jeans and a red jersey. The urge to vomit had receded, but in its place emerged the aches and bruises and pulled muscles from the match, and he was debating whether he should go back to the pub and ask to call his parents when a voice said, somewhat impatiently, 'Shift over a bit then, will you?'

When he turned, the girl was standing at the parapet beside him, leaning over to look down into the pool of shadows where the water sounded in its flowing like the piteous whisperings of the drowned. She scrutinized it briefly, as though she wished to be let in on whatever had drawn his fascination, and then, evidently unimpressed, seemed to wait for him to offer something worthwhile in its place. Carwyn drew himself up straighter, feigning nonchalance, feigning sobriety. 'I saw you at the match.' He wondered if he sounded as drunk as he felt.

'Did you?' she said, and it was clear from her tone that the question was rhetorical. She laid her hands on the rough stones, a pair of silver bracelets chiming softly on her wrist, and up close there was a ruddiness about her – not the slender, fey, translucent being she had seemed in daylight, but the beginnings of an altogether sturdier back-country woman showing through her waning girlhood.

'It's late, what are you doing out?' he asked.

'I got the wrong idea of someone.' Again, her bluntness declared that avenue of conversation closed. She slipped off one of her bracelets and rotated it distractedly between her fingers.

For an uncanny moment, he could see them standing there as

an observer might — two tiny figures on a bridge among the last few lighted windows of the village. Every street lamp dark. And all around them, midnight country where serrated silhouettes of peaks and ridges carved into the heavens, so the sum of all creation seemed contained in that topography with they two at its epicentre.

To break the silence, Carwyn took the stubby earthen figurine out of his pocket and set it on the parapet. 'What do you think that is?'

She picked it up and held it to the light from the pub windows and then put it back again with a brief shiver of revulsion. 'It's horrible. Is that your lucky charm?'

He laughed. 'It might be now, the day I've had. I don't know, it was in a stream up on my parents' land. I think it's old. I like the feel of it.'

'I don't,' she said. 'You know, people used to throw their valuables in streams and wells. Tools, coins, jewellery, things like that. It must have meant something to someone once.'

'What for?'

'A sacrifice, I guess. An offering. Because the water was so vital to them.' They listened, for a moment, to the Colwyn as it burbled underneath the bridge. 'Or they might have thought the water was a *thin* place, where their gods were.' With that, she took off her other bracelet and cast them both one by one into the river. They caught the light as they flew, turning, through the air and then, without even the smallest splash, the Bible-blackness of the current swallowed them and they were gone.

Carwyn looked at her as if she might be just some figment of his drunken state. It felt like he had witnessed an unravelling in the sturdy fabric of reality that underlaid his universe. 'What did you do that for?'

She shrugged. 'To see if it still works.'

They stood and talked for hours, until the last window darkened and the only light came from the moon and constellations, and it seemed there was no living soul in all the world but them. It might have been the colouring of hindsight, but there was an ease about their conversation – a sense that they had known each other many years and could share secrets in this strange nocturnal no man's land that never would be uttered in the light of day. He did not know if she remembered him at all, and was afraid to ask, for it might break whatever spell was on them. Afterwards, he would remember the impression that the black and towering landscape gathered closer in the dark. Listening. And after they ran low on things to talk about, they still were not inclined to part and stood in bashful silence, basking in the other's company. When the night chill crept down from off the mountains, she stepped in close against him shivering. He put his arms around her shoulders, and she told him, 'To be clear, I'm only cold. I'm done with boys for good.'

He thought to say, 'We're not all bad,' but then decided that it would have been at best a hollow boast, at worst a lie. Instead, he only held her, saying nothing, and they did not part until the village had begun to stir and the first light of dawn was bleeding into the complicit sky.

Over the course of many weeks, he did his best to play the part of courtly suitor. It was a role for which he found himself to be in every aspect comically unsuited, like when a pasty, ginger-headed lad had been cast as Othello in the school production. While the village boys went out in the belated rural imitations of the current fashions – wide-collared shirts and Levi's jeans and George Best haircuts – Carwyn's clothes were plainly functional and smelled perpetually of sheep. A couple of the older boys had motorbikes. Carwyn had a five-mile walk down country lanes. Try as he might to look presentable for Rhian – he would fix his hair and scrub himself until his skin was raw before he left the farm – it was the height of summer, and he arrived without fail sweating and dishevelled, looking not unlike a scarecrow that had run a hundred-metre dash. Where his rivals might have offered grand bouquets of roses from the florist, he brought scrawny sprigs of clover and hedge mustard and bell heather, picked at random on the way. The rituals of courtship were obscure and alien to him as the most arcane ceremonies of the Druids.

Rhian, for her part, was equally unlike a damsel in a tower. For starters, she was almost never home. She lived in a stone terraced house behind her father's garage, and she seemed to view the place as a bird might its nest – somewhere to roost at night until the time came to be fledged and then migrate to distant, warmer shores. And yet at once she was entirely rooted in the landscape. For all the allure of leaving, walking barefoot on a beach while the sun set fire to the Aegean Sea, or living as a punk in Camden Town, or wandering rootless all across the world, she told him later that she could not quite conceive of any life beyond the mountains. They were the anchor points of her existence. Without them, she said, some deep part of her feared she might find herself adrift, thrown to the mercy of new currents and new predators, a goldfish suddenly released into the open sea.

A few years later, on a snowy morning when they smelled of smoke and kerosene, she told him that she used to view the steady flow of wooing princes mostly as a source of entertainment rather than affection, and their visits were transactional, small acts of rebellion against her father's strictures. With time, she had become adept at calculating the bare minimum of her time and attention she might barter for a film, an ice cream, a trip into town. He guessed they must have each found her a changeling, malleable to their company, but distant, frosty, and then gone when next they came to call for her. She grew bored of their invariable sameness. What she liked most, she said, when there was nothing she desired from them, was just to hike alone up to the tŷ unnos or sit atop the mossy, ruined keep on Dinas Emrys, even on a rainy day, and eat her sandwiches in reflective seclusion while the weather rolled across the miles of rugged land.

He could remember very vividly the first night he came calling at her house. It had been one of those rare August afternoons that feel as if the summer might stretch on forever, the thought of school and rain and winter distant as the memory of dreams, and the future lying bright and boundless at his feet. He had been making hay down in a neighbour's pasture in the valley, where fieldmice darted in the cut grass and the air was thick with flying gossamers of chaff. The crop that year would be a good one. Strands of it had lighted in his hair and collar as he rode atop the rusted tractor, crowning him with gold, and after, with the sweat of honest labour on his brow and money in his pocket, he could think himself the king of all that he surveyed.

He walked to town through banks of wildflowers, the berry brambles twining all among them and the boughs of apple trees all groaning with the weight of fruit. Iridescent dragonflies and bumblebees the size of hens' eggs buzzed around him as he passed. The wild abundance buoyed him. It seemed the world conspired in affirmation of his burgeoning youth. His nain would have read signs and auguries in every leaf and petal, every fly's trajectory, every rabbit's step, and found them all encouraging. By the time he fetched up at the outskirts of the village, though, his doubts began to make their voices heard. At each shopfront and car window, he paused a beat to smarten his reflection, but between one and the next it seemed some lick of hair would spring back out of place, and he came face to face with more than one perplexed old lady into whose front parlour he'd been staring with a look of intense concentration. In his restlessness, he had eaten a few too many blackberries along the way. His stomach gave forth guttural digestive noises with each step. The fine handful of cornflowers he'd picked had wilted in the evening heat, so that they looked like stolen offerings from a grave, and he discarded them beneath a hedge at the end of her street. He thought of turning tail and heading home.

From inside the house he thought he heard the slamming of a door. The sound of muffled, unintelligible voices raised in argument. It seemed to come from different places, and indeed, he glimpsed them moving in the windows, upstairs first, and then below: one smaller, slimmer silhouette, and following behind the broad and hulking figure of a man. He found himself conflicted. The greater part of him was firmly in the camp of minding his own business. Whatever family dispute was going on was no concern of his, and besides, how would he intervene? And yet, the child he had been still persisted somewhere at his core. He thought of his feet planted firmly on the dirt floor of the old, abandoned house, stick in hand, with the girl's raging, ogrish father bearing down towards him like a fighting bull, and he imagined himself in the same position now. Culhwch undaunted at the giant chieftain Ysbaddaden's fearsome court.

But then several things happened at once. The cottage's front door opened with such force that it seemed it would be splintered on its hinges and Rhian came storming out. She crossed the yard towards him, pulling on her shoes and jacket with a graceless, hopping gait, and he could tell that she had recently been crying; but there was a fiery, elemental fury to her – not in flight but leaving on some urgent errand. Barely a second later, her father appeared in the doorway, but did not advance. He was not quite the dark, colossal beast he had become in Carwyn's memory – a little smaller than a giant, slightly greyer at the temples, somewhat rounder at the belly – but he was still a formidable figure. He flung a boot after his daughter, shouting, 'If you go now, don't come back,' and then he slammed the door and disappeared into the house.

Carwyn thought of retreating out of sight, pretending that he'd only just arrived, or fleeing altogether and returning on a calmer day, but it was too late, she had seen him. 'What are you doing here?' she asked impatiently. She palmed a rivulet of tears from off her cheek as if its presence there offended her.

He looked about for something that might save him, but found nothing helpful. 'I was just—' he stammered. 'I was just passing. I was just on my way home.' He pointed in some vague direction.

For a heartbeat she stood regarding him, her eyes still red from crying, her brow just slightly furrowed, as if by looking hard enough she might read the direction of his thoughts. She picked a strand of hay out of his collar and released it to the breeze. Then she said, 'Take me with you.'

She spent the best part of a week up on the farm, and it seemed to them the overdue continuation of the time that was cut short when first they met. His nain and taid and parents asked no questions, but treated their houseguest with stiff, unpractised hospitality, as they might have a foreign dignitary or a wandering minister. Carwyn slept out in the long barn with the sheep and dogs, because his visitor was in his bed – made up by his mother with fresh sheets and blankets saved for best. It would have been scandalous, now grown as they both were, to share a room. Even to sleep with only the yard's width between them felt frighteningly intimate. He stood, as night fell, in the doorway of the barn and watched the light in his own curtained window, sensing that a threshold had been crossed and a stark line of closure had been drawn indelibly beneath his childhood.

When he came in for breakfast the first morning, he found the kitchen changed beyond all recognition: Nain's finest china laid out on a linen tablecloth, and vases of wildflowers that his taid had picked on his evening walk; a rack of toast, and eggs in dainty cups, and Rhian at the centre of it all like a crowned Prifardd at the Eisteddfod, looking slightly awkward with a sprig of campion in her hair while Carwyn's father ceremoniously poured her tea. She was not, perhaps, the match his family would have wanted for him – no farm she could inherit and combine with his, no flock, no youth spent so entirely with sheep that she would need no teaching in the matter. A summer fling, but not marriage material, for she would only move away and leave him pining. But damned if she did not look *right* there somehow at that table.

After they had eaten and the morning's chores were done, they went out walking, and he took her to the limits of the farm. To the summer meadows where the birds sang and the flock cropped lazily among the wildflowers. To the field where the stream ran glistening in its bed of stones, and still, in those days, offered up its treasures with some regularity. And down to the stone wall beside the lane, and to the shearing pens, and to the fairy wood with its old rusted, padlocked gate. Up, then, to the highest pastures where the grass was short and sere and grew begrudgingly between the scatterings of rock. The day was bright and warm, but at that hour a band of something neither fully mist nor cloud clung to the contours of the hillside, and climbing through it was like trespassing into the borders of the afterlife. She took his hand, and he could feel that she was shivering. The air was damp, and the view curtailed and milky, indistinct. He had to trust that his feet knew the way, for in that opaque world a wrong step would be easy and might send them hand in hand over a precipice or loose a slide of jagged stones to bury them. She said, 'It's like we're ghosts.'

And then, somewhat abruptly, they emerged above the clouds into the pure and brilliant sunshine. They were both giddy from the altitude. The view as much as the exertion made them stop to catch their breath. They passed along a ridge, an island in a sea of fog that seemed to stretch on infinite in all directions, and their only company was the mighty peaks that pierced the white and a lone buzzard wheeling in the blinding sky.

He had bent to pick a Snowdon lily and was placing it behind her ear as delicately as his clumsy fingers would allow when her grip suddenly tightened on his arm and she said, 'Carwyn.' At first, he almost misinterpreted the gesture as the prelude to a kiss, but when he turned to her he saw that she was looking past him, fearful. It made his heart lurch, too, when he saw what had frightened her. Below them, in the mist, there stood a pair of gaunt, gigantic figures. They were dark and indistinct, obscured as they were by the fog, and as it rolled and shifted, so did they. Their shapes bled into and out of one another, making it seem one moment there were two, then one, then a vast and swarming congregation, then two again. Something uncanny in the way they moved, although, if pressed, he would have been unable to say what – only that its wrongness unsettled some deep part of him. Strange, sun dog rainbows haloed them. The mist that cloaked them robbed them of their scale, so that they might have been ten feet tall and close, or fifty feet tall and further away, though in that moment he could not say which would have been worse.

Instinctively, he stepped in front of Rhian. There was nowhere else to go, nowhere to hide, the ridgeline bald and narrow and the only way down past the looming spectres in the fog. He bent again to where he'd picked the flower, and this time he came up with a stone. No plan in his mind. No logic, even, in that instant. Only the stubborn will to stand and fight whatever came. He took aim at the indistinct monstrosities and raised his arm to throw.

To his surprise, one of the giant figures did the same. Behind him, Rhian had begun to laugh, and when his mind arrived a moment later at the same realization, he did too. They both waved, and the shadows in the mist waved back. For a long time, they both stood breathless, laughing and embarrassed and relieved. She told him they could never again look down on people who had long ago believed that there were giants haunting these high slopes, for they had believed exactly that themselves, and when he agreed she stepped in and embraced him. For a moment he could smell the flowers in her hair. He could feel the spot where she had printed herself on his cheek. And in that instant, in their private world above the clouds with their hearts still racing from their fright and the sunlight fresh as the first pressing of an apple, he felt sure again that she was the most wondrous being in creation.

In the evenings, after Rhian went inside to bed, he sat out in the yard as the moon crossed the mountains and tried to carve a love-spoon for her. He could see the finished work in his imagination. A thing of ornate intricacy, like the arm-length ones that hung above the parlour fireplace – moving chains and knots and daffodils and dragons all carved from a single piece of wood. The courting tokens of his grandparents and their grandparents and of others long before them. It took shape with agonizing slowness from the sycamore stick he had carried on the day they met, which seemed with hindsight singularly badly chosen for the purpose – full of knots and whorls and awkward kinks – but he persevered. The more difficult the making, he persuaded himself, the more heartfelt would be the gift. Too crude, perhaps, to bear the lofty name of art, but no less meaningful for that. There was a satisfaction in the process, too, the shaping of an object into something else, a pleasing comfort that might not have been unfamiliar to the stone age boy from Mr Morgan's class. Each night when he at last retreated to the barn to sleep, it was transformed a little more from what it had been when he started. A little further on in its transfiguration from branch into spoon. And the more it took its shape, the more concrete the sense became that the love-spoon was exactly what the piece of wood was always meant to be; that the tree had grown with this purpose in mind. His chisel strokes were not creating but revealing.

And so it was with disappointment that he viewed the finished article. It was a little shorter than he had first pictured it – about the length of his forearm and as broad as the palm of his hand. Each time he felt that it was done, something compelled him to make one final small adjustment to perfect it, and the process of trimming and correcting had left it intricate but ugly. Eventually, he hid it in the barn, not willing, yet, to just throw it away, but neither wanting anyone to ever see it.

After dinner on the fifth day, Rhian asked if he would walk her home. She seemed not to relish the thought of leaving any more than he did, and indeed, the past few days it had begun to feel as though she'd somehow never go. They had both allowed themselves to bask in the illusion that their lives might stay exactly so forever. But the walk back along the valley road was filled with hope. They talked of when they next would meet, and what they would do then, and how they might recreate for themselves a future in the image of those glorious August days. The sky was rose gold. Swallows swooped and dipped out on the lake, and the sheep of all the valley flocks called peacefully to one another from the hillsides. It was not cold, but Rhian walked with Carwyn's jacket draped around her shoulders. If he could choose one moment to exist in for eternity, he would have been hard pressed to find a better one.

When they arrived back at her house, it was beginning to grow dark. There were no lights in any windows of the cottage. She kissed him on the cheek at the entrance to her yard, and afterwards they stood grinning shyly, furtively at one another in that way that only teenagers are capable of doing, until she turned without a word and went inside.

The double doors of Rhian's father's workshop, padlocked from the inside with a heavy chain, stood ajar just enough to spill a crack of yellow light across the drive. It looked almost welcoming. As Carwyn passed, he peeked in and could see a group of men in overalls around the glow of an old miner's lamp. There were some that he knew from the farmers' auction, and a couple from his evening at the pub – perhaps a dozen altogether.

'—somewhere down by Birmingham,' a man was saying. He was the village undertaker, Carwyn recognized. 'I'd have preferred if she could stay close, of course. But the house prices are just a joke here now – it was that or living with her mam and me for ever. Funerals are no business for a girl of her age anyway.' He turned to Rhian's father. 'Is yours still causing trouble?' Carwyn's ears pricked up at this. He stopped and backtracked a few steps to listen in.

'Just like her mother was. I'm sick of trying to argue with her.' The hulking man rocked in his chair and took a deep swig from a brown glass bottle. 'Can't bloody tell her anything – she'll do the exact opposite of what I say.'

'Boys again?' a man in wellingtons and a wool jumper asked, a note of sympathy in his voice as if they'd had this conversation many times before.

Rhian's father nodded. 'Boys.' He jerked his thumb over his shoulder at the door, and Carwyn felt a stab of panic, thinking for a moment that he must have been discovered at his eavesdropping, but nobody looked up. 'She's off now with another one. Some farm lad up the valley this time.' Scoffs and tuts and rolling eyes at this that made him bristle. 'An education's what she needs. Off to university in Durham in the autumn, with a bit of luck. She'll thank me for it one day.'

The grocer said, 'It's not right, is it? If you want a better future for your children, send them out of Wales.'

'And who's replacing them?' the undertaker asked rhetorically. 'Bloody English pensioners, that's who. People who couldn't give a ha'penny shit about this place. It's like you were saying before, Siôn. They're buying all the houses cheap and driving prices up and then leaving them empty till they want to come on holiday.' He glanced towards the door and the anger on his face made Carwyn draw a little further back into the safety of the dark.

'I was down the Llŷn the other day,' someone agreed. 'There's whole villages down there completely deserted. All second homes. No shops, no pubs, no nothing.'

Rhian's father leaned into the lamplight. He seemed made all of rugged angles and hard shadows. 'What can we do about it though?' He switched to English and adopted a surprisingly convincing RP accent. 'A petition to the Welsh Office, perhaps?' Louder laughter broke out now. One man even slapped his thigh.

The undertaker chuckled bitterly. 'To be honest, I'd as soon see all those empty houses burnt.'

Rhian's father grinned. 'That's not a bad idea, Ed.' He raised a jerrycan and shook it, and the sloshing of the liquid in it was drowned by a drunken cheer from all the gathered men.

THE HILL IN THE DARK GROVE

Their laughter followed Carwyn down the drive and out of the gate. In his elation, he could not have been less interested in their grievances or their bravado. He walked home singing 'Bread of Heaven', feeling he had cracked the mystery of a happy life.

He was still singing when he came into the farmhouse kitchen. Rhian had not been gone more than an hour, but already he was pining for her company. His own home felt lacking and forlorn. His parents and his grandmother were sitting at the table, drinking mugs of tea while the news crackled from the radio.

'Where's Taid?' he asked, not wanting to provide an opening for the questions that would inevitably follow now he was alone.

His nain got up and hobbled to the sink, where she rinsed out her mug alongside tins of hoof-care spray and jars of worming pellets. 'Go and get him, would you? He's not back from his walk yet, and it's getting cold.'

'He's probably fallen asleep out there again,' his father added.

He was glad of an excuse to go outside again. He took his time. Past the battered wire chicken runs where the hens cooed softly from their roosts. Past the corrugated tin and slate and rough stone buildings of the yard, the night already creeping fully formed from underneath their eaves. Past the wooden farmyard gate tied shut with twine, where he could see right down the valley to the hog's back outline of Moel Hebog haloed in the last fire of the sunset, and then out into the fields. Asleep, he thought. His taid would be asleep again, as he had been so many times before. Sat down to rest and nodded off and lost track of the time. He heard the keening of a night bird, and for a reason that he did not understand he thought of the cyhyraeth – the portent, which was heard by those about to die. He shivered and picked up his pace.

His taid was sitting cross-legged at the top end of the lower field, gazing out towards the last faint embers of the sun, and Carwyn called to him as he mounted the stile, but he did not respond. The old man sat enraptured, staring down the hill as if a shimmering procession of the Tylwyth Teg had come up from the trees beyond the padlocked gate and left him deaf and dumb with awe. The breeze carried the phantom odour of his pipe smoke; the smell of mountain heather; the bleating of ewes. Carwyn stopped in place astride the wall, struck suddenly by the eerie stillness of the scene. 'Taid?' he called again, more hesitantly this time, but still his grandfather sat motionless. His two collies, Hemp and Brychan, sat close, attentive, keeping guard. There was something of the monk about his posture – something of the old hermits who were said to mummify themselves alive – and for a moment he could almost have believed his taid was in a state of deep and transcendental meditation. But before he had descended from the stile and crossed the few short paces of the field, Carwyn could tell with every fibre of his being he was dead.

It was not the glassy blankness of his dry, unblinking eyes, nor his mouth that hung agape, trailing a silver ribbon of spittle, nor the waxen, candle-coloured pallor of his skin that was the giveaway. All these things Carwyn saw and catalogued and pushed to some back corner of his mind to later haunt his grief, but they were not the markers of death's passage there. Rather, it was the impression of utter absence. He could not feel the slightest trace of his taid's presence on that mountainside – the seated, lifeless form simply did not contain him any more.

It seemed a husk, an empty shell, a cast-off like the shed skin of a snake. Neither did his ghost seem still to linger close at hand, and Carwyn stood beside his body stunned at how completely every trace of him seemed to have vanished from the world. His mind clawed fruitlessly for any piece that might remain, and found not one – a photograph or two, perhaps; a clutch of trinkets; his contributions to the drystone walls; some scribbles in an auction stock book. Not a single thing that would be left to stand to mark his presence on the earth once those who could remember him had followed into death. His grandfather was solid gone. A memory, growing fainter, and then nothing.

He felt no shock, no fear, no sadness, but stood with his beloved old taid's corpse beneath the cold, indifferent stars and catalogued the details of the moment with a strange dispassion, like an anthropologist or an accountant. The grief would hit him later, inescapably and at the strangest times – at the farmers' auction, or in the bathroom, or on the night before his wedding – and when it came it was a foretaste of the steady, growing losses he would feel as one by one his other loved ones passed away, but in that instant he could not produce a single tear. How monstrous he had felt, then. He'd wept for dogs and lambs and rugby scores, and here he stood like stone beside the empty ruin of his taid, feeling numbed and shell-shocked by the sheer futility of it all.

It was a fitting end, he supposed, and how he might one day be glad to go himself. There seemed a privilege in it – to die out in the sun on land you owned with just your flock and dogs and mountains in attendance. He wondered if old Taid had known the end had come. Hobbled out into the fields to be alone the way the farmyard cats would seek a quiet spot to die in private. An echo of Nain's stories where aged warriors would lash themselves to stones so they could perish upright, outdoors, on their feet. But there was, too, in such a death, a horrid loneliness. He stood and tried to gauge the view that must have been his poor taid's last – a panorama of bare slate and scarp and scree and empty sky, and droughty grass and drystone walls that all seemed to conspire to draw the eye towards the little scrap of woods beyond the overgrown and rusted gate, with nary another human soul upon the whole vast face of it. Alone, alone, alone, for miles. The sheep stood cropping all around in mute assembly.

VI

Vine

REAPING

At reaping time, they led the bound boy to the gathering place. He was a fair youth, unmarred by the grim disfigurements that were so widespread then as to draw little notice: pox scars, warts and buboes; hunchbacks and broken limbs set crudely; even the occasional wandering leper exiled to the colony at Llanfaes. His sisters had braided his golden hair with buttercups and daisies. The women showered kisses on him, and the older men plied him with ale, and when they tied his wrists to lead him up the mountain, he went with them gladly, staggering and singing.

A bright procession danced uphill through meadows lush with late-September flowers, and these were plucked and added to the decoration of the boy until he might lie down and be mistaken for a garden. Some of the revellers beat a tabwrdd or blew clarions so that rapturous music heralded their coming. The boy's mother walked beside him, weeping, but it was not clear if her tears were of grief or joy or some measure of each.

Of late, this had become their way of giving thanks. It had begun some years before with sheaves of wheat left on the ancient barrow in the clearing as an offering of gratitude – a *light-hearted echo of a memory of a tradition from their grandfathers' grandfathers' time. But so effective had it been that the next year they offered up a tithe of all their crops, and for the harvest after that they took a sow and slaughtered it, and afterwards there was great merriment and feasting. The next year, their lord brought one of his wolf-hounds. They did not regard these practices as pagan, any more than when they baked sweet buns at Easter or went wassailing to celebrate the birth of Christ. Their faith was built upon subsuming older rituals.*

Most crucially, it seemed to work. When word came that the coastal towns were ravaged by a pestilence, they did not sicken. While drought shrivelled their neighbours' crops, their fields were blessed with rain, but when a flood drowned the next valley, theirs was dry. When the soldiers of King John came rampaging across the River Conwy, Prince Llywelyn drove them back. To stop now would invite catastrophe.

They referred to the god of the clearing only euphemistically: the Antlered One, the Watchful One, the One-from-Many. Sometimes obliquely by the place it dwelt – the Stones, although by then the only ones still visible were the crumbled, mossy ruins of the fallen chapel. They spoke of it as interchangeable with their familiar Christian God. Or rather, they applied the terms and trappings of their Christianity as a disguise, as though the elder deity had donned the interloper's skin and carried on elsewise unaltered. Half suspecting them to be wild heathens anyway, the bishops and the abbots of the lowland priories did not intrude. They shivered down there in their draughty chambers, happy not to know and not to wonder what the distant music from the mountains meant.

In September something started living in the attic. Neither of them ever saw it, but they knew it by its smell – an acrid, urinous musk that seeped down through the ceiling hatches, like the deep scent in the dens of nesting animals. At night, they heard it moving, sometimes skittering, sometimes slithering, sometimes tramping with a heavy, almost human tread. When it was still, they felt its presence up there, the way prehistoric people might have sensed a lion or a cave bear prowling somewhere in the karsts and warrens just beyond the reaches of their firelight, and the sensation was entirely physical – a rising of the hackles and a prickling in the fine hairs of the arms and neck. A marten or a stoat, they told each other, maybe more than one. Carwyn went up by torchlight several times into the old, oppressive darkness, setting traps and plugging holes and checking for the telltale signs of vermin, but he never found the slightest trace. The traps remained untouched, the poisoned bait uneaten. Even the mice seemed to have disappeared.

Eira took, for the first time in all her life, to sleeping at the foot of the bed. The barnyard cats claimed her spot in the kitchen, and even the bold, crepuscular chickens no longer ventured from their roosting boxes after dark, so that, beyond the thickness of the farmhouse walls, the night pressed down on them with leaden, smothering silence.

He had begun to dig again. Surreptitiously at first, stealing moments here and there between his chores so Rhian would not worry, but latterly to the exclusion of all else. The days were already starting to shorten, the dawn arriving on the mountaintops a little later and a little further south each morning, so that the entire landscape was a kind of sundial. Often he was out before the cockcrows, taking Eira and his pick and shovel down beyond the trees into the bottom field. He was certain of a find of the most monumental import lying buried just beneath the soil. It seemed a duty to reveal it. From the first trench he opened back in April when he found the head, he had begun a series of test pits in a large circle just beyond the mound's base. Two or three a month since May at careful pace. And to prove his instincts true, each one he excavated was a treasure trove – bringing up first tiny artefacts of bone and beads and arrowheads, and then larger objects standing there in situ, each one taking days of excavation. The mound was surrounded by a ring of jagged megalithic stones.

It was a morning of glorious Indian summer. The dry, oppressive heat of August, unlike any August he had known, had given way to weeks of pleasant weather. The sky was the colour of cornflowers, and what few clouds passed overhead were small and cottony, without the threat of rain. The daylight had a golden quality. Down in the valley, several of the trees had begun their transition into autumn, but the flowers and the animals were bursting back to life as though a second spring might follow. Purple heather clothed the mountainsides.

He woke to birdsong from the open window, and from where he lay he watched the dark sky brighten as the land unfolded in the dawn, the night's fog retreating to the dripping hollows and the mossy stream-beds, and it seemed the world was being made

THE HILL IN THE DARK GROVE

anew before his eyes. All his imaginings could not have conjured any finer view. This was his country. His. Rhian was still asleep, and for a moment he considered waking her to share the sunrise as they used to when they first were courting, but decided against it. Her face was serious with dreaming. Instead, he padded barefoot round to her side of the bed, past Eira who lifted her head and wagged her tail as he went by, and turned off the alarm. The cockerels would soon wake her anyway, he reasoned to himself with some success. He told himself it was a kindness to let her lie in. But deep down he knew he only wished to be alone a little longer, another hour undistracted at his work.

As quietly as he could, he gathered up his clothes and tiptoed down the creaking stairs, with Eira following sleepily at his heels. He dressed in the kitchen, as he had begun to every morning. Most days now he forewent brushing his teeth – another couple of minutes saved – though they'd begun to hurt. His breakfast was a glass of milk, a slice of toast wolfed down in haste, and when he caught sight of his own reflection in the toaster, he looked ragged and peculiar, a stranger even to himself. Then he listened in the hall to make sure Rhian had not woken, and went out into the crisp Eryri dawn.

His tools were in the workshop, and the geese and hens all stood and watched in silence as he crossed the yard. Some old part of his brain formed of long habit listed out the usual duties for the day: Crovect the ewes for ticks and blowflies while the weather was still dry and the treatment wouldn't wash straight off them in the rain; begin selecting lambs for market; put out hay and silage where the grass was sparse. Most years, both he and Rhian could smell the approach of winter – could hear its portents on the wind or feel the chill in their old bones as it drew near – and autumn would be spent in frenzied preparation after the relative calm of summer. But now, these tasks seemed trifling and vestigial. He'd do them still, of course, but later. They would have to wait. From the deep shadows of his workbench, the stone head eyed him with its cold, inscrutable expression.

The fields were rough and scrubby as he made his way with Eira down towards the woods. Beneath his boots the blades of grass felt strangely coarse, cropped almost to the roots by the sheep in their hunger, and here and there tall stalks of thistle sprouted insolently, unkempt as his beard. They looked not right to him somehow. Their leaves too sharp; their heads too large; their colouring too vivid, as though made as thistles ought to be instead of as they were. The flock, too, had grown wild and wary. Where once fat ewes and lambs would have come running for feed, they now went scattering at his approach. They looked rangy and lean.

Even Eira seemed to sense the change, or else be changed by it herself. She stayed close at heel instead of casting out alone, racing off ahead as she had loved to do. When Carwyn lifted her over the gate that led into the bottom field, he noticed the first strands of grey among her fur, and he paused to ruffle her old head and tell her what a lovely dog she was. Ten years old – too old to be a working dog much longer, but it might hasten her senescence to be kept at home. He picked her up as he had done when she was just a pup and marvelled at how age had ambushed both of them.

Down through the woods, the excavation had progressed with startling speed. It awed him every morning when it first came into view, seeming each day to be a bit further along than he

THE HILL IN THE DARK GROVE

remembered, as if others were continuing his work while he was gone. On three sides, slopes of scree and boulders rose towards the distant peaks in silhouette against the dawn, and at his back the patch of woodland crowded close so that the clearing lay in a secluded grove. He had burned away the ferns and dug away the topsoil in a ring around the central mound, and what was left might have resembled the foundation of a building site, were it not for what stood revealed before him.

It was a circle of standing stones, twelve in all. A ring of them encircling the mound where now his trench revealed them. They were not quite as tall as he was when he stood up next to them, a little broader than his shoulders at their widest point, and tapering towards the tip like arrowheads or thorns or shark teeth sprouting from the earth. He wondered if their shaping was deliberate, for no two of them were quite alike: some squat, some slender, some askew; some fiercely sharp and others blunt. At once unique and as unsettlingly similar as a family standing petrified. They leaned at drunken angles, so that at first he thought they must have shifted in their long interment, but when he had unearthed them all he saw their placement was precise – socketed in place with smaller rocks, and slanted slightly outward from the centre – and the effect was like a jagged crown to place upon the head of something ageless and colossal.

He stood dumbstruck as he did every morning in the early chill, the sun not yet risen and the dew still glistening and the trees behind him dripping with the dampness of the night. A headache grated in the sockets of his eyes. With just a fingertip he touched the rugged surface of the nearest megalith, and the dizzying question of how long ago another hand had touched it struck him. A hand older than bronze and iron. Older than the wheel. He wondered if the owner of that hand would recognize him as a kinsman. But no. They would not even recognize the world itself, for it had changed enough to drive them mad: their home obliterated by the steady march of time, their loved ones dead so long their bones had turned to dust, their language and their gods forgotten save for a few fading echoes. Their landscape altered by millennia of strangers until the only constant was the mountains. And the stones.

So regular was their arrangement that when he had uncovered the first three, he had been able to extrapolate exactly where the next would be before his spade had even touched the earth. The stone circle, the mound within, was exactly ninety of his old-man paces around the perimeter. About thirty up over the top from one side to the other. There was a proper order to these things. He had found the edge, next he would move inwards to whatever might be buried in the tumulus. He saw himself not as a vandal or a grave-robber but as a sort of archaeologist, and the treasure that he sought was one of knowledge, understanding, revelation. It had stopped occurring to him altogether that he might be doing anything unusual. The importance of his labour felt self-evident. 'Anyone would do the same,' he said to Eira, or himself. 'Anyone would *need* to know.'

There was something unsettling in his excitement, too. He felt as though he were revealing things that were illicit or forbidden. A clear effort had been made to bury the entire construction. He could think of no natural reason that it should have been interred while all the others he had heard of stood in situ. And then later – perhaps thousands of years later, judging by the rubble of the chapel that he cleared away – there had been a failed attempt to Christianize the place. Had those early monks been as enchanted by it as he was now? Perhaps they, too, had stumbled on it hidden in this fold of mountain. And what of the first builders who had quarried out these shards of rock and hauled them halfway up a mountain to this wild and unforgiving place? They must have weighed a couple of tons apiece. There was a vaguely sinister aspect to the sheer gargantuan effort involved. It begged another simple but disquieting question. What for?

Some days earlier, he'd brought a brush and scrubbed the centuries of soil from off the menhirs. Scoured the dirt out of their jagged contours. They were a dark conglomerate of a type he did not know. Not slate nor granite but a rough accretion of small lumps and pebbles that his taid would have called puddingstone when he chanced on a piece for walling, and Nain knew enigmatically as breeding stone or growing stone. It sometimes multiplied at night, she used to say. Or changed its shape by creeping increments when nobody was watching. In some deep recess of his pounding head, he found one of her stories of a field in Llanfihangel where a pair of breeding stones still stood, and when a third appeared it would foretell the ending of the world.

He recalled conversations with his fellow farmers from the days when they were young and many, before they had begun to slip away into infirmity and death, replaced by a new, unfamiliar generation. Some had a standing stone or two out on their land, just humble things: a cairn, a cist, the robbed-out traces of an ancient burial. They said they were a group of revellers turned to stone for dancing on the Sabbath, or a thief who stole a Bible from a church; or else they were cast from a distant mountaintop to prove the strength of giants; they were the places where the fairies lived. Some roamed around at night when everyone had gone to sleep. Of course, nobody was so superstitious as to give real credence to the stories – they were just passed around as curiosities, or cautionary tales to scare the grandchildren, or local colour for the tourists.

But nonetheless, they left a mark. A little voice of doubt against the modern, certain scepticism. When Carwyn was a boy, one of his school friends had a field where an enormous slab of granite was engraved with rings and cup-marks, and for several yards around it nothing ever grew. He saw that with his own eyes and could not account for it. There was a broken cromlech in old Brynmor Jenkins's summer pasture, overgrown with grass and nettles until it had nearly disappeared from view, its capstone smashed and fallen in. He always left the hay unmown there. He used to say that he would not go near it after dark. In '83, Tom Roberts from Ysbyty Ifan took his tractor out to move a fallen monolith that legend claimed had untold riches buried underneath. It had been a fine August day when he set out, but by the time he neared the stone a violent storm whipped up, the sky aflame with sheets of lightning and the thunder loud enough to shake the ground, and hailstones big as hens' eggs lashing down upon the tractor cab. Tom must have died ten years ago, thought Carwyn, in a Bangor nursing home, but he had sworn to any who would listen that he never would disturb the stone again.

In other times, those stories might have given Carwyn pause. Whether real or simply superstition, there were certain things one did not trifle with. Rhian would have called it erring on the side of caution. There was a power in something so ancient and unknowable, and to poke around in it seemed unwise. When he was near the stones, his arm-hairs stood on end, his toes and fingers prickled, one leg sometimes went numb. He tasted metal. He might even have blacked out briefly once. One moment he was on his hands and knees, scouring away the loose soil with a trowel, and the next he was lying splayed out on his back, his ears ringing and his head propped awkwardly against one of the leaning menhirs, with Eira nosing at his face and pacing back and forth beside him, whining with concern.

The circle, though, it spoke to him. That is to say, it spoke to him the same way as the carved head did – in his own inner voice, with his own thoughts. It spoke to him of comfort and familiarity. He had been born and bred in a land shaped by ancient stones: the interconnected rows and rings and monoliths, tumuli and dolmens; the crumbled ruins of the chieftains' strongholds perched on lonely crags, and the many castles of King Edward; the vast slate quarries and their spoil tips that still scarred the landscape. It spoke to him of universal symbols that he understood implicitly. A circle like the seasons by which he still lived and worked; a circle like the cycles of the flock; a circle like the sun, the moon, eternity. It spoke to him of reassuring permanence. The stones represented something that endured, that would not rot or burn or melt away, perhaps placed there by people who felt just as he did that their very way of life was under threat and wished to mark their presence ineradicably on the changing world.

Today, he would begin to excavate the central barrow. It was about the size of a small cottage, bounded by the stone circle and covered by a layer of blackened ash from where he'd burned the ferns away, and pockmarked with small pits where he had dug a foot or so until his spade met stone (among them the first hole where he had found the head). He unrolled a blue tarpaulin at the foot of the east slope. There, he knelt down stiffly, laying out his tools: a pick, a spade, a trowel, and then used a heavy brush to clear away some of the ash. His headache waxed and waned. Eira no longer joined him in his digging. She remained outside the circle looking back towards the woods, and sometimes she would growl or whine as though things sensed but not quite seen were watching from the tangled undergrowth.

He had barely been about his work five minutes when he came upon an artefact. It was a bead of vivid-yellow seashell, pierced through with a tiny hole and worn white on each side where it must once have rubbed against its neighbours on a string. He wet his thumb to carefully wipe the dirt from it and held it up to see it better in the daylight, then secreted it in a back pocket of his overalls. Behind him, Eira barked – unusual for her, he thought – but when Carwyn followed her gaze to the little patch of woodland he saw nothing. She must have seen a bird, perhaps. The starlings had begun their flocking early this year, and every evening their enormous, shifting murmurations throbbed and undulated in the valley sky. He said, 'There, girl, tell them what's what,' but otherwise paid her no mind.

Shortly after that his trowel revealed a length of pale clay-pipe stem and a badly rusted disc of metal that he guessed might be a button. Perhaps only a few centuries old. And then another. Then a horseshoe and a silver buckle and a rotted, fragmentary tongue of leather. He had sat back to examine them when a breath of wind sent something else entirely tumbling into his lap.

It was an empty chocolate wrapper. His puzzlement gave way to mild annoyance, and at first he presumed it must have made its way up from the rafts of litter left behind by day trippers down on the lake, or been carried on the breeze from hikers up Yr Wyddfa, but when he looked he saw another lying not far down the ring of stones. Further still, there was a cardboard sleeve from a six-pack of beers. He heaved himself back to his feet, his old joints creaking, and noticed a bottle balanced jauntily atop one of the menhirs. Eira turned to watch him clamber from the trench, but did not follow when he made his way around the circle, grumbling as he picked up the debris.

The trail of rubbish led a little way uphill to a secluded corner where the woods gave way to mossy boulders and a fresh slide of loose scree. Carwyn's anger grew with every step. It was as though he had discovered strangers rooting in his private drawer or peering in his bedroom window every night while he and Rhian were undressed. He found the shards of a smashed bottle, then a pile of intact ones. Then the bent foil tray from a disposable barbecue, black and greasy with burnt fat and smelling still of meat and char. And finally, the circle of a campfire and a rectangle of flattened, yellowed grass where a tent must have been pegged overnight. His hands were clenching and unclenching slowly. Blood beat loudly in his ears.

When he got back up to the house, Rhian was loading hay into the trailer.

'What's wrong?' she asked, a bit too hurriedly. There was a look of nervousness about her that he was not used to seeing and he did not like, for it seemed clear he was the cause. She was never one to tread on eggshells until recently.

'It's bloody kids. Camping. *Trespassing.*' He almost spat the word, and for a moment he seemed a stranger even to himself. 'In the bottom field.' He threw the armful of litter into the black bin beside the gate and slammed the lid shut after it.

Rhian paused astride a bale and gave him a questioning, sympathetic look.

'What are they all *doing* here?' The question was rhetorical, of course, but there was genuine exasperation and bafflement in his voice. Indeed, it seemed to him the insult was worse than the mere act of trespass. It was not so many years ago that they had tolerated the occasional camper on their land, and even then, the visitors had few qualms about littering. But this, it felt like an act of aggression. An expression of hostile indifference. A sign that, bit by bit, these new, outlandish strangers would keep coming, and they had neither respect nor veneration for the things that he held dear.

She nodded sadly. Shrugged. 'It's worse every year.'

'They just come and treat it as their weekend playground. It's like a theme park for them, like Disneyland with sheep and mountains. First sign of a sunny day and they're bumper to bumper down there on the road –' he gestured violently – 'and nothing left behind but all the shit they can't be arsed to take back home with them. They've no consideration for the fact that people live here. Why can't they just fuck off?' He was aware that he was swearing, and that it was unlike him.

'"Come to beautiful Wales and see the lovely scenery,"' she agreed, '"but bugger it and chuck all your rubbish out of the car window on your way home." They'll be gone soon, love, try not to worry. As soon as the weather starts to turn, we won't see them until next summer.' She picked the bale up by the twine and manhandled it awkwardly onto the tailgate of the trailer, and he helped her push it the rest of the way in.

When they were done, she looked around and asked, 'Where's Eira got to now?'

Carwyn pointed to where the old collie rolled contentedly in a long, green streak of goose shit at the gate. He said, 'Come and have a look at this.' There was a sly, conspiratorial half-grin on his face.

She followed him down through the dew-damp morning, treading in the ways that he had beaten through the brakes of oddly shapen burdock leaf and thistle, with Eira staying close at heel. The sheep watched them, gaunt and listless. Out of the valley, they could hear the distant drone of the occasional car down on the road, the last of the fair-weather visitors out with their camper-vans and kayaks and their camping gear. There was a chill in the bright day that seemed to foretell the end of their coming. He helped her over the gate at the woods, and she asked why he had not unlocked it, nor trimmed back the weeds that wove so thickly in between its bars that it could scarce be budged. It was a question he could furnish with no satisfactory answer. Only that it felt better to keep it closed. Felt safer that way.

Then through the copse of oaks that crowded green and gnarled and ancient round the narrow tunnel of a path. Every branch and trunk and stone bedecked with vivid moss as if it might soon spread to smother all the world. How strange it seemed to have her company. When he was alone, the woods could do odd things. Out of the corner of his eye, a knot of bark looked like a wizened face, or the straggling roots of creepers seemed to take the shape of figures, and tall, watchful shadows loomed among the trees. But with Rhian there, the forest ceased its tricks. He felt a boyish shiver of excitement at bringing her here, and it was with no small measure of enjoyment that he heard her gasp of wonder when they broke again into the daylight.

'Bloody hell, Carwyn.' Rhian stood blinking for a moment. The understatement of it made him smile. 'So this is what you've been doing all the time.'

He stepped proudly into the trench. 'Not bad, is it? What do you think it is?' The tumulus stood stark and denuded behind him.

For a long time she stood and looked hard at it, and her face took on an expression that he had not seen in all their years together, and whose meaning he was unable to read. Squinting, with her thumb held out, she tried to gauge the way the stones lay in relation to the red and risen sun. 'Twelve of them. A calendar, maybe?'

Carwyn looked at her as if she had declared it was a shoehorn or a microwave. 'A calendar? What for?'

With careful steps, she walked a short way round the outside of the trench. 'It might be they were plotting the positions of the sunrise, or the phases of the moon, or both. To know when certain animals would be migrating, or when certain plants would grow, or when they needed to stockpile for winter.' With this last, there was a barb implied, thought Carwyn, but she seemed suddenly uncertain and went on, 'Or, I don't know, a monument? A tomb? A temple?'

He nodded. 'That's what I thought, too. But for what? I was

thinking, isn't it strange the way that people try to pen in what's most sacred to them? You once said to me we used to worship trees and rocks and rivers – like how God's supposed to be everywhere, they say. But still, we build a church to keep Him in, and He's *more* in there than He's outside, isn't it?' He did not wait to see if she agreed. 'And before that we built the little chapels in the holy places for to keep Him in, and before *that* we built all kinds of shrines and temples. And first of all, we built these mounds and circles for our gods to live in. Places where they would be stronger, where we could go to visit them, where they would be *contained*.' Domestication, he thought – domesticating deities the same way as the first farm animals were tamed. There was a wild and agitated look about him. He felt he was within an inch of some essential axiom. 'Ancient, isn't it?'

Rhian glanced at Eira, who had stopped again a cautious distance from the circle. It seemed to him they both were staying back, and it annoyed him in a way that he could not account for. She said, 'It's more than ancient. Carwyn, we have to tell someone. The university or someone.'

'We will, we will. I just need to understand it first. I need to know what's here.' For a moment, he imagined the embarrassment of being wrong. Of going off half-cocked, only to find no one was interested in his ten-a-penny standing stones, his maybe-empty mound. 'It's something big though, I can feel it. Look at these, just from this morning.' He gathered all the objects he had laid on the tarpaulin and held them up in his chapped hand for her to see.

There was an underlayer of concern beneath her fascination, he could see it plain as day. In all their years together, he had never known her be so guarded with him. 'These are treasures, Carwyn.' The word was oddly childish, somehow, for these little scraps, yet that was undeniably what they were. 'You've got to tell someone. Those metal detectorists who found that Viking hoard down Hereford way, remember that? They went to jail for not declaring it. These things belong in a museum.'

'All right, Diana Jones.'

'I'm serious.'

'So am I. They belong *here*.' The sudden violence of his tone made Rhian take a step away from him. Let her fear him, then, if that was what she wanted. Let her have her silly worries. He had toiled for this, and he would not let the glory go to some or other pompous academic. He felt as if the words that now came boiling forth had been amassing in his chest for weeks. 'I'll be buggered if I'm going to let them stick all this in a glass cabinet for bored schoolkids to file past and forget about a minute later. Do you think the ones who left their empty bottles here last night would queue up at a museum to see it? And that's even if the bastards put them on display. Someone put hours of work and love into these things. Do you think that's what they made them for? They belong to the land. They're part of it. They're *mine*.' The world swam briefly in his eyes, and he leaned on one of the menhirs to steady himself.

She threw up her hands in exasperation. 'Do what you bloody want, then,' she said. 'I'm not going to interfere. But I don't want to be a part of it. I've got a farm to run, if you're too busy here to help me. I seem to be doing all the work myself now anyway.'

Without waiting for an answer, Rhian turned to leave, and she had disappeared into the woods before Carwyn could call after her. He watched her go and said, as much to himself as to her, 'We won't have a farm if I don't finish this. Whatever's here, it's make or break for us.' Eira cocked an ear, but when he reached a hand to beckon her for patting, she would not approach.

For the best part of the next hour, he rooted in the deepest part of the long barn, in the webbed and dusty shadows that in some long-vanished time had been a stabling for horses. High in the corners, swallows had once made their dried-mud nests, and little clusters of their droppings lay beneath, but the birds themselves were gone. He supposed an archaeologist could find in here the evidence of every generation since the farm was built. Let them have this instead, he thought, and leave his stones.

Rhian's attitude had rankled. He had thought that after all these years together, she would understand. 'Tell someone!' he muttered to himself. He would, of course he would – what good was finding something so important if he kept it to himself? Why did she think that he had shown her in the first place? But timing mattered, too. This was not something to be squandered while it was yet in the ground, only to have legions of journalists and students and New Agers swarming over it like ants on jam. He would uncover it himself, and when he did, he would control the access – charge admission, maybe. Then they could come and study it and gawk at it, and they could pay him for the privilege. But they would have to wait.

Eventually he dragged into the brightness of the yard a roll of razor wire and two of barbed, a tub of coloured paint he used for smit marking the flock, and a stack of plywood boards that bore Plaid Cymru posters down beside the lane every election season. Eira came trotting out behind him, her tail wagging. She seemed oddly brightened now they were back at the house. He rummaged in the pockets of his overalls and came up with a bone-shaped biscuit, which she caught in mid air when he tossed it. Her coat was sleek and black and lustrous in the morning sun. Not a trace, in this light, of the grey he thought he'd seen.

He leaned the signboards up against the wall to paint them, and while he worked Rhian came in with the hay trailer and washed her hands under the spigot by the porch and crossed over to the patch of dirt and canes they thought of as the vegetable garden. She did not speak to him, but cast him mute, resentful glances. This was the form their arguments had always taken. They did not shout or curse each other or slam doors (or worse, he thought; he had known couples aplenty who did worse), but aired their disagreements in the form of vengeful silences. Meaningful looks. He wondered sometimes if this would have changed if there had been a child. A child needed instruction, explanation. Perhaps they would have both picked up the habit of communicating their displeasure in clear words if they had raised a child. A memory came unbidden, slyly, catching him off guard. One sunny morning taking bin bags full of unworn baby clothes down to the charity shop in Llanberis. He'd left them out on the pavement. Could not bring himself to go inside and face the awful, silent sympathy when they were opened. The thought was wretched and bitter, and he scoured away a single tear that he licked from the back of his fist.

It took all afternoon to carry out his plan. At every stile where footpaths crossed into his land, he first prised out the step. Then he wove tangles of the vicious wire about them so that anyone who tried to pass would be cut to shreds. Nearby each, he hammered signs into the ground which read, in foot-high, blood-red letters:

CADWCH ALLAN – KEEP OUT

EIDDO PREIFAT – PRIVATE PROPERTY

DIM MYNEDIAD, DIM GWERSYLLA – NO ACCESS, NO CAMPING

Each one a variation on those themes, until the words outgrew their literal meanings and became instead expressions of more general, primal concepts. This territory belongs to me, and you set foot here at your peril. Afterwards he ran all the remaining coils of wire around the gaps in the hedge down along the lane, in case of errant hikers tempted to explore, and while he worked a flock of starlings thousands strong made roiling, psychedelic shapes above his head. He saved the last of the razor wire to top the coping of the drystone wall around the bottom field, and here he placed the final sign:

PERYGL – DANGER

What danger it might be, he did not specify. He was not sure he knew. A wave of pins and needles prickled from his fingers to his shoulder, leaving in their aftermath that strange metallic taste.

In any case, his efforts seemed to work, and for the next few nights they were no more disturbed by trespassers. The traffic in the valley quieted. The day trippers grew fewer and farther between. The coldness between him and Rhian thawed, and when the news came that old Brynmor Jenkins had died in his sleep, they wept together at his lonely funeral. In the car on the way home, she said, 'There's hardly any of us left.' And she was right – the people they knew and who knew them had dwindled to a handful. They drove the rest of the way back in morose contemplation, feeling mortal and alone.

The night of the funeral, he dreamed with unusual lucidity. He dreamed that he awoke in bed at some ungodly hour of black and moonless darkness, so absolute that he only knew where he was by the feel of the bedclothes, and the breathing of Rhian beside him and the snores of Eira at the foot of the bed, and the surreptitious stirrings of the something in the attic. Even the face of the alarm clock had gone dark.

In the dream, he lay there for what felt like an eternity, thinking with half-awake detachment that he must have gone completely blind. But soon there came a faint glow at the window. He rose unsteadily, noticing with uncanny vividness the feeling of the floorboards under his bare feet, the way his breath condensed on the small windowpanes. He smelled the faint odour of smoke. The dark outside hung rich and thick as velvet, and the yard and all the outbuildings and all the land beyond seemed vanished traceless in its depths.

Yet in the distance he could see a light. At first, he thought it was a pale, bright star, but slowly it began to drift across the sky, and he realized that it was moving down from off the mountain, flickering and growing larger as it came. He could see the silhouettes of objects that it passed: a hawthorn tree, a boulder on the scarp, a gatepost. It moved along the topmost wall of one of the high pastures, and then came up and over it unsteadily, and crossed the field. Then up over another wall, and on downhill.

The understanding struck him in the way of dreams – imparted with the sudden certainty of revelation. It was the trespassers again. Without a shadow of a doubt. They must have seen his signs and efforts to resist them and come back to taunt him further. He charged down the steep stairs on sightless instinct, while Eira woke and followed without hesitation. Then barefoot out into the pitch-black yard, barely noticing the sharpness of the gravel underneath his feet, and as he swept out of the gate he seized a vicious shard of coping slate from off the wall and raced downhill across the fields. The earth and sky were featureless, and were it not for the feel of the grass or the coolness of the breeze he might have been suspended in a void of purest nothingness.

He caught sight of the light again as he came through the narrow squeeze-stile into the low pasture. It was a couple of hundred yards ahead of him, a sallow candle-flame moving towards the woods, where in its flickerings he could discern the phantom boughs of trees, the tall thistles, the baleful eyes of the flock. He felt the brush of Eira's fur go past his ankles as she cast out low and soundless in pursuit.

Even in the dream, he was panting and breathless, feeling winded, feeling old. A stitch of pain sawed up under his ribs. He was at the gate now. Eira whined and waited to be lifted over. The light of the trespasser was deep in the wood, moving ghostly between the stands of oak and throwing pallid, monstrous shadows up into the canopy. He climbed the gate with Eira under-arm and set her down and raised the lump of slate above his head. In the dense and seething darkness, the woods seemed to gather close about him in anticipation. Nowhere left for the bastards to go, he had them cornered.

With a surge of violent adrenaline, he burst into the open of the hollow, poised to enact a swift and brutal vengeance on these troublesome intruders. But there were none. A sliver of moon the colour of bleached bones now grinned above the crags, and stars in foul and unfamiliar constellations bright enough again to see by, but save for the crown of stones in their trench around their barrow, he and Eira stood alone.

It was Rhian nudging him awake that roused him from a deep and clinging slumber. The alarm had not gone off, she told him, the cheap batteries he'd bought had died, and when he rolled onto his back he saw she was already up and dressed, and the day outside was near full risen.

'What's wrong? What is it?' He thought to scold her for letting him sleep late, but he was glad of it. There was a chill about the morning, and his neck felt stiff, and his joints ached, his head thick and groggy as it always was these days when he slept too much or not enough. Eira had come up on the bed beside him. He stroked her head and picked a prickly burdock seed out of her fur.

'You won't believe this,' Rhian was saying. She looked stunned and shaken. She had his clothes laid out, and hurried him as he got dressed but would not tell him what the rush was. 'I've never seen anything like it.'

Neither had he.

The lane below the farm was covered with dead starlings. Covered with them. They lay broken all across the tarmac as if they had fallen from the sky. Their little speckled, iridescent bodies were arranged in every attitude of death: some with wings spread, beaks splayed, feet clenched; some perfectly intact and others shattered. At least a hundred of them, maybe more.

'They're only in the road,' she said, and she was right – not one in the hedges nor in the fields on either side. If they had somehow dropped dead in mid flight, they ought to have been scattered everywhere.

'D'you think a car could have hit them?' he said. 'Those flocks are so thick, maybe these ones couldn't get up out of the lane quick enough.' That'll be the bloody tourists as well, he thought, who used these quiet country roads as though they were a racetrack, but he did not say it.

'Could be. Or maybe they were in a dive and couldn't pull up, I don't know. You've seen the way they flock. And look – some of their beaks are broken.' Several of them looked as though they must have hit the ground head first, at speed. 'It's awful, Carwyn, the poor things. Can you deal with them? I can't stand to leave them in the road.'

She went to fetch him a wheelbarrow and a shovel, and while he waited he paced up and down the strew of tiny bodies, wondering what would be next. A plague of frogs, or lice, or locusts? *The killing of the firstborn sons?* piped up a traitor inner voice not quite his own. His feet were sore and stinging, and when he sat down on the verge to take his boots off and examine them, he found a thorn stuck in the skin between his toes. High in the silvery overcast, a V of geese flew southward.

Once suitably equipped, he began the grisly task of gathering up the starling carcasses out of the lane. The shovel must have stood a long time in the sun before the sky had clouded over, for when he grasped it by the metal collar it was hot enough to burn his hand. He scooped the birds in lines like shovelling snow. They made a high, unsteady pile in the wheelbarrow, and when he went back up the rough and rutted driveway to the farm, he had to take care not to let them topple off the sides.

He decided he would burn them – make a pyre out past the barn, as he had in '01 when foot-and-mouth had struck, and half the country smoked and stank with nightmare bonfires like sacrifices to some foul and gluttonous divinity. And with that thought, another came to him, and Carwyn's gaze followed a breath of wind downhill towards the wood. What could it hurt, he thought, to do it in the circle? It seemed as good a place as any. Better, even – the ground there was already burnt from when he cleared the overgrowth. Almost immediately he sensed the absurdity of the idea. 'You silly arse,' he said aloud. That rebuke got him several strides across the yard before the urge became insatiable, growing like the semi-conscious certainty that he had left the water running or the oven on until there was no option but to go and check. The circle. Burn them after nightfall in the circle, on top of the mound. That was the thing to do.

The rain began in earnest as he turned the wheelbarrow of dead and ruined birds around.

VII

Hydref

HALLOWS

The novice hurried downhill through the sheeting rain. Only when lightning lit the heavens and picked out in stark relief the crags and outcroppings above him could he make out the path ahead. It was surely his imagination, but it seemed their shapes were never twice the same. Between the flashes he ran blindly, trusting in the Lord that he would not rush headlong from a precipice or twist his ankle on the jagged ground or meet with some unholy creature in the dark. At least the storm would keep the wolves away. These highlands seemed to be infested with them, for at night their howls could be heard all around, and every day at matins, though the monks kept watch, another chicken or a goat or even one of the disciples would be gone.

When finally he passed the splintered palings of the monastic encampment, he was soaked through and shivering. It was a cluster of rough huts of daub and wattle squatting on the valley floor a harsh place even by the monks' austere standards. No fires burned. No candle, even, so that in the rainswept night it might have been mistaken for a ruin lying desolate. Bodfan, the Saint, kept vigil in a doorway. The man looked gaunt and crestfallen, as though he had been waiting for this evil news. He was brought up a prince, but there was nothing princely in his bearing now – his beard bedraggled and his Celtic tonsure grey, his back bent and his cheekbones hollow. Since they'd arrived the building of the chapel had been like a millstone hung around his neck.

The task had consumed him, and he would not allow himself to be dissuaded nor hear any counsel to the contrary, for he insisted that the place appeared to him in dreams and visions. God had sent him here to claim it. At his urging, they had built a hermitage of woven willow fronds, but on the second night it stood a fearsome gale uprooted it, and in the morning it was gone without a trace. Next came a timber oratory, roofed with thatch, that lasted seven days before a toppled brazier burned it to the ground. The Good Lord disapproved of their poor craftsmanship, the Saint had told them, but the older men, Ceitho and Meilig – haunted by the Saxon massacre at Bangor-is-y-Coed – grew certain that the ground was foul.

Illuminated by the lightning, Bodfan beckoned the young novice in. They ducked out of the rain into a cramped and draughty hovel where the other monks lay sleepless on their beds of straw. Even in darkness, he sensed they had already guessed his tidings, but he could not summon up the words to tell them. Weeks of toil. The chapel built of stones they carried up in baskets from the lakeshore. The carvings sculpted by a craftsman brought across the sea from Laigin. The nights spent feverish with prayer. Nothing to show for any of it now except a heap of broken rubble. Before anyone had spoken, Brother Seiriol began to weep. On Winter's Eve, Nos Calan Gaeaf, they went up to survey the bitter wreckage of their efforts, and they buried the head of their statue of the Christ while Bodfan croaked a prayer, and afterwards they gathered up their few possessions and set off defeated for the coast.

Rhian was awake before the cockerels, when the stars had not yet faded and the Milky Way still blazed above the mountaintops. The heater in the bedroom must have gone off in the night, for it was cold enough that she could see her breath, but she had no desire to cwtch up close to Carwyn for a bit of warmth. To do so felt repellent somehow, as it used to when they fought. But they had barely fought in years. Eira had come up on the far side of the bed and now slept curled beside her master. She twitched and whimpered in a dream.

Carwyn was lying with his back turned, snoring softly, perfectly still, but Rhian was struck by the unsettling impression that he was not really sleeping. Something felt feigned about the rhythm of his breathing – too measured. His stillness felt too stiff, too rigid, as though maintained by a deliberate effort. His posture did not feel relaxed but tensed up like a spring. She imagined if she crept around to his side of the bed, she would find his eyes were open, and the thought made her shiver. He was not sleeping, only waiting. Watchful.

For a long time, she tried without success to go to sleep. She lay there in the dark with her arms at her sides and the blankets pulled up tight under her chin, but her joints ached in the cold and she could not find a position that was comfortable, and so instead she made herself get up. The days were warm still at this time of year, but in the night it could be bitter, as if the winter crept into the world a little at a time, under the cover of darkness. When she looked back at Carwyn, he was fast asleep, of course, one arm crooked over Eira. She chided herself for her silly apprehensions. Then she wrapped herself in an old dressing gown of his that hung on the back of the door (and that still smelled of Carwyn in a way the man himself did not seem to this morning) and went downstairs to make herself a cup of coffee.

She stepped into the yard to drink it, where the frost still glittered on the slates and in the grass. Besides the stars, the old bulb above the front door was the only light, and she stood in its glow clutching the mug like a totem in her hands. Beyond, the night was lingering. How curious it was, she thought, that some nights – for no reason you could put your finger on – something about the darkness made your hackles rise. Broomstick nights, her granny used to call them. The mountain air was soured by a faint but greasy charred-meat smell of smoke and smouldering wool.

Carwyn's digging bothered her, nagged at her in a way she could never entirely silence in these moments. She counted back – six months now and no sign of stopping. Getting worse, in fact. And try as she might to convince herself that this was just an old man's hobby, a harmless, even healthy curiosity to keep the mind and body active, she was not persuaded. He had changed. Obsession was the word that came most readily to mind. It was the guileful way he went about things now. He was not the type to have affairs – that was a worry she had never had in forty years of marriage – and to say he wore his heart on his sleeve would be an understatement, for he wore it in his every look and gesture. But when it came to the digging, he was secretive, evasive. She sipped her coffee, but it had gone cold. She poured the rest away into the drain beside the door.

When she went back into the house, Carwyn was sitting at the kitchen table. He was already dressed and had prepared himself a bowl of plain porridge which he ate mechanically, without enthusiasm. Eira waited patiently to lick the bowl clean after he was done. As Rhian passed on her way to the sink, she bent and kissed him on the temple, and he gave her back a tired smile. 'I'm sorry, cariad, I think you'll have to take the lambs down to the mart today. I'm not feeling too good.'

She looked at him with furrowed-browed concern. He hadn't missed a livestock sale in all the years she'd known him – even in the spring of '92 when he had fallen from a ladder in the long barn and gone down on crutches with a broken leg. He's ill, she thought with unexpected relief. He's just ill, that's all that's wrong. She felt his forehead with the back of her hand. 'You don't seem hot.'

He set his bowl down on the flagstone floor between his booted feet, and Eira set about it happily. 'That's good, then. But my throat's on fire, and I've got a splitting headache. I barely slept a wink. I'll just finish this and then I'm going back to bed, if you're all right to manage it without me.'

That explained the strangeness in the night, she thought. And why he seemed aged lately, too, all of a sudden, as though several years had fallen on him all at once. It worried her in a vague, nagging way. Reminded her of how their livelihood demanded vigour, and that the day when one or both of them would find themselves too old was closer than they dared admit. They had reached that stage of life when every sickness, every stutter, every stumble could betoken something ominous and irreversible. 'Do you want me to ring the doctor?'

'No,' he said, 'I'll be all right. A day or two in bed and I'll be good as new. D'you mind?'

She told him that she didn't mind at all, hoping she sounded more sincere to him than she had to herself. She fetched her dog-eared notebook with its ever-growing tally of their outgoings, thinking at first to ask him to update it for the week if he felt well enough, but when she turned she caught his fleeting look of pained annoyance as though this would be a hindrance to his urgent plans. Six months ago, before all this, she would have argued. No, not even that – would not have needed to – he would have offered without waiting to be asked. 'Just rest,' she said instead. 'Get yourself better.' She slipped the book into a pocket of her dressing gown.

When she was dressed, she called to Eira and the dog came with her only grudgingly, glancing back at Carwyn as if guilty about leaving him behind. She would work for Rhian, and she was always obedient, but not in the way that she loved to work for him. Rhian was always left with the impression that the dog was doing her a favour – helping out of obligation rather than enthusiasm.

But they worked well together nonetheless, and within an hour they had selected fifty-seven likely-looking lambs to sell. Stores, they would have to be, sold cheap to go and finish fattening on another farm before they could be butchered. The first real income in months, and still not half of what their sheep would normally fetch. They had grown poorly this year, and when she felt their backs, their bones were sharp and angular beneath their coats, and they seemed scrawny and malnourished. Whatever curious malaise was blighting them, she could not fathom it: they had been wormed as usual; the vet had been and taken blood and found nothing amiss; the weather had been more erratic these past years, but not as extreme as she feared it soon might become. And so she could not quiet the thought, as she and Eira loaded them into the trailer, that some greater ill had settled on the farm. She worried about Carwyn – she could always tell when he was sick by looking at his eyes, and he had not seemed sick to her this morning. She worried about the debt collectors – how long until they would be back again? She worried about the lambs – not ready by a mile, but they would have to do. The bills had to be paid. When she got into the pickup, she held the door for Eira to jump up beside her, but the dog regarded her a moment with her wise old head cocked to one side and then went trotting back towards the house.

She had never much liked the auction mart. It straggled along both shoulders of an empty stretch of road through ugly, marshy flatland near the coast, and though some of the mountains that she knew from home were still close by, it unsettled her to see them from the other side. They looked distorted, wrong, from here, like catching sight of your reflection in a spoon. Even the sun seemed not to sit right in the sky. She pulled into the already-busy car park past the dereliction of an ancient drovers' inn that must have marked the spot where mountain folk had brought their flocks since the days of William Morgan's Bible, and yet no market town had grown around it. There was the mart, the inn, the rusting remnants of a petrol pump and nothing more. It was a place to come and leave again, and not to put down roots.

A red-haired lad in overalls came sauntering from the shadow of the auction sheds to wave her to a parking space. The last in line, beneath a hissing pylon, where weeds sprouted from the asphalt and a row of tractor skeletons waited to be stripped

THE HILL IN THE DARK GROVE

for parts. She was out of practice with the trailer and had to back in several times before it lined up with the pen.

The noise and smell assaulted her before she even stopped the car. She had lived most of her life near livestock, but here their stink was of a wholly different order to the mountain air up at the farm. The bellowing of sheep and cattle by the hundred – an endless purgatorial lament – and the reek of their dung and their feed and of diesel fumes and the dead-seaweed smell from off the beach. It was viscous. She felt she could have run her finger through the air and it would come up black. But by the time she'd signed the stock in with the auctioneers, she barely noticed it. How quickly we habituate ourselves to awful things, she thought.

She waited. The lambs had to be checked and weighed and listed, sorted into lots. An hour or two, perhaps, before her sale. To kill the time she wandered up and down the rows between the livestock pens, through eerie twilight underneath the corrugated hangar roof, the day scarce penetrating through the building's open sides, so that the animals and people coexisted vaguely in the shadows. She saw poorly in the half-light. Some acquaintance called a greeting to her, and she waved, but who it was she could not say. The red-haired boy passed by her on a narrow catwalk set atop the pens, as nimble as a tightrope acrobat, and further in the darkness others to-and-froed above the stock – counting, checking, barking figures to each other in the noise. She could hear the auctioneer's voice, too, distorted over a loudhailer. A babbling, gibbering ululation like a speaker of tongues. And above it all, the lowing of cattle and the bleating of sheep and the grunting of pigs and the hushed conversations of men. Rows upon rows upon rows of them. She was struck, suddenly, by a sense of them all waiting, oblivious, to be sold and butchered and devoured, and of herself alone possessed of this foreknowledge of their fates. It granted not superiority, but rather kinship. We are earmarked, each and all of us, she thought, for the great slaughterhouse of time, and know no more than these poor beasts do when or where or how the killing blow will fall.

There was a rich vein of hypocrisy, she knew, beneath her pity. This was the culmination of the process that was her and Carwyn's life and livelihood; but she had, by and large, kept this part mostly from her mind. At the farm, she could tell herself their role was one of care and husbandry – midwife one day, nurse the next; protector, doctor, loving parent each by turns. When lambs were born, she would rejoice. When they grew fat and strong, she watched them proudly. When one of the flock died at home, she grieved. When Carwyn loaded them into the trailer and she stood at the farm gate and watched them disappearing down the lane, she felt the sadness of their loss, but it was the sadness of seeing one's children off to their first day of school. She did not allow herself to think of what became of them, not because there was a wrong in it, but because the next stage of their journey was for someone else to oversee. Someone who had not watched them grow.

She reached over a gate to feel the hips of one lamb and another, and was disheartened that they felt fat and muscled – not at all like her own handful did. Part of her had wanted to believe that the year's troubles were not particular to them, and that the other flocks might have been struggling equally, but she could tell at once this was not so. The flystrike, the strange listless wasting, none of that was evident among these others. The plagues, it seemed, were being visited on them alone. A boil-faced man in a flat cap and wellingtons and shirt and tie patted the gate and said, 'They're sold already, I'm afraid.' She thanked him absently and wandered on.

Down concrete alleyways awash with straw and urine, she came to a row of corrals with gangly feeder calves. Then cows and heifers sorted into lots. And finally, almost back where she had started, to the prize bulls. The show winners, their pens just a low breeze-block wall away from the one where her own lambs waited. Sickly stock beside these wondrous specimens. There was a majestic, auburn-coated Limousin, Cwmorthin Ned; a Hereford named Nasareth, heavy with ribbons, with a weary, seen-it-all expression in his piggy little eyes; an enormous Angus with rosettes along the bars of his gate, and a sign identifying him as Penmon Gladiator. Magnificent beasts, all of them – a fortune's worth of champion breeders – and all would be a shoo-in for top billing were it not for the last bull that Rhian came to. The last was in a different league entirely.

Arwr was his name. The champion of champions. He was a polled Welsh Black, standing in the dusty rays that filtered through a plastic skylight in the roof, and even there he seemed as dark as a December night. A mighty thing, he was. Long as a car. Broad as a wardrobe. A being of lean muscle, barely contained so that beneath his glossy, spilled-ink flanks each overlapped the next like they might otherwise outgrow his skin. Rhian reached through the bars to stroke his lustrous mane of curls and wide, wet nose, and his colossal head dwarfed her pale hand. It frightened her to be so close to him – whispered to some old, deep region of her brain that this was danger, this was death. The flimsy metal gate would not contain him if he had a mind to charge.

He regarded Rhian dolefully, and she could see herself reflected in his melancholy eyes, two shining galaxies of the profoundest sadness, as though he had foreseen the future and had found it bleak beyond imagining. Rosettes and ribbons from his victories adorned his bridle like the pagan offerings that might have decorated shrines: Best in Show at Anglesey, Best in Show at Eglwysbach, Best in Show at Royal Welsh. Bright tokens of the faithful's veneration. All part of the same human urge, she thought, that makes us decorate a Christmas tree or throw confetti at a wedding or place flowers on a grave. He seemed not to belong here in this cement pen, but to a time when snow covered the mountains all year round and aurochs roamed the windswept tundra in vast herds while men painted their fury on cave walls. He might have been a god to them. A mythic, snorting, bellowing deity – bringer of thunder, bringer of virility, bringer of war. But he was calm and still and docile, now. She stood enrapt and scratched the thick curls on his brow and could not shake the feeling that he pitied her.

She had once spent a Christmas with her grandparents down in the Rhondda Valley when she would have only been but five or six. They had lived in an old miner's cottage with the looming silhouettes of pit machinery and spoil tips all around it on the blasted hills, and not too many years or miles from there a slag-heap just like those had liquefied and surged down like a tidal wave into a school. She dreamed, still, sometimes, of those children buried at their desks.

Grampa Nevett was a lay preacher, a long, gaunt, balding man with wire-framed spectacles who smelled perpetually of coal-tar soap, and even in those days he seemed a relic of a bygone time. He still worked a full week down the colliery then, twelve-hour shifts deep in the bowels of the earth, but on Sundays he'd go up and down the valley with a horse and trap, peddling fire and brimstone to the miners and their families. His knowledge of hell was personal, he used to say. He and the Devil worked in close proximity. She could imagine when her father was a boy, her grampa had been joyless and severe (when he was there at all), and that his parenting had shaped the man her father would grow up to be. But he had softened, in that way grandparents often do, and when little Rhian came to visit, he was always spry and kindly and indulgent. He and Granny Nevett spoiled her rotten.

It had been the evening of Boxing Day, and Christmas still lay steadily against the house. The kitchen smelled of mince pies and of ginger wine, and seemed to echo still with last week's carollers. She had been sitting at the table playing with a plastic horse while Granny in her gingham pinny stirred a pot atop the stove and Grampa read the Bible in his rocking chair. The decorations she had made hung from the ceiling beams and mantelpieces so that the cottage was awash with raucous colour in the drear midwinter night around it. The place looked ready for a feast.

It was getting late – long past her usual bedtime. From time to time her granny would come over with a spoonful of her cooking for Rhian to taste, though dinner had been hours ago, and little Rhian took this duty with the utmost seriousness. Or else Grampa would send her off on little errands, fetching things around the house, and afterwards he'd set her on his knee and rock the rocking chair. Both he and Granny watched the clock. She sensed they were awaiting something, keeping her awake especially, though for what she could not guess.

And presently there came a jingling of bells. The distant crunch of many boots across the frozen common. Her first thought was that Father Christmas had returned, and she could scarce contain her joy. A *second* Christmas – could it be? She jumped up from the table, sending a bowl of oranges and walnuts scattering, and went tearing to the door, which she threw open with the quick, uncanny strength of five-year-old anticipation. A blast of icy air swept in and caused the fire to dance and throw wild shadows in the grate. It took her a long time to understand what she was seeing.

The moon shone warmthless and bone-white above the spoil tips on the hills, picking out the scene in silhouette like paper cutouts. The distant frame and winding gear of a pithead lift; the chimneypots of cottages across the village green; the mismatched wheels of a child's homemade gambo. And then a huddle of dark figures hastening across the frosty grass in mute procession – some with Davy lamps and some in stovepipe hats so that at first she thought they must have been carol singers come a few days late. But leading them was something that she could not fathom. A looming shadow, narrow as a man but taller by half, and draped in a white shroud like a child's costume of a ghost. It swayed and lurched along before the congregation. The tinkling of tiny silver bells preceded it.

A cloud passed across the face of the moon, and for a nervous moment all was darkness. Little Rhian stood framed in the doorway, shivering and squinting out into the night and starting to feel frightened now, but hopeful nonetheless that this strange visit might mean presents, might mean fun. But when the moon broke free again, it brought only a vision of sheer horror.

The shrouded giant leading the procession had the face of a

white horse. Only as it drew closer, she saw with an awful jolting, weak-kneed feeling that it was not a face but a skull. It was brightly beribboned and painted with colourful symbols, red and green, but all leached to black in the moonlight, and worse, somehow, for all its gaiety. The silver bells along its bridle tinkled coldly as it came. A wintry, deathly music. Blind, bulbous, luminescent eyes were set in its dead sockets, and its dark nasal cavity gaped, and its grinning, lipless mouth snapped open and shut rhythmically as if it whispered to her in a voice she could not hear. She had started, without knowing it, to back inside. Her eyes, though, did not leave the terrifying apparition.

Around it, she caught glimpses of its followers – men in topcoats and hats and flat caps like the mourners at her mother's funeral. When she had backed far enough inside, she slammed the door and latched and bolted it, and pressed her little back against it. 'Something's coming!' she hissed. 'It's a monster. It's a ghost.' She began with frantic urgency to turn off all the lights so that the fiend might not see in, and in a moment they were left with just the flickering firelight, and all was silent save her panicked breathing and the jingling of bells.

They were right outside now. She could see the windows darken as their shadows passed before the moon. And by and by there came a rapping at the door. It had been an ordinary knocking, probably, but in her memory it sounded like the tapping of dry bones, a hollow, grim, cadaverous sound like something old and too long dead come creeping from its dusty tomb. She buried her face in her granny's skirts while Grampa Nevett unfolded himself from his rocking chair and stalked across to answer it. 'Don't let it in,' she pleaded, but he did not seem to hear her. He appeared aged – more gaunt and drawn and sunken-eyed in the glow from the fireplace. He had to duck beneath the paper decorations strung between the ceiling beams, and when he reached the door and called, 'Who's there?' his voice sounded to Rhian for the first time like the voice of an old man. Her granny held her and hushed her and told her it would be all right.

What happened next was something she had not expected. The voices at the door began to sing – an eerie, faltering chorus, and there was something of the draughty chapel pew about it, but also something of the raucous village pub.

> *Wel dyma ni'n dwad,*
> *Gyfeillion diniwad,*
> *I ofyn am gennod*
> *I ganu.*

She understood the words, and at the same time did not. 'Here we come, dear friends, to ask for permission to sing.' But the meaning underneath them had been chillingly clear to her. They wanted to come inside. The dark figure of a man went flitting past the parlour window, and she could hear his footsteps going around towards the pantry door. The latch rattled. 'Don't let them in, Bampa,' she begged again, and Granny stroked her hair distractedly.

It was her grampa, now, who sang:

> *Ma'r cŵn a ma'r catha*
> *Yn cilio ta'r tylla*
> *Wrth glywad shwd lisha*
> *Nos heno.*

'The dogs and the cats are running to their holes at hearing such voices tonight.' And though his voice still sounded older than Rhian had known it, he did not sound afraid. He sang as he sang hymns every evening coming home along the lane from the colliery. A pale face appeared in the dark outside the kitchen window, and little Rhian screamed and set to bawling, and Granny let her go and took a broom and shooed the man away. He backed into the shadows, while the party at the front door answered.

The unnerving sing-song exchange went on this way for what seemed like an hour. Each time the awful phantoms just outside the door would sing an exhortation to be let inside, and each time Grampa Nevett would sing back some clever reason why he could not let them in. He must have been making them up on the spot. A ritual was how she came to think of it, but at five or six years old, it had been only terrifying.

She hid beneath the kitchen table, and the cowled, horse-headed spectre stalked around the outside of the cottage. Its blind marble eyes peered through the frosted windowpanes. Through her tears she saw its odd, inhuman puppet gait, and underneath its shroud its form seemed stooped and hunchbacked, as though unfurled it might stand taller than the house. She tried not to imagine what might be beneath that winding sheet, and the images came to her instead in nightmares later: a giraffe-neck of bones, curled like a finger; the shrivelled body of a horse contorted into human shape; something more terrible, even, than the grinning, ribboned skull that had to be covered lest it drive the looker mad. Above the song and the sound of herself crying, she heard the tinkling of its bells, the clacking of its jaw.

Outside the visitors sang mournfully:

> *Mae'n gaseg lwysgedd, wisgi.*
> *Mae miloedd yn ei moli.*
> *Ei phen hi'n gnotog enwog,*
> *O foddion llawn difaeddu.*
>
> *She's a lovely, lively mare.*
> *Many thousands praise her.*
> *Her glorious, ribbony head*
> *Is filled with enchantments.*

And then at once they were inside. She remembered her grampa standing aside in the doorway, suddenly no longer Christian with his hymns and Bible and starched suit, but complicit with this pagan spirit of the fields. The horse-thing swept in past him with an icy draught where flecks of frost flew glittering in the moonlight, its white sheet billowing, the fire blowing out and pitching the house into darkness. Little Rhian ran, terrified and shrieking, and the tall, dead thing pursued her. Tears and snot streamed down her face. She tripped and bumped into things that she could not see.

In her grandparents' bedroom, she tucked herself into a corner by her granny's lace-topped washstand. A moment later, the thing's bony, painted face came stooping through the door, its movements hideous and snaking. The bells on its bridle tinkled softly as it stalked into the room. It paused at the foot of one iron bedframe, its milky eyes seeming to search. Then, silhouetted in the moonlight, it came on. Between the feet of the two beds. Past the framed embroidery on the wall that read, *Christ is the head of this house; the unseen guest at every meal; the silent listener to every conversation.* She clasped her hands across her mouth to stop herself from screaming.

But then it did something distinctly unbefitting the decaying, deathless relic of a terrible and ancient god. It stumbled on the lino floor and kicked the chamber pot from underneath her granny's bed and swore, and its voice was a man's. Its shroud had got caught on the bedpost, and the hem lifted up enough for Rhian to see it had a pair of muddy boots on underneath. She had watched, at first paralysed with fear, and then bewildered, then amused, as the confusing apparition struggled to untangle itself, turning and cursing and clawing at the sheet. It wrestled singly for a moment, the horse skull jolting wildly. And finally, the figure inside freed himself, emerging from his wrappings in the moonlight like a moth from its cocoon, and Rhian could not help but giggle when she saw him.

It was her daddy. The dead horse had been her daddy all along. He stood there puffing, red-faced (and perhaps a little drunk, she would think later), holding his strange vestments as if glad at last to take them off, as if they had been burdensome to carry and their shedding had released him from a fugue. Then he squatted heavily and beckoned her from her hiding place, and she came out trailing spider-webs and with her face a mess from crying, but wearing an expression of relief and laughter now.

'I'm sorry if I scared you, del,' he said. His massive arms enfolded her and when he let her go again her tears had soaked the shoulder of his overalls. 'What a brave girl you are.'

He had knelt with her perched on his lap and shown her all the workings of his frightening disguise: the horse skull mounted on a long pole, like a grisly hobbyhorse, with a string so he could snap its jaws open and shut; the eyes filled with cloudy glass; the ribbons each contributed by women from the village. It was scary still, up close, but in a different way. No longer a living monster chasing her, but one of those adult peculiarities that she was still too young to understand, the way a child might catch an early glimpse of death or illness or divorce. Mostly, though, she found it fascinating. Magical, almost. To find that something that had seemed so supernatural was merely a contraption made of simple parts.

When they went back into the other room, a party was already under way. Grampa Nevett had brought out the beer he had been brewing in the garden shed, and poured it liberally, his Methodist severity forgotten. The costumed men were drunk as lords. Her granny served up mince pies and Caerphilly cheese and pickles, and peppermint ice and dates with marzipan, and in the middle of it all a fat, glazed ham that had been roasting since that morning. A swarthy, bearded fellow in a dainty bonnet and a dress was sweeping out the glowing cinders of the hearth, ready to light a new fire for the coming year. Rhian made her way to Granny through the raucous crowd of people crammed into the little cottage. 'You didn't have to terrify the poor girl like that,' Granny scolded, but before her daddy could apologize, Rhian said, 'I was only a *bit* scared.' By the time the visitors with their eerie figurehead had staggered out into the freezing dark again, she'd fallen fast asleep.

She remembered asking her granny about it the next day while she was hanging washing, half believing it might all have been a dream. She had woken in the pale, crisp light of late morning, and the cottage bore no trace of any late-night revellers. The windowpanes were bright, and it seemed impossible to her that a dead horse had come a-tapping at the glass. She had felt almost embarrassed when she asked.

But it *had* been real, her granny said. And she was sorry it had been so frightening, but that was all part of the fun. Rhian's daddy had been frightened too when it first came to him, and so had Granny when she was a little girl herself, and so had *Granny's* granny, on and on into the inconceivable past. She was called the Mari Lwyd – the Grey Mare, the Pale Horse – and she'd been visiting in the bleakest depths of winter for as long as any living person could remember. So long, in fact, that no one knew exactly how it started or what any of it meant, although Rhian would much later come to think it bore the hallmarks of some long-forgotten pagan ritual: a celebration of fertility and death entwined, and the innate wildness of horses, and the stone age cult of skulls.

'She was a mother horse,' Granny said, and the story she told was roughly this. 'It was the night Jesus was born – a cruel winter's night in Bethlehem, and Mary and Joseph with nowhere to go but a stable, and the baban Iesu on his way.' She talked through a mouthful of wooden clothes pegs while Rhian listened perched on an upturned bucket. The sheets on the line were already beginning to harden in the cold. 'And in that stable was a mother horse lying in the straw, heavy with foal and ready to give birth herself, just like Mary was. But there wasn't room in that stable for two mothers, you see. So d'you know what they did?' Rhian shook her head. 'The men of Bethlehem tied ropes around that poor mother horse and dragged her from her birthing bed. Heaved her out into the freezing cold to die.'

That was an image that came back to haunt her – the pregnant horse, aching with foal, screaming and whinnying and white-eyed as she was dragged into the night. It left a sour taste to the Nativity. And later she would wonder if there was a deeper symbolism to it: a lingering memory of the old religions being callously thrown out to make way for another's birth. Those upheavals made deep wounds that, even two thousand years on, could leave scars in the oddest places. And those old injuries could fester.

'So ever since,' her granny said, 'that poor dead mother horse has wandered through the night, looking for a house to welcome her. That's how my granny told it to me, anyway. And God willing, someday you'll tell it to your own granddaughter, too.'

The purgatorial dirge of the livestock auction had grown louder. The mighty Arwr still stood dolefully before her, as though he had been waiting for her reminiscence to conclude, and his great ribboned head looked heavy with a ponderous epiphany. Along the row of metal and cement, two youths were leading the first of the bulls out of its pen, off to the ring, and it went with them docile and plodding and tame.

To get a breath of air, she left the chaos of the livestock barn behind and crossed a weed-choked gravel yard to what was generously termed a cafe. It was a squat grey prefab structure with metal cages on the windows, set beneath a nest of loudly humming power cables. There was a dustbin at the door filled with the detritus of meals; a rotating sign that read *Hot Food*. She found herself a seat in a far corner, clearing a space among the empty trays, and ate a floury bacon roll slathered in sweet brown sauce, both dry and greasy at once, washed down with scalding tea out of a polystyrene cup. The food was comforting and she felt better, being away from the claustrophobic riot of the hangar. She would stay until it was time for her lots.

Geraint Jones from down the valley came in just as she was finishing her tea. There must have been a sudden downpour, because he stood and shook the rain from his waxed jacket and his cap before he paid for his paned and made a beeline for Rhian, a look of happy recognition on his weathered face. 'Ti'n iawn, Rhi?' he said cheerfully, pulling up a plastic garden chair. 'Not seen you since old Brynmor's funeral. Sorry we didn't get a chance to chat – I'd have had you round for dinner.' He took a sip of tea and winced and blew on it, and the cup looked like a thimble in his hands.

'You know how it is,' she shrugged. 'Not much time for socializing these days.' Saying it aloud made her acutely conscious of how much she missed their dwindling circle of friends. So much of one's identity was lost when there was nobody to share it with. 'How are you keeping?'

'Not bad,' he said. 'Just sold a lovely pair of breeders and a few clean lambs from last year's crop.' There was a bashful pride in his expression, as if not wishing to dwell on his success. Or not wishing to *look* like he was dwelling on it. 'Have yours gone yet? Some bugger's brought theirs in in a right sorry state.'

'Not yet.' She realized that she had crossed her fingers out of habit. Her knuckles looked gnarled and arthritic like her granny's. Their lambs would sell, she told herself. Sell cheap, perhaps, but they would sell.

They went through the ritual of friendly trivialities: the weather, politics, the price of lamb; births, marriages and deaths. Rhian was glad of some familiar company, even aged and stooped as Geraint was compared to the young, strapping man that she remembered. She supposed she looked the same to him. An old woman, now. How cruel time was. There was an agitation in his affability, though, as though there was something important that he could not bring himself to say.

'How's Carwyn, by the way?' he asked eventually. 'He's not—' He put his hand on hers, and she drew it back reflexively.

He's digging, she wanted to say. He's out there digging as we speak. And though the thought was unkind, she could feel the ugly truth of it. She said, a bit too hastily, 'He's fine.'

He nodded but seemed unconvinced. 'Only, when I saw you both a few weeks back, he didn't seem himself. A bit off, you know? He just seemed – I don't know – a bit thin. A bit tired.'

'He's fine, honestly now.' Without quite knowing why, she felt an anxious, sinking feeling as she told that lie. She wondered briefly if a part of Geraint's question was asked in the hope for Carwyn not to be all right – for her to be an eligible widow with her own flock and an enviable swath of upland pasture – a handsome prospect for an ageing widower still renting scattered grazing parcels here and there. Almost instantly she felt ashamed of the uncharitable vanity of such a feeling, but there was an odd sense, too, of bobbing in a rough sea while the lifeline thrown to her went floating out of reach. The silence stretched just long enough to be uncomfortable. She glanced up from her hands to find him looking troubled. 'He's fine,' she said again. 'Not much time for socializing these days, you know how it is.' This time it felt a little better.

They talked a while of other things, until when Rhian asked what time it was an hour had passed. She was still excusing herself – brushing the crumbs from her coat and downing the last dregs of her third cup of tea – when there came a sudden flurry of activity. A swell of panicked shouting carried from the mart pavilion, and then someone was screaming. The other patrons in the cafe got up and rushed to the windows, one boy of about ten in a bronco hat climbing onto a table to get a better view, while a couple of the men went hurrying out of the door.

Rhian and Geraint exchanged a questioning look. The shouting coming from the livestock shed had become general, mingled now with the frantic cries of animals, and it spread through the packed hangar like a conflagration. They went out into the drizzle, where people had already begun spilling from the shelter of the vast roof, seeming not to know whether to flee or stand transfixed. Several climbed onto the hurdles to see above the crowd; a man in overalls stood calling for his children; milling people spread into the road, and their dazed, shaken faces looked to Rhian like survivors in the aftermath of a disaster. The hanging cables overhead hissed menacingly in the rain.

Geraint led the way against the press of auctiongoers pouring from the hangar, and Rhian followed in his wake. Her first thought was that there must be a fire, but she could not smell smoke. They fought their way into the dark of the pavilion, and here the terror of the animals was deafening. She had not the faintest clue how she might make herself of use in an emergency – only that she wished to help. She was aware, as well, that her own fifty-seven lambs were penned up in there somewhere, and she would get them out if she could reach them. They were her first priority. The people could fend for themselves.

The crowd thinned as they neared the middle of the shed, and down the parallel rows other good Samaritans had come running. Ahead, she saw men standing on the catwalks and the barriers, struggling frenzied in the dirty rays that filtered through the skylight. They were haphazardly and ineffectually armed with anything that was to hand: one with a piece of scaffolding and another with the metal stand of a floodlight; a few with canes and crooks; one with an extension cord he wielded like a whip. For an absurd moment, they reminded her of the stick figures from a cave painting. All of them were shouting, some waving their outstretched arms as Carwyn sometimes did when herding, and there was an almighty bellowing and crashing and a clang of metal gates. And above the frantic livestock in the pens, she saw the back of something black and lustrous surge and buck in fluid stills.

Geraint had stopped in his tracks. Before she could see more, he turned and shook his head and ushered her away, and he looked pale and stunned. There was a different sort of hurry now as they retraced their steps. When they came out again into the overcast of day, he bent and vomited and sat down in the gravel. Someone was on the phone to the police. There were already sirens coming down the road.

Rhian had not got so good a look as he had, but what she had seen came back in awful, jarring snatches: Arwr the bull loose from his stall and wild with fury in the narrow walk between the pens; people grappling with him from the dubious safety of the barriers, beating at him fruitlessly like clumsy matadors; a pair of shears protruding from his shoulder, and the sheeting blood as black and glistening as molten tar. And mercifully, only glimpses of the rest. Arwr's owner lying on the ground beneath the beast's enormous, snorting head and trampling hooves, one side of his chest grotesquely flat, deflated, holding up his hands in blind surrender. She saw it with the numb detachment of a nightmare, and the memory felt already distant.

She was saying something, repeating the same phrase over and over without thought. 'He's dead,' she was sobbing. 'He's dead. He's dead.' The bull had tossed him, and he somersaulted limply in the air like a rag doll with half its stuffing gone, bending in more places than were joints. An eye bulged in the mangled wreckage of his face. And yet his hands still clawed beseeching at the wrath set loose upon him, as though his shattered body had not realized that it was done. 'He's dead,' said Rhian, almost willing it to be reality. She was still saying it when the police arrived.

It took most of the afternoon to get the auction clear. Firefighters came with silver blankets, and Rhian sat in the pickup cowled and shaking. Old Geraint stood across the car park in the glow of flashing blue and orange lights, his eyes glazed and vacant. She did not see him leave. They brought the man out on a covered stretcher, one arm dangling boneless from beneath the blanket, and some time after that a tow-truck came and winched the hulking carcass of the bull into a skip. Then one by one the other cars and lorries went away, until she was alone.

The sun set foul and sickly yellow on the salt marsh, and by nightfall she felt steady enough to drive home. She went the whole way at a crawl, not even changing gear, her headlights full and casting grotesque shadows in the winding lanes. She could not shake the feeling that it was her fault the man and bull had died – that whatever blight had settled on the farm had travelled with her and would taint all she touched with its contagion. She would stay at home, she thought, and keep the scourge contained. When she pulled into the yard, the house was dark. She let the unsold sheep out of the trailer and then went inside and wandered up- and downstairs, switching on the lights and calling out half-heartedly for Carwyn. She was too numb and weary to be worried. In truth, she did not even need to search. She knew already where he was by a deep, gnawing intuition. He was still out there digging.

VIII

Tachwedd

SLAUGHTER

The legions had departed. When Macsen Wledig had gone south to Gaul, they followed him with gratitude, only too glad to leave behind the cold, the wet, the wilderness. Their mighty forts and palaces stood silent, dripping, empty like the aftermath of some great cataclysm that had struck dead their inhabitants but left them otherwise untouched.

It was the herdsman's youngest daughter who first noticed that their neighbours' room was oddly still. They had all been living since the Great Abandonment in a deserted villa near the lake – several families of settlers come down from the old vicus of Segontium to farm. They were rugged and hard-working folk. By sunrise, there was normally a bustle of activity: animals to feed and water to be fetched and cook fires to be tended, children playing in the fallen leaves along the shore, the old yellow mongrel dog let loose and barking. This morning, though, an eerie quiet lay upon the place, as though the cold mist creeping from the water's edge had swallowed every sound and rendered mute the house's occupants.

The girl went to the door and called out but received no

answer. She wrapped herself more tightly in her woollen cloak. There was an ashy scent of cinders from a fire that must have burned out in the night, and it mingled with another odour that she did not recognize but found instinctively unpleasant – a rich metallic smell, like rusted iron. A long-handled dolabra stood against the wall, its axe edge and its pick edge both matted with blood and hair. She guessed (or hoped, perhaps) that someone had been using it to slaughter goats. Calling out again, more loudly now but with a hint of hesitation in her voice, she pushed aside the wicker door and waited for her eyes to grow accustomed to the darkness.

Up on the mountainside, the naked man was woken by her distant screams and knew his work had been discovered. The thought gave him a pleasant frisson. An echo of what he had felt the night before – the thrill that drove him. They would search for him, as always, but he did not fear them as he used to. He too had been a farmer once, and knew their ways. He found that he could disappear into the clouds, into the caves and crevices and boulder fields where their hounds would not follow, and they would think him a lemure or shade come out to haunt them. The patresfamilias would scatter beans at midnight, and the women-folk would beat bronze pots to drive away the spirits, and a few nights hence he'd venture down to strike again elsewhere. He curled himself into the caved-in passage of the barrow like a hibernating snake, the rich, black dirt of it embedded underneath his gory fingernails where he had clawed his way by hand into the frozen ground. The cold no longer troubled him. From deeper in the earth, the whispering began again.

She watched the winter come with growing dread. There was a leaden certainty, deep in her stomach, that it would be worse than any that preceded it, and she took to gauging its approach by superstitious auguries: how frantically the squirrels hoarded, how brightly the haws in the hedgerows grew, how early and how often the migrating flocks flew overhead. The animals and plants could sense it somehow, and their urgency brooked little reassurance.

November swept into the mountains in a shroud of heavy overcast that never fully lifted. It rained with grim intensity and without warning, and even when it stopped, a dampness hung perpetually in the air. The treetops in the valley turned to russet. On the precious few dry days, there was frost. The trackways of sheep stood out green against the silver grass, and tourist guidebooks might have called it 'picturesque' or 'atmospheric', but to Rhian all these signs foretokened only hardship.

She worried about Carwyn. Missed him, even. It seemed they seldom spoke now, and saw little of each other, like ships passing in the night. For months, the change in him had been so gradual she scarcely noticed it, but these last few weeks it was quickening. When he crawled into bed each evening, he seemed to her a different man, gaunt and sallow and fretful. His breath smelled. His once-neat beard was an unruly tangle. He spoke of strange things, as if to himself – of the dark mound he was exhuming in the hollow, mostly, but also of more abstract topics that she found increasingly unlike him and alarming. How they alone were holding out against a tide they could not stop. How, on these drear days when clouds descended on the farm, they existed in a liminal space neither wholly earth nor sky, and he had glimpsed things in the mist that he could not describe. How things used to be better when there had been local gods who occupied themselves with no more than a single valley or a mountain or a lake, for a god who ruled alone over the universe could hardly be expected to attend to so remote a place as this. At night she lay awake and fearful while he thrashed and muttered in his sleep.

'I think you need to see a doctor,' she told him one morning. It was a day of ceaseless drizzle, and he had come back from the auctions with a pair of handsome tupping rams whose cost she did not want to estimate, ready to be loosed upon the breeding ewes. There was a swagger to these animals. They seemed to know what duty lay ahead.

'What for?'

She realized she had not thought of how to broach the subject. Had been putting it off, in fact, for fear of how he might respond or what the doctor might reveal. 'You're not yourself. You don't seem well.'

A look of convincing perplexity passed across his face. 'Ond dwi'n iawn. Dwi'n wych.' He danced a little jig to demonstrate.

'You *look* ill, Carwyn. I know you can't stand doctors, but I'm worried about you. Will you go for me, if not for yourself? Just to humour me?'

It was only there an instant. A flash of hateful fury in his eyes, gone a fraction of a second later, but she saw it and it frightened her. The rams tugged at their bridle-ropes, eager to be about their business with the ewes, and Carwyn held them patiently. He grinned a lopsided, indulgent grin. 'Waste of time, love, honestly. I'm better than I've felt in years. It's these boys that'll need a doctor when they're done – they're going to be exhausted.' Pulling on his flat cap and waxed jacket, taking up his stick, he led the rams out of the barn.

Rhian spent the next days helping with the tup. Carwyn seemed genuinely to improve, throwing himself into the work of breeding so that he had little time for digging, and it began to feel like the last few months' troubles had just been a phase, or stress, or half imagined. She sorely wished she had some means of divination to confirm or lay to rest her fears.

One afternoon before dark, she went out for a breath of air and walked the wide perimeter of the farm. The rain had lifted, but a thin fog had come down in its place and left the landscape vague and formless. She wandered through it hooded, following the damp stone walls, for every time she strayed into the open she seemed to get turned around. More than once she felt sure she had headed straight across a field, only to find herself back at the gate she'd entered by. Nothing was in its proper place. The stream was in full flood, and on the other side she found a gathering of ewes, their backs stained bright with raddle where the rams had mounted them. Come April, they would lamb. In with fireworks and out with fools, that was how Carwyn's mother used to put it. There seemed far fewer in the flock than there ought to have been.

At a dismantled stile, she passed one of the signs he had erected, warning dire punishments to any who strayed across. Seeing them always jolted her – the same feeling as drifting off to sleep and stepping out into a sudden nothingness. They stood now, fading and forlorn, awaiting the return of tourists in the spring. Who was this angry man who used to be so welcoming? It had not been so long ago that he would stand and chat with the occasional hikers, campers, passers-through. Only the dog walkers had bothered him. She leaned and looked across the sweep of hillside, remembering the two lost hikers he had brought into their kitchen on his birthday, and she was surprised at how much longing and nostalgia such a recent time could hold. Now these black walls in the mist felt solid and impregnable, with her, Carwyn and Eira on one side and all the world on t'other.

Coming uphill again towards the house, she heard a cawing, and in a tangle of barbed wire she came upon a near-grown lamb, still living, with its eyes and tongue pecked out. It stood there blindly grazing as though utterly untroubled by these losses, and she could see the stalks moving in their vacant sockets when it raised its bloody head at her approach. Atop the wall nearby there sat three ravens. Their tattered feathers ruffled in the breeze, and they eyed Rhian with a spiteful, nonchalant intelligence. She had asked for an omen, and there could be few clearer ones than this. She shooed them, but they did not go.

That night, she felt fragile and shaken. Carwyn made dinner, and they sat down to eat together for the first time in a month. He had something of his old self about him, joking as he cooked, and though he still looked haggard, his demeanour reassured her that a corner had been turned. The table had been set with candles, cleared of all the mess of bills and threatening letters. Lamb, of course, was on the menu. A juicy leg with mint sauce and carrots and potatoes, and he made up for his lack of culinary skill with effort and enthusiasm. Eira sat beside the stove, gnawing contentedly on a long bone.

Afterwards they lay in bed and listened to the drumming of the rain upon the roof slates and the rustling in the attic. 'It's going to get better soon,' he said, 'I promise. We're going to have a lean few months without the auction money, but come the spring, all this will have been worth it.' He laced his fingers through hers, looking at her earnestly. 'Do you trust me?'

She wanted to, how desperately she wanted to. Perhaps just wanting was enough. 'I do.'

'I've just been feeling at a loss. Getting old, I suppose. Everything's changing so much faster than it used to. These people everywhere, and they're not like us like they used to be when we were young. They want our lamb and our landscapes, but not our ways. When I went into town the other day, I didn't hear a word of Welsh.' His grip on her hand tightened gently. She could feel his hopeful look, but kept her eyes downcast and could not meet his gaze. These were not sentiments she had ever imagined he would harbour. 'How many kids speak Welsh today? If we'd had our own, it would have been different.' That hurt her deeply. They *had* had their own, even if she never spoke a word. Carwyn himself had been the one to point that out when she had been too deep in grief to see it. How could he be so cold about it now?

'And all these bloody politicians down in London making rules for us who don't know the first thing about the countryside or how it works.' There was more sadness than annoyance in his voice. 'I know I've not been pulling my weight, I'm sorry. But the digging, it just feels important. The people who built that, they were farmers, shepherds, mountain people just like us – *Welsh* people. Some of the very first Welsh people, maybe. And however many thousands of years later, here we are, maybe some of the very last.' He gave her an apologetic smile. 'I know you think I'm daft, but it's important to me. I'm on to something big, you'll see. It's going to save us.'

There was a long and pregnant silence. She did not answer, but turned off the light and straddled him and wept with tired relief, and afterwards in fitful sleep she dreamed of ravens on a barren mountainside, picking clean her bleached and scattered bones.

She spent the next week willing the world back into a fragile semblance of normality. Carwyn's eccentricities were chalked down to forgetfulness, or stress, or ageing – perhaps even the creeping onset of dementia. How bad must things have got, she wondered, for that to feel like a reassurance? The chickens still came scratching for their feed, rangy and balding and beady-eyed, but still reliable companionship. There were cabbages and leeks and parsnips in the vegetable patch that needed tending, though they grew now in grotesque and stunted shapes that disconcertingly resembled hands, faces, homunculi. Cooked, they tasted sour or musty or insipid. Or, bizarrely, of completely different vegetables. No matter. 'If it doesn't stick in your throat, it'll not stick in your arse,' her father would have said.

In the iron overcast of morning, when the sky seemed to press ever lower on the mountaintops, she checked the progress of the rams, and dagged the tails of the ewes to make them easier to mount, and turned a blind eye to the dwindling numbers of the flock. At first she counted them, finding one or two fewer every day, and when this trend began to feel disturbing she stopped keeping tally; but soon the shrinkage was unmissable even without a count. Escaped, she reasoned – they must have been finding a way out up to the higher pastures, and would return to lamb come spring. Carwyn had clearly been neglecting his routine of wall repairs.

On a Monday, she slept well past sunrise and awoke to voices in the kitchen. Carwyn and a woman deep in conversation, and in her still half-dreaming state she felt an abrupt, palpitating certainty that he was having an affair. That this, all along, was the true cause of his odd behaviour, his constant absences, his change. And he had brought this mistress now into the very bosom of their home, to make his infidelities official. She threw on one of his white woollen turtlenecks that still smelled of lanolin ('Where did you park the U-boat?' she had asked when he first wore it), then brushed her teeth and splashed cold water on her face, and catching sight of herself in the bathroom mirror she was struck by what a poor competitor she would make to a romantic rival. How *old* she looked, when it was only yesterday she had been twenty. Had her hair always been so grey? Her posture so stooped? Her cheeks so sunken and her teeth so long and yellowing? What a source of needless misery it was, she thought, to see ourselves only through our own uncharitable eyes.

But, coming down the stairs, she saw the woman sitting at the kitchen table was a police officer – a radio and handcuffs hanging menacingly from her coat. There was a threat implicit in that uniform, something that spoke to an ancestral mistrust of the troops who had been sent to smash the Merthyr Rising or deport the Merched Beca or to pay the traitors' tail pounds at the Penrhyn Strike. Although she knew that she had done nothing wrong, a wave of irrational fear went through her.

The woman greeted Rhian with a tired, apologetic smile. Aside from the impression of her strict attire, she did not seem the least bit frightening. She had the air of someone with more pressing matters to attend, and she sat perched awkwardly beside the overflowing paperwork, taking cautious sips out of a steaming mug that dwarfed her hands. The bull. She must have come about the bull.

'You haven't seen this lad, have you, del?' Carwyn asked Rhian as she ducked into the kitchen. He handed her the policewoman's phone. 'He doesn't ring any bells for me.'

She took it clumsily, this object she was unaccustomed to, and by the time she looked at it the screen had gone dark and she had to ask the visitor to bring the picture up again. It showed three handsome young men with their pints upraised in the beer garden of a pub, all smiling with their arms around each other's shoulders in the sunshine. Then, swiping to one side, one of them in a suit and tie. Swiping again – the same man playing a guitar. Again, this time with a pretty young woman and a child of two or three. Then another showing him with several others at a wedding. 'No, nor for me, I'm sorry. What's the matter?'

'He's been reported missing,' the officer explained. An unpleasant swell of static that might have contained a choir of voices buzzed briefly from her radio and then returned to silence.

'From here?'

'No, no. Not necessarily. He could be almost anywhere really.' Her tone was weary and placatory, as though she knew she was too busy to be wasting other busy people's time. 'The last his family knows, he planned to go wild camping somewhere in

Eryri or the Rhinogs at the weekend, but nobody's heard a peep out of him since.'

'Oh gosh,' said Rhian. 'I hope he's all right.'

'We're not too worried yet. You know how it is with these people – they come over from Birmingham or Liverpool because it looks like a nice day and they think they're going to climb Yr Wyddfa in flip-flops and a T-shirt.' She shook her head ruefully, and her expression left no doubt this young man was far from the first to embark unprepared on such a reckless errand. 'The mountain rescue teams in Aberglaslyn and Llanberis have already been out looking. They get one like this every couple of days. They'll find him. He'll have a cold and miserable few nights and learn his lesson, or he'll turn up at home tomorrow saying he's been fine but couldn't get a signal. I've just been going door to door in case he's sheltering in a barn or something. You'd be amazed.'

When she thought about it later, Rhian could not put a finger on exactly what it was, but in that moment some profoundly ugly feeling made her want to study Carwyn's face – examine him for any trace of guilty knowledge of the missing man. Her intuition flared, just briefly, and then quieted again. He knows, she thought, he's done something, but a glance at his eyes immediately reassured her. This was Carwyn. This was her husband. This was the man she'd known and loved and trusted all her life. A gentle, caring man who wept whenever one of their lambs died. A bit changed lately, granted, and always late with paying bills, always slapdash when it came to paperwork or tax returns, but not a criminal. And absolutely not a murderer. He caught her glance, and the expression in his eyes was one of utterly sincere worry. 'Come on,' he said. 'We'll go and have a look.'

They searched the house and then the yard and then the outbuildings, making gloomy small talk as the policewoman shone her torch into the attic ('Phew, something nesting up there,' she said as she climbed back down, waving away the musty reek), the hayloft, the cobwebbed, junk-strewn corners of the long barn. In Carwyn's workshop, the torch beam swept across the carved stone head, and in the fleeting light it looked to Rhian like it wore an awful, knowing grin, but when the torch shone full on it she saw that it was as it always had been. Eerily expressionless. They took the officer up to a windswept vantage-point where she could see out over all the farm. She surveyed it with a pair of Carwyn's binoculars. 'Those woods down there,' she asked eventually, 'are they part of the property?'

'They are,' said Carwyn, but before he could say more the heavens opened and sent all three running to find shelter. They made their way back downhill through the downpour, soaked and laughing bitterly with disbelief at the sheer suddenness of it, and at her car the policewoman thanked them hurriedly and told them not to wait, and not to worry. 'Poor bugger,' Carwyn said as they stood dripping in the hallway, 'I hope he's not outside somewhere in this.'

Rhian agreed and had begun to ask, 'Where's Eira?' but no sooner had the question formed than the drenched dog came scampering through the door and shook the raindrops from her fur. Outside, the morning had grown ominously dark.

December crept into the house unnoticed. For near three weeks, the weather kept them more and more indoors, and Carwyn took to reading, voraciously reading. This barely literate mountain man, who hitherto had been no more acquainted with the written word than leafing through a farmer's almanac or auction catalogue, began devouring dense, impenetrable volumes overnight. When he had finished everything in his grandmother's old collection, he ordered more by post. Academic papers and used textbooks with clear plastic overcovers and blue library stamps from the universities of Chester and Bangor and Aberystwyth. 'Spatial Distribution of Prehistoric Monuments in Wales', 'A Study of the Reuse of Passage Graves', 'Death in the Neolithic: The Role of the Child'. 'Sacramental Cannibalism in the Pleistocene'. 'Anthropophagic Dreams'. They lay untidily around the house alongside copies of the Mabinogion and *Bullfinch's Mythology* and *Llyfr Taliesin*, all marked with dog-eared pages and torn scraps of envelopes. They disturbed her in a vague, sordid way, as if she'd come across a stash of his pornography. She read the lines he'd singled out, but could discern no common thread to link them, nor any reason why he might have felt them worthy of particular attention.

She forgot all about the policewoman's visit. The face of the missing young man faded completely from her memory, so that she might have passed him in the street and would not know him, and no more news and no more questions came about his whereabouts.

They spoke little, and when they did, Carwyn talked in riddles and morose philosophies. On an envelope on the kitchen table, he scrawled, 'Are the gravestones we put up in cemeteries a continuation of a need to mark our sacred sites with standing stones?' She threw it in the bin without wanting to ask him what he thought the answer was.

'We're old,' he said one night. 'We're dying. How long might we have? Ten years? Ten years if we're lucky.'

She would have liked to disagree with such a bleak prognosis but found that she could not.

'I was thinking,' he continued, and there was a subtle slurring to his words, as if he had been drinking, 'what's going to be left of us after we're gone?' The rain drummed on the roof slates while he waited for an answer, then supplied his own. 'What's left is what we build. The people who built the circle knew that – look at it, still standing after all this time. But what's left of my mam and dad? My nain and taid? Nothing. They've been forgotten, and the way they lived has been forgotten.'

This time she did speak up, and forcefully. 'What's left of them is *you*, Carwyn. Not bloody stones. *People*, all the people who they made a difference to and left a mark on. Everybody who remembers them.' They used to have debates like this for fun, but tonight she saw a leaden and unyielding seriousness in his eyes. His lips were thin and cracked and humourless. He frightened her.

'And who's going to remember us?' he asked. A gust of wind howled down the chimney. The rain seemed to intensify, a sleet-edged squall that lashed against the windowpanes and set them rattling in their sashes. Try as she might, she could not think of a response.

That night, staring up into the fluid darkness in between the ceiling beams, the thought occurred to her that she might take some time away. It was a series of ideas that coalesced into decisions, then into a plan, the process too vague and gradual to define, like trying to determine the precise point where a stream becomes a river. It was a product more of feeling than of cold evaluation. A growing certainty that she would simply have to go, just briefly, for the good of them both, though if someone had pressed her for detail she would have been unable to provide it. Carwyn had simply changed, in myriad small ways. His peculiar obsession with the buried stones was part of it, of course, but it was harmless on its own. An old man's hobby. What concerned her was the souring of their lives, the growing rift between them. Even the mountain air no longer tasted like it used to. The farmhouse smelled of strangers' homes. Hindsight made her wonder if she was a fool not to have got out sooner.

Hindsight was a traitor anyway, she thought, lying awake and cold and restless while he slept his strange, taut, coiled-spring sleep beside her. Her life so far had not been over-generous when it came to second chances. What if she had married Billy Owen when he went off to become a barrister? What if she had taken up the scholarship at Durham University? What if she had travelled Europe with a backpack and a badly tuned guitar? You're never too old, people so glibly said, but there would be no going back to try again. And she was not sure she would want to even if she could. For now, there was only forward. Hindsight was just a multiplier of regrets.

In hindsight, the last day that Carwyn Gwynnant truly was himself had been a Thursday. It passed, as such things almost always do, without much notice. The most remarkable thing about it was the weather. A double sun dog came up with the dawn – an eerie halo hanging in the mid December sky – and they remarked that it would once have been regarded as a portent of a bitter winter. He seemed contrite this morning, almost bashful, as if he'd read the run of her recent nocturnal thoughts and they had shaken him. Their plan had been to scan the breeding gimmer ewes for pregnancy, and Rhian steeled herself for anything from disappointment to disaster. The flock had suffered terribly with liver fluke a week or two ago and lost a great deal of condition, but they were still hardy animals. Carwyn was decontaminating the old run of metal gates beside the rented ultrasound machine, burning off the mites and tangles of fouled wool with a gas wand hosed up to a propane bottle. She hated that contraption – it always looked to her like some abhorrent piece of weaponry, as deadly to its wielder as its targets, and there was not a single time he used it when her mind's eye didn't see him going up in flames.

There was a moment when she looked away to make sure Eira had the ewes in check, and in that very instant came a deep and resonant boom. Her heart lurched. She jerked her head to look, already certain she would find him blazing there, engulfed in oily fire and roaring as he burned alive. But he was fine. He stood looking slightly puzzled, and there was time for their eyes to meet before the booming came again. Thunder. A long roll of it this time, so near it made the hillside tremble, though the sky was a pale, wintry blue and the day crisp and rainless. A tang of ozone lingered in the air.

They continued with the scanning, then, perplexed but undeterred, and she felt buoyed by the results they saw. She worked the gate at the end of the run, marking the hip of each passing ewe as Carwyn called the numbers of embryo sacs he saw: blue for triplets, green for twins, yellow for a single. The barren ones she marked with red to go for sale or slaughtering. She couldn't quite believe what she was hearing – twins and triplets almost every one, the dry ewes few and far between. A bounteous breeding year by even the most optimistic standard.

He came up to her grinning when the last of them was through. 'I told you things would turn around.'

She nodded, wondering how it was possible, feeling that there must be some mistake. Perhaps the ultrasound machine was scrambled by the thunder. And yet, when she looked at the flock, the signs were there to see with her own eyes: they *had* been looking better lately, healthier; their bellies had begun to round out subtly; their udders hung a little lower; they hadn't bothered with the rams for weeks.

'We didn't need to rent that bloody scanner after all. You can see it.' He looked at her, and when she did not answer he said once again, as much to himself as to her, 'You can see it, can't you?'

Their astonishment was broken by a sudden fall of hail. It sent them scurrying for shelter, Eira yelping, but no sooner had it started than it was already over, as though it had all fallen from the clear sky at a single stroke. All afternoon the hailstones lay unmelted in the frosty grass, as big as marbles. The thunder came again at nightfall, a hollow, echoing rumble that rattled all the crockery in the house and loosed a slate which skittered down the roof to shatter on the doorstep. Carwyn brought out a patchwork quilt his nain had made, and as they spread it on the bed with Eira curling up on it at once, Rhian allowed a hopeful note to creep into her thoughts. At midnight, a torrential rain set in.

The next morning, she began to feel a little better, willing to believe the strangeness of the last few months had all been just another passing episode. They'd seen their share of ups and downs before. Blame this one on age, or stress, or lack of sleep – chalk it up to Pluto in the Twelfth House, even. There was comfort in an explanation, even when it was absurd. The infestation of misgivings that had settled somewhere just beneath her ribcage was still gnawing at the edges of her thoughts, but with an effort she could drown it out. Carwyn breezed into the bathroom whistling while she washed herself perfunctorily at the sink, and he stood urinating with the cheerful air of someone looking forward to the day ahead. A year ago, that would have irked her ('Can't you wait two ticks, you bloody mochyn?'), but this morning it seemed wondrous.

He made for them a celebratory breakfast: plump sausages and strips of bacon fried until they crackled; poached eggs fresh from the coop; baked beans and laverbread and buttered toast and tea. 'We're going to be all right, you know,' he said, and his voice was bright and certain. 'It's working. It's *heard* me.' His face had lost the haunted aspect that so worried her. He still looked gaunt and dirty, but today it was an altogether vigorous dishevelment.

She did not ask what he meant, nor was there time to wonder, for he continued with his jovial prognostications while he cooked up second helpings. In truth, she barely took in what he said. It was enough to bask in his fine mood – become so rare that she had feared it lost entirely – like feeling the first sunny day of spring after a gruelling winter.

Too full to eat another bite, she pushed the last few scraps of bacon to one side and whistled. But in answer there came only unexpected silence. No scampering of running paws, no swish of wagging tail, no eager panting. 'Where's Eira got to now?'

At first, she thought his look of puzzlement was simply at the obviousness of her question, as though she might turn and see the little collie at her side. 'Eira?' He looked out into the dreary morning and then back at her, confused. 'What do you mean, "Eira"?'

'Eira, Carwyn! *Eira!*'

Concern, now, as he sat beside her and laid his hand over hers. 'We haven't had old Eira for years, del. Wyt ti'n teimlo'n iawn? Christ, we must have buried Eira back in '87.'

'You're pulling my leg,' she scoffed, but felt a tremble in her voice. 'She slept on the bloody bed with us last night. Her bowl's there, look.'

But it was not. The little nook beside the oven where Eira used to sleep before she took to joining them upstairs was empty. No bowl, no doggy bed, no bag of food.

She drew her hand from under his. More seriously this time she said, 'Carwyn. I'm not in the mood for joking. Where's Eira?' She enunciated each word with a slow firmness that sounded more accusatory than she had intended. Blood pounded in her ears. She felt as though she had to either faint or vomit, so she gripped the table-edge and swallowed hard to force the urge away.

All the while he met her gaze with worried patience, and the look chilled her all the more, for she could find in it no hint of humour or deception. 'Do you want me to phone the doctor?' She could see in his eyes the very fear she felt for him – was this the start of some insidious decline? It outraged her to be thought of that way. A poor senile old dotard. *He* was the one who had spent six months grubbing in the dirt while the farm foundered. *He* was the one who would be starving on the street in rags if she was not around to shop or pay the bills or do his laundry. *He* was the one who didn't even know they had a dog, for goodness' sake.

She shook her head resolutely, and the shaking seemed to loose a thought: 'We've hundreds of sheep on this farm, Carwyn. Are you trying to tell me you've been chasing them up and down a mountain all this time without a dog?'

'Of course not. Not *inside* dogs though – a pair of yard dogs in the kennels down at Ifor's. We bring them up when there's flock work to do.' He gestured vaguely at the window. 'Look, have another cup of tea. Stay here in the warm today. I've got some things I need to see to, but I'll manage on my own. Try not to fret about all this. It'll come back to you.'

Rhian nodded, but she was only half listening.

'I'd better get on while it's dry. You'll be all right, now, won't you? I won't be far.'

She nodded again with a weak smile, and he kissed her distractedly on the cheek as he gathered up the muddy canvas bundle of excavation tools and ducked out of the door.

Some of the shock subsided with his parting, leaving in its place a sense of grim bemusement. There were two options, as far as she could see, neither of them reassuring: either one of them was losing it, or he was lying. She struggled to believe the latter. For all his flaws and foibles, he had always been a hopeless liar. (He's different now, though, said a quiet voice of doubt at the back of her mind, but she pushed it away.) The former, then – she knew damn well it wasn't her. She might sometimes lose track of the days of the week, or walk into a room without a clue what she went in there for, but this was altogether different. Eira was their dog, not thirty, forty years ago, but *now*; she clung to that with a fierce certainty. If she was wrong about Eira, she might as well throw away everything else she knew and start again.

For the first time that morning, it occurred to her to worry about Eira's safety, and the realization made her feel ashamed at being so caught up in her own cares. She wondered if there might have been an accident, or if Eira's ripe age had finally caught up to her, and weighed the possibility that Carwyn's story might have been a misguided attempt to spare her feelings. They had lost many dogs before, but each loss was sharp-edged and cruelly unique. Sorrow was not, in her experience, a thing that became easier with practice, and nor did the foreknowledge of its coming blunt its bite. In her mind, a pet was borrowed happiness that someday had to be repaid in grief. Eira, though, she had loved Eira more than all the others. Her loss – if she was lost – would be a heavy one to bear.

Faintly, it occurred to her that Carwyn might have been responsible, but she chastised herself immediately for even letting in the thought. Ridiculous to think that he would ever hurt that dog. Ten years or so before, a thoughtless walker let a black lab loose among the ewes at lambing time. This was the countryside, the idiot had reasoned – the ideal place to give the dog a run around out in the open air – and the dog, not knowing any better than its master, did what dogs were born to do. The scent of the new lambs had piqued its curiosity, and when they ran, its instinct to give chase and hunt them drove it wild. By the time the man caught up to it, the damage was already done. It was a bloodbath. The owner stood and shouted at it from the gate, but the dog paid him no heed. He seemed stunned that this gentle animal, well trained to sit and stay and come when called with no distractions in the living room, could be an altogether different beast when loosed on fleeing, bleating prey. In the end, Carwyn had heard the barking and come running down and prised its jaws from one ewe's throat (getting bitten himself in no small measure). Six newborn lambs lay ripped to tatters all across the field. One ewe had died of fright, another two miscarried the next day; one had its ear torn off, one's leg was gouged clean to the bone. A dozen more had fled into a narrow gully where they smothered one another in their terror.

When Rhian arrived, the man was falling over himself with excuses and apologies: 'He's soft as anything, daft as a brush. He wouldn't hurt a fly. I'll pay whatever this has cost you.' He fumbled in a pocket for his wallet and came up with several notes.

Carwyn, though, was not so easily appeased. He was shaking with fury, gripping the dog by its collar with one hand and casting the money down into the mud with the other. The thought of it had been insulting, he had told her later, like offering to pay a parent after running down their child. 'I ought to shoot the thing,' he spat, and both Rhian and the walker could see that this was no idle threat. The man fell to his knees while Carwyn stormed back up the hill to fetch his gun. His wrath seemed elemental, and the walker must have felt this too, for he made no move to leave. Futile to try to outrun it.

A long time passed. She waited there with them beside the grisly scene, and when Carwyn did not return she told the man that he should go and not come back. She found Carwyn in his workshop, cradling little Eira on his lap with tears streaming down his rugged face.

* * *

She searched the house, calling Eira's name, and then went out into the yard and found no trace of her there either. Only the barn cats and the hens, who kept a wary distance as she moved among them. A chill breeze bore the scent of smoke, of hearths and garden rubbish. Bonfire season. Woodpiles stocked against the coming winter.

Not for the first time, she was unable to shake the sense of a colossal, brooding presence underneath the mountain. Bared by the cold and blackened by the rain, the crags towered watchfully around her. On days like this, when the tourists had gone and the locals had retreated to their firesides, it was not so easy to disbelieve the old stories of hags and ogres and giants that used to haunt these high passes. It was a landscape where one might meet gods.

She ducked into the long barn, where a tiny, unseen, rustling creature fled at her approach. Light fell thinly through the narrow slitted windows, glassless like the loopholes in a castle wall and moaning with each breath of wind. This was her home, her workplace, but she felt that she was seeing it for the first time the way a stranger might. An eerie, claustrophobic place. The stone walls flecked with hay and dung and snags of wool. The space they now used as the shearing floor, but where hung chains and hooks that hinted at its prior usage. Dust drifted from the dark above the beams to settle in her hair as she proceeded deeper. Eira used to play in here when she was just a pup – pursuing swallows, mice, or semi-feral cats among the heaps of old equipment, and a part of Rhian half expected she might find her there this morning.

In the nearest stall, she lifted the dustsheet that covered a precarious stack of pails and buckets. A curled dead spider, weightless, fell onto her sleeve and she brushed it away reflexively. No Eira hiding there. The next, a big chest freezer and shelves groaning with their winter pantry of boxes and tins. Traps to keep the rats away. Ladders in the next stall, and a rusted roll of fencing wire, and spare parts for a tractor they no longer owned. The last stall had been piled so high and deep with a miscellany of cast-offs that, for fear of dislodging an avalanche upon herself, she had to bend and peer underneath, pulling out loose items where she could to clear her view. A half-full spray can of adoption musk; a ram harness and a box of tupping crayons; a pair of footrot shears. And then a boot.

It was a hiking boot, a man's, and barely worn except that a walk's worth of mud and grass clung to the treads. She looked again under the stack but could not see its partner and sat for a moment puzzled, turning it over in her hands. Not Carwyn's size, nor the kind of thing she'd ever seen him wear. Too new. Lost-and-found, a helpfully naive voice of denial offered – in the early nineties they had opened up a field to campers, and the sheer number of things that they had lost or left behind had been astonishing: wallets, watches, glasses, shoes. ('How can you forget a *shoe*?' they used to wonder, laughing.) But this was not a relic of that time. Whose, then? The fine hairs on her arms stood up. With a shiver of disgust she kicked it back under the pile and let the sheet drop over it.

The air in the barn had grown close and smothering despite the cold. Rhian stumbled out into the drizzling, milk-white overcast, unsure of what she would do next except that she needed to get away. She needed to get her thoughts straight. Things had not been right for months, but now they all seemed to be coming to a head: Eira disappeared, Carwyn's strange new manic cheerfulness. His *constant* bloody digging. The words 'nervous breakdown' came to her. (Did they still call it that?) Something up here was clouding her wits, making her thinking slow and foggy and perpetually distracted, uncertain of herself and what she wanted in a way that she had never been before.

He was coming up the field towards her and she met him at the gate to tell him of her plan: a break, some time apart, just for a week or two; she had some money put aside for an emergency and this was it. She scrutinized his face for a reaction. Anger, disapproval, wariness. But to her surprise there was only concern and acquiescence, and perhaps – only perhaps – a little eagerness. 'It's a good idea, del. It'll do you good, I think.' He laid his hand on hers atop the gate. Her fingers pricked with pins and needles.

'Are you sure you can manage?'

He puffed out his cheeks, tallying the coming tasks. 'Quiet time now, isn't it? The lambs are out to keep. Bit of ditching to clear, a few walls to mend.' She noted that he did not mention digging. 'I'll cope.'

It took her a moment to summon up the nerve to ask the next question, whose answer she was unsure if she truly wanted: 'Carwyn, there's a boot in there. Where did it come from?'

'A boot?'

'A walking boot. A man's.'

His brow furrowed, and then a sudden look of realization dawned in his face. He snapped his fingers. 'Those campers – do you remember? Those bloody trespassers a couple of months ago who made that mess. They left it in the field, the silly buggers. Someone must have had a wet foot. Serves them right. Come on, we'll get your bags packed and I'll drop you down to Betws.'

The charitable side of her, still mostly in charge, was grateful for how quickly he had understood. And she thought she had detected something of the old Carwyn – a hope in his eyes that she might yet escape whatever was consuming him, even if he could not. There had been a fleeting, pleading look that seemed to whisper, 'Go while you still can.' And yet, another part of her could not help feeling he would be glad to be rid of her, glad of the opportunity to carry on his work in peace.

IX

Rhagfyr

DIMINISHING

The only sounds to be heard were the howling of the blizzard, and the crunching of the laden ponies' hooves, and the sobbing of the seven women. An avalanche had closed the pass behind them, so their brothers and their husbands would not find their trail until the spring. No rescue would be coming. Their abductors were a contubernium of cavalry auxilia, clad in threadbare skins over their loricae and bearing the long moustaches and fierce tattoos that marked them out as fellow Celts, though they spoke a guttural dialect the women could not understand. The captives were tied to the rear horns of their saddles like pieces of cargo, fastened there alongside cooking pots and blanket rolls and satchels overflowing with other plunder. The falling snow accrued on them so quickly that, were it not for their struggling, they might have been the carcasses of hinds dressed for that evening's dinner.

They were headed for the river crossing at Canovium – a word the women recognized – and there seemed to be a heated disagreement about how to reach it with the weather worsening. The long way round the coast was safer, but a short cut through the Miners' Pass would halve the distance. A note of fear had crept into their arguments. The raised line of the roadway was already barely visible. With every hour of fading daylight, they found themselves climbing ever higher, ever deeper into the forbidding mountains.

At sunset, they came upon the tattered ruin of a marching camp. It would have made a poor defence as it now stood – its ditches filled with drifted snow, its palisades askew and rotten – but it was at least a respite from the biting wind. The women huddled in their shawls while the auxiliaries pitched their tent and gathered kindling from the birds' nests that filled the watchtower, and soon there was a generous fire. This process cheered the men, who grew less fearful and more vulgar. They looked frequently towards their captives, and there could be no doubting their intention, for they leered and gestured to their genitalia and laughed uproariously. Their only hesitation seemed to be deciding which of them would take each woman now, and in what order after that. They bartered over them like herdsmen at a marketplace. It was not long before the first got to his feet.

They spent several days at the camp, hemmed in by the snow which lay against the walls so that they dwelt in a depression that their warmth had melted. The women grew emaciated while the soldiers ate unsparingly of meat and puls. The women's eyes were blacked and noses broken where they had resisted. Beneath their cloaks their arms bore multicoloured bruises. Outwardly, they became docile and compliant – no longer spitting, biting, hissing curses while the men grunted atop them – and when the moon rose on the eighth day, they found that they were untethered and unwatched. Their captors must have deemed them pacified.

When the first man staggered from the tent to urinate a steaming hole into the snow-bank, one of the women cut his throat with a falx from the auxiliaries' tool bag. They daubed their faces with his blood. While he lay gurgling, they took a mattock and bound strips of cloth around its end and lit it like a torch, and as they worked the chieftain's wife climbed to the creaking watchtower and threw down crows' nests which the others piled around the tent. It ignited with surprising suddenness. One moment only smouldering, then ferociously ablaze. The men's cries mingled with the war song of the Ordowici, and the very mountains seemed to raise their voices in approval.

She had stayed a week in an austere bed and breakfast in Betws-y-Coed. It was run by a stern and strait-laced woman of uncertain age, who seemed a relic from a bygone time when guest houses were the preserve of well-to-do old spinsters, hostile to the very thought of hospitality: breakfast served at seven sharp; front door locked for the night at half past eight; lights out at ten and not a minute later. Her bedroom was a single on the second floor, scarcely bigger than a linen cupboard. It was daintily pink and cluttered with a baffling array of fussy frills and ornaments that made her feel as though she were a troglodyte at a tea party. In such prim surroundings, she was acutely conscious of her roughness – her face scoured by the mountain winds, her hands gnarled and inelegant, her clothes so deeply impregnated with the smell of sheep that she might nearly qualify as one by scent alone. She spread a towel on the bed each time she sat, as her grandmother used to, though she could not say whether she feared she might spoil the neatness of the place, or that it might spoil her.

The view, though, was a fine one. Below her window, past the steep slate garden steps where a great many gnomes had congregated, the little high street ran one-sided, busy with last-gasp winter visitors in brightly coloured coats. Across the road, someone was hanging Christmas decorations from a lamp-post. It was a stark relief to find herself back in a world of people. There was a reassuring sense of banal normality, of everyday routines continuing unchanged, of once again belonging to a cogent time and place that had of late felt sorely lacking at the farm. She could see the Pont-y-Pair where it arched ramshackle high above the white and raging torrent of the Afon Llugwy, and the rapids' spray hung misting in the air and made the whole town damp and blackly slick in perpetuity. Beyond, dark pinewoods climbed the far side of the gorge, pierced here and there with jagged spurs of rock and draped in ever-shifting cloud so that she often was content to sit and look and try to think of nothing but the scenery.

That was easier said than done, for little else was left to her aside from contemplation. In the mornings, she would walk along the icy pavement past the hiking shops and souvenir shops, and shops selling all manner of expensive woollen gifts for tourists that bore little relation to anything the locals knew. She stood for hours at a time on the footbridge above the station, watching children riding laps aboard a miniature steam train. Her days became an exercise in the avoidance of intrusive thoughts.

There was an irony in that, she was aware, for thinking, after all, was her entire purpose here. Just to get some space and clear her head and go home with some new ideas for how to make things work again. The atmosphere up there had grown too suffocating. Sitting in the window of a cafe by the park while dogs played fetch out on the frosted grass, she thought vaguely about divorce and was surprised at how little appeal the prospect held for her. It could be done, of course, if it should come to that. She had known couples who divorced when well into their seventies, and they had come out better for it, lighter afterwards as if emerging from some bitter chrysalis. But as hard as she tried, Rhian could not imagine charting such a course herself. Its promise was a bleak and lonely fate. Half of the proceeds of the farm that she had loved since still a girl might buy a poky flat in Rhos-on-Sea, where she could spend her fading years attending jumble sales and coffee mornings with acquaintances whose only commonality was that they were alone. Daytime television. Bingo. Learning needlework or chess. She knew such grim imaginings were born of pessimism – even cowardice. That life post-Carwyn could be anything she chose to make of it, but even the most cheerful visions left her unpersuaded. God help her, she would miss the bugger's company too much.

In many ways, her love for Carwyn had begun as a rebellion against her father's expectations. Go off to university, and marry well, and get out of the mountains. The latter most of all. With the benefit of many decades' worth of retrospect, she could see now that those demands were not for cruelty or pushiness or greed – merely that he wished for her a gentler path than that which had been set for him. Perhaps he'd felt a duty to her dear departed mother to ensure she would do well. She wondered, too, if even that was just a scapegoat for her own fears of inadequacy. What if when she made it to this ideal life, she found she could not manage it, or that it was not what she wanted after all? To have a goal not yet fulfilled was sometimes better than achieving it.

Her dad had burned the first house in the winter of '79. She had not long been out of school then, working shifts behind the bar at the Tanronen, and he'd come in with half a dozen mates all soot-blacked and singed-eyebrowed and reeking of paraffin, drunk as lords already and in festive spirits. By their attitudes, one might have thought them heroes fresh from glorious battle, but to Rhian they seemed only foolish, like a gang of misbehaving schoolboys proud of their hilarity. It wasn't long before the landlord threw them out, telling them in the bluntest terms that he'd call the police if they darkened his door again, and they went out hooting and jeering and bestowing unflattering epithets upon him. Bradwr – traitor – was the kindest of them. For others she could find no equal in a language so polite as English.

In the next weeks, he became a kind of soapbox preacher, holding court out in his garage and receiving converts who arrived with cars in need of mending, then left afire with smouldering resentments kindled into flames. That spring's disastrous devolution referendum – four-to-one against – was proof of rampant English dominance. Plaid Cymru's leader contemplated suicide. Thatcher's pre-election promise of a Welsh-language television station had been swiftly dropped as soon as the last votes were counted. There were twenty thousand English second homes in Wales, empty ten months of the year, while fifty thousand locals were on housing waiting lists. The young were being driven out of their ancestral villages. It was, he said, a cultural genocide by stealth – forcing a generation far afield into a grey and pacified diaspora. Snapping, she had finally asked him, 'What does it matter to you, if you want me to leave anyway?' and the answer hung loud but unspoken in the air.

Carwyn had been a godsend then. A calm and gentle contrast to her father's rages, steady when her life at home felt volatile, a constant in a world in flux. They were not yet a couple, but those were the days when they had first become inseparable. Most nights when she finished at the pub, he would be waiting by the bridge to walk her home, and he'd enfold her in his sheepskin coat while he stood shivering in her driveway, pointing at the stars while both made flimsy pretexts not to part. The farm was an escape for her. A place of orderly routines with direct, tangible results. Clearing ditches or repairing walls or taking fodder to the flock out on the snow-bound mountainside took on a meditative quality. She was a natural, he told her. And she felt it.

It had been Christmas week when Operation Tân arrested Carwyn's family. Two jam-butty police cars turned up without warning in the yard, carting off not just his parents and his frail, widowed nain, but also their few books, their records, boxes full of calendars and correspondence. They were held all day and all night. Separated and interrogated by a fierce sergeant fresh arrived from Belfast, who was implacable in his belief that they were terrorists complicit in the recent spate of arsons. Ten holiday homes burned to date and counting. The man was under orders to crack down on nationalists and agitators, which by his definition meant all those deemed too conspicuously Welsh. The Gwynnants were entirely innocent, of course, and let go without charge, but Rhian's blood boiled. The next day two more families were raided. The crisp December air began to smell of revolution.

She recalled with some particularity just a few days later coming home to find her father and his friends hunched round the kitchen table in their overalls, jabbing with their oil-stained fingers at a disarray of maps and papers like impoverished generals on the eve of war. They all fell silent at her interruption, but she waited in the doorway for them to continue. It was clear

THE HILL IN THE DARK GROVE

from her demeanour that they'd have to go on with her present or else be the ones to leave.

'When?' she asked.

'Tomorrow night.'

'And it's definitely empty?' There were nods to this. 'I'm coming, then. And Carwyn, too.'

In the moonless dark of Christmas Eve, they urged her father's Chrysler Sunbeam down the winding backways to Ffestiniog, following the tail-lights of his van through driving snow. She had to wrestle with the wheel, her heart jolting a little every time the tyres lost their purchase on the road. A Clannad folk song vied with vicious static on the radio. Beside the lane, the snow lay in churned, browning drifts so high the walls were buried to their tops and the ridge of Moelwyn Mawr loomed lifeless in the swirling dark. Carwyn had made a show of needing some persuasion, but Rhian had a suspicion that he would have shinned up Tryfan in his underpants if she had asked him nicely. Their breath blew out in plumes to mingle on the windscreen, but they did not speak, save once when Carwyn said, 'This is a bad idea,' when the first lights of the village came in sight.

And she had *known* it was, that was the thing. She eased the Sunbeam round a bend in high gear, slipping, thinking of where she might be instead – home, perhaps, for Christmas break from university, or living in her own place where the sweat of her brow paid the rent – but found she could conceive of no more fitting place than this. They passed houses decked in Christmas lights, but it was late. A television flickered in one window. Two cars were parked outside the Pengwern Inn, their headlights off but curiously free of snow as though they had their engines running and their heaters on. A trio of unsteady drunks trudged down a side street. Ahead, the van came to a halt.

She exhaled a tense and trembling sigh, her breath a cloud of vapour. 'Right, then. Are you fit?' The question was addressed to Carwyn, but she was unsure what her own answer would have been.

The house was ordinary, and that galled her. It stood alone between two rows of terraces – a rough stone cottage with a modest garden at the front, a good slate roof, a view towards the peaks of the Arenigs. The kind of house that she or Carwyn might have realistically aspired to own. She seemed to glimpse in it a stolen future. They crunched out of the car towards the empty drive, her father's towering figure waiting there already (he had been big in life, but in her memory he was colossal), blowing in his fists and stamping to keep warm. The house was dark and silent. No smoke rising from the chimneys, nor a light in any window, nor a single shred of festive decoration. It might be occupied a few weeks out of every year, her father's friends had told them. Otherwise forgotten.

Carwyn put a hand on her shoulder, and when she turned to look at him, she saw he was afraid. He said again, 'This is a bad idea. Come on, we should just go.'

Rhian's father fixed him with a grin. 'I don't like you, boy.'

He swallowed drily. Said, 'I'll take that as a compliment.'

Fear caught her then, belatedly. Her heartbeat thudded in her ears. 'You're *sure* there's no one here?' A bottle with a wick of rag that reeked acerbically of kerosene was pressed into her hand, and distantly she felt her cold-numbed fingers close around it.

The way she remembered it, several things seemed to happen simultaneously. Her dad strode past her as he launched his bottle at the door, and in her mind, the sound of breaking glass was deafening. At once, a sheet of flame roared up the house. Some primordial part of her recalled a thrill of vindication at the sight of it, that purging, cleansing, righteous conflagration. One of the other men had smashed a downstairs window and was setting light to the net curtains. A second flung a waxy cylinder tied in a condom through the hole, and she found the sight ridiculous. There was a moment when she thought the fire would not take. Then the house went up with an almighty suddenness that she would not have believed had she not seen it. She felt a rush of hot air strong enough to step her backwards, and when she opened her eyes again it was entirely ablaze. Carwyn stood beside her stunned and rooted, the fire casting wavering shadows on his face that made him look by turns much older and much younger than his years – a flicker of the boy he'd been, a flicker of the man he would become. The bottle in her own hand was forgotten in her awe. It dropped into the snow unlit.

Before there was time to absorb it all, the sirens came. They must have known, she later thought, they must have been there ready, waiting. Blue lights flashed across the night sky, where they caught the rising smoke in strobing pulses, spilled across the snow-white street like muted lightning. The first unmarked police car screeched around the bend and bore down on them at ferocious speed. From down the street, she heard the dire wailing of another. Then a third. All this in no more than a moment. Her father and his friends had made it to the van, vaulting the garden wall backlit theatrically by the burning house, and it was with a sense of nauseous panic that she watched them tear away in both the vehicles. Two of the police cars followed close behind. There was nothing she could do but watch the furious procession disappear into the night.

'Come on,' Carwyn was shouting in the roar of flames. 'Come on, we need to go!' He grasped her sleeve, but she could see already silhouettes of running figures in the street.

'Not that way.' Instead, they struggled down a narrow, smoke-filled passageway to the back of the house – a square of garden, chairs stacked at a table covered with tarpaulins for the winter. Behind came many footfalls, frighteningly close. The sound of someone slipping, cursing, pressing on. The fire had spread up one face of a fir tree so that it stood half ablaze and half green and untouched, like Peredur's tree in *Y Tair Rhamant*. In that tale, it had been a sign to mark the hero's passage to the Otherworld, but if this one marked just such a point of no return, it went unheeded.

They scrambled breathless underneath it, through the fence, and as she reached the other side a rough hand seized her by the ankle. It sent a jolt of terror through her like a current. She kicked blindly at it, clawing her way forward. For a moment, she could not see Carwyn, and she felt a sudden certainty that he too had deserted her. But then he was again beside her. He gave the hand a mighty boot and it released its grip and sent them tumbling down a steep embankment while the shouts of disembodied voices hounded them. One of the house's windows shattered. An ancient hawthorn hedgerow parted for them in the sweep of torchlight, opening their way into a tangled brake of briar and deadwood. Then across a frozen stream where tiny waterfalls of icicles hung motionless. They ran until they could hear nothing but the crunch of their own footsteps and the hammering of their own hearts, harried and jubilant.

'I think we've lost them,' Carwyn said eventually, and Rhian panted, 'Good. Now we can freeze to death in peace.' Her panic had subsided and left in its place a fury at her father. How could he just abandon them? And take their car, to boot, and leave them stranded? It would not occur to her for years – long after he had died – that he'd been leading the police away. A cruel defect, she thought, that so much of the gratitude she felt towards her loved ones had remained ungraspable until they each, in turn, were gone.

They circled through a wood so that the fallen leaves would break their trail. Up beyond the snarl of branches, they could see the house still burning, and the arcing spray of water from a firehose, and lights in every window all along the street. The trees ended abruptly, giving way to a windswept void of dark and cold that stung her face. She felt the landscape out there in the blackness. Heading back uphill, they helped each other climb an ice-slicked wooden gate and crossed a rugby pitch so slanted and stippled with molehills that the forwards might need crampons and the backs a topographic map to find the try line. The snow lay powdery and deep upon it, glittering. Rhian agreed with Dylan Thomas's assessment – that snow was *better* somehow, purer, more exciting, in the eyes of youth. All the snow she had known since that night had been a mediocre imitation.

Next, into the churchyard, where the drifts had covered half the crooked tombstones and completely plastered one face of the church. They pushed their way in through a side door that was thankfully unlocked. Carwyn heaved it closed behind them and stood shivering against it. In her memory, his teeth were chattering. A powdering of snow clung to his hair, his lips, his eyelashes, and he had looked to her like Dwynwen's lover Maelon turned by a pedantic god into a block of ice. She felt the cold herself as well, without the false heat of adrenaline. Stinging, bitter, whispering of death. He said, 'Bit chilly,' and the understatement made her laugh.

The church was cavernous and dark, only the distant glow of fire and police lights through the stained-glass windows for illumination, casting a faint kaleidoscope across the whitewashed walls. There must have been a carol service hours before, for there were branches of yew and holly strung about. A hint of oranges appended to the old familiar scent of must and age that made her think all churches (unlike people's houses) smelled alike. Pigeons cooed up in the rafters. She found a box of matches on a candle rack. Her numb and trembling fingers struggled to strike one, then to light one of the votive candles in its coloured glass. Someone had left a blanket folded on a pew, and Carwyn draped it tent-wise over both their heads so they could huddle face to face, cross-legged underneath it with the candle in her hands. He leaned his brow against hers and she closed her eyes and felt the warmth of his breath on her face.

The tiny, flickering candle thawed them in their makeshift tent. Within the unforgiving church they made a sanctuary for themselves, perhaps more sacred. That night, she thought, though did not know it at the time, would form the blueprint of their life together – a pocket of small light against a cold and hostile world. She kissed him gently, and the kiss grew urgent of its own accord, as though it had been years in waiting. It was a kiss that eclipsed all of the others she had ever known. Its electricity seemed still to crackle in the air after their lips had finally parted. 'Nadolig Llawen,' she had said, 'Merry Christmas.' Her head settled onto his shoulder. It became balmy, humid from the melting snow upon them, and soon she fell asleep. For the first time she could remember, she had felt completely safe.

There was a comfort in the memory even now, even after Carwyn's worrying decline. She held tight to it, as if hoping that by force of will she might impose the simple passions of their youth upon these bleaker days. He had been that young man once, she reasoned. Perhaps some sliver of him lingered yet. Old again, Rhian licked her finger and collected the last crumbs of carrot cake from her plate, finishing them with a smear of buttercream. She drank the dregs of her artisanal tea – gone cold during her lengthy reminiscence – and replaced the cup alongside the bewildering array of miniature pots and sieves and strainers. As Victorian as the waiter's perfectly pomaded beard, and yet unfathomably modern to her unaccustomed eyes. 'It's trendy now,' he had explained with an apologetic shrug. So it was true, she thought, that times long past could come around again in ways that one might not expect. Things reappeared in cycles.

That night, she woke up shivering. It took a moment to remember where she was, why she was in a different bed, why Carwyn was not with her. The room smelled cloyingly of pot-pourri. A winter moon shone through the floral curtains, bathing her in pallid, warmthless light by which her ghostly exhalations rose and dissipated. Swaddling herself in the duvet, she sat on the edge of the bed and waited for her body to adjust to being upright. The heating must have gone off. She reached across to feel the radiator and found it ice cold, the thermostat turned all the way to five where she had left it. The clock on the wall had stopped its ticking. 'Go home,' she whispered to herself. 'You don't belong in this world any more.'

Still shivering, she pulled the curtain back an inch or two. Outside, the night was eerily unmoving. Not a passing car nor a local staggering home from the pub nor even a breeze among the branches to disturb the utter stillness. The moon above the pines had halted in its orbit. She could hear the rushing of the river, but it sounded oddly muted, as though dampened by the mist that rose out of its rocky banks and shrouded everything around. Nothing stirred. At first.

The thing came shambling up the street below her with a hideous, spidery gait. She only glimpsed it for the briefest fraction of a second, from the corner of her eye and mostly obscured by the angle of the building, but that was enough. *More* than enough. The curtain fell mercifully back into place. 'That was a dog,' she said aloud. 'It was just a mangy dog.' In her mind's eye, she saw its frail, emaciated limbs; its long and withered face; its wisps of lank white hair. She lay paralysed in bed believing she could feel its gaze fall on her window. The air in the room seemed to grow denser, pressing in on her eardrums. Time elongated. There was a moment of frenetic, maddening certainty of the kind only truly possible at night that some foul thing that Carwyn had dug up was here to drag her back. She listened, waiting for its dry tread on the stairs, but there came only silence. She watched the doorknob, half expecting it to turn, but it did not. Then she felt whatever it was move away across the bridge and pass into the misty pinewoods on the far bank until it was gone. The radiator came to life with a series of soft metallic creaks and groans. The clock resumed its ticking. The rushing of the River Llugwy grew steadily louder, and the moon and stars continued in their course across the sky. 'It was only a dog,' she whispered again. She wished for Carwyn, she wished not to be alone.

It was already light when she got out of bed the next day, feeling slow and heavy and thick-headed. The nightmare – it *had* been a nightmare, of course, she could see that clearly in the rational light of morning – had disturbed her sleep. Normally, when she had bad dreams she could cwtch up to Carwyn. He would grumble reassuringly, still half asleep, and fold his arms around her while she laid her head against his chest and listened to him snoring. If last night was a foretaste of how divorced or widowed life would feel, she had already had her fill of it. She examined her weary reflection, wondering what her younger self would make of who she had become, but much to her surprise she could find no recriminations in the answers. The fiery girl she used to be was not a solitary creature. For all her untamed introversion, she could no more have envisioned casting out into the great wide world all by herself back then than she could now. It was, if she was truthful, why after all her long years she still lived in walking distance of the house where she was born. Not out of fear or lack of curiosity. There were people who could set up home in a new city, a new country, a new continent, and she bore them neither envy nor disdain. She simply felt she was among a lucky few who came into existence right where she belonged. Hefted, as they would say of the sheep. Generation after generation brought to graze on the same pastures every spring for centuries until they were imbued with an instinctive sense of place, belonging to the mountain just as it in turn belonged to them. How much did landscape play a role in the formation of a person's character? Did the familiar sight of rock and earth and water randomly configured by the chaos of creation leave an imprint on the mind? She could not speak for others, but she knew what her reply would be.

And when she stood back and surveyed the sweep of memory stretching from this morning to that long-ago girl running from her father's cottage with a tin of pear halves and a pocket-sized transistor radio, she found Carwyn entwined through all of it. She remembered the bruise on her father's knee where Carwyn – just a little boy – had hit him with a branch. That night on the bridge still cringing at the thought of some lad's clumsy pawing in exchange for two cheap bracelets, Carwyn had wanted to stand with her and nothing more. She remembered the way his hands smelled after shearing; she remembered the bits of hay she had to pick out of his hair; she remembered the prickle of his beard. There was no home she could conceive of where he was not present. They had changed beyond all recognition. They had known days when they had not liked each other. They had faced rough times and frightful hardships, but even at their lowest point, there was no struggle that was not made easier by facing it together. No burden that would have been better borne alone.

* * *

THE HILL IN THE DARK GROVE

In '86, she had been Rhian Gwynnant for a mere three years. A friend returning from a lengthy absence might have noted subtle changes: seen a ruddiness in her complexion or a spark of mischief in her eye, or heard a note of newfound optimism in her laughter. The farm had worked its way under her skin. It imposed a set of altogether different priorities than those of village life, and she took to them like a duck to water. Her days were not dictated by a watch, but by the weather, which had seemed to her a fundamental and profound improvement over the idea of trudging to an office every morning, where she'd sit contractually shackled at a desk until she was allowed to leave. At the farm, she woke with the sunrise, with Carwyn. Then, each day, they would go out together into the fresh air and work until their legs grew tired and their backs ached, bound by nobody else's schedule. It was not without its hardships, but it was about as idyllic a life as she had ever dared imagine.

The previous summer, when the flock were sheared and dipped and the last spring lambs weaned, they spent their evenings swimming in the lake – bracingly cold even at the height of August – and afterwards they lay bare in the grass on the shore and watched the stars come out. In October, Carwyn's parents moved into a bungalow down in Beddgelert. His father still came up to help with tupping, but they had the farmhouse to themselves. It became for them a recreation of the sanctuary they had built together in the church – somewhat bigger than a blanket and a candle, although fulfilling the same purpose. That winter they were snowed in for the first time. They took turns to carry armfuls of hay out to the pregnant ewes in the long barn, and after dark with drifts lying head-high against the house they curled up in an armchair by the fire. She read him *Wuthering*

Heights that winter, picturing herself as Cathy, wild and free and sometimes cruel out on her windswept moor. When she finally closed the book as spring came and the snow began to melt, she had asked Carwyn what he thought, and he had pondered with a look of intense academic consideration before replying, 'I was mostly thinking you look like Kate Bush.' She had chased him round the house for that, swatting at him with the paperback until they both fell into bed in fits of laughter.

In her mind, she thought of that night as the moment of conception, though it was only one of many possibilities. Back then, they had been at it not like rabbits but like hares – a pair of undomesticated, solitary creatures clashing nightly in their fierce couplings. Some of her memories were surely compilations. They had spent one morning taking down the lambing pens and sweeping out the barn, the hay strewn with the buttony placentae of the ewes (their collie, Seren, used to eat them with great relish, potently nutritious as they were) and full of heady reproductive scents. Each time her gaze met Carwyn's, they would grin at one another, suddenly grown bashful, full of optimism for the future that awaited them. How certain she had been that everything would go to plan. Not out of naïveté, she reassured herself. There had simply been a persuasive sense that all was falling into place precisely as it ought, and indeed, it was hard to shake that feeling even in the face of the catastrophes to come.

'86 was a year of rain. On this day, though, the downpours were fleeting, every shower punctuated by a spell of brilliant, blue-skied sun, and when they'd eaten a quick lunch of bara brith spread thick with homemade butter while they waited for the rain to pass, they ventured out to walk. The lambs were bounteous that spring. Impossibly white and clean and healthy, with their little tails awag as they went frolicking across the meadows. The lanes were lined with daffodils. A carpeting of early bluebells thicker than she'd ever seen transformed the valley woods. It had appeared to her as though all nature was conspiring to some common end, with her and Carwyn part of it, greater than the sum of themselves.

They stopped at the low-hanging bough of a tree overlooking the lake, worn smooth by many sitters. Even now, she could recall the conflicting emotions of that moment: worry and unreadiness, and quiet self-assurance. Inexperience and new maturity. A deep sense of intuition, and embarrassment she might have got it wrong. And most of all a curious, unshakeable sense that she was no longer alone in her own body, though she was aware of how ridiculous that would have sounded without retrospection's proof.

It took time to summon up the nerve to broach the subject, not for fear of how he would react, but because voicing it might somehow render it more real, and to his credit he had not tried to press her to speak and only waited patiently until she could begin. 'Carwyn, I think I'm—' She laughed and could not bring herself to say the word aloud. To say it would have felt like dragging out a pleasant dream into the light of morning, withering it before it could be enjoyed. 'I mean it's much too early to tell, but—'

He wrestled with a smile and lost and let it break across his face. He said, 'I know. I think so too.'

She remembered feeling that they both stood at a threshold

or a precipice where their old lives would soon be shed like winter fleeces. 'Can we do it, Carwyn? Are we ready?'

When she examined his expression for a shred of doubt, he pantomimed a comical expression of panic, which relieved her. 'God, I don't know. I hope so. Don't people say it's one of those things that no one's really ready for until it happens?'

'And then they find that they were ready all along?' she finished.

There was more optimism in his nod than confidence. 'Yeah, maybe. Or else we'll pick it up as we go. Learn on the job. Like shearing.' He must have sensed that his reply had been unsatisfactory, because he went on, 'Whatever comes, we'll handle it. Not just this, I mean – everything. I'm not saying it's all going to be smooth sailing, but no matter what, we'll always manage so long as we've got each other. We can do it.' His hand closed over hers and squeezed it gently. Did he sing to her, or had that been a dream? She thought he had. He twined a bluebell in her hair and said she was Blodeuwedd in full flower.

It began to rain again as they looked out across the lake, grape-sized gouts that broke the water's mirror calm. The curve of the tree limb pressed their hips together, and Rhian shifted to take something hard from Carwyn's pocket. The ugly clay figurine. It made her shudder. She cocked her arm to cast it out into the depths as its primordial maker might have done, but Carwyn stayed her hand, saying, 'Let's hang on to it. We might need it for luck. I've got something else for you instead.'

He dug into the jumble of his overalls and came up with a sliver of carved, polished wood a little shorter than his hand. His face had reddened slightly. 'It's not quite the way I pictured it when I first started,' he explained. 'I could never seem to get it even, so I had to keep on trimming it.' With an apologetic grin he laid the tiny object delicately in her palm. 'I thought I'd better give it to you now before it's small enough to be a splinter.'

It was true the love-spoon was not like any she had seen before – a miniature compared to the great two-foot-long ones hanging in the farmhouse, as much akin to them as a teaspoon was to a shovel. But it was a work of art that paled even the most elaborate of the others. The head was teardrop-shaped and beautifully curved, pierced with a latticework of holes as fine as lace. It tapered to a handle not much wider than a pencil, which seemed made of an impossible entanglement of knots and chains and daffodils, until it culminated in a hollow heart wherein a smaller heart hung unattached but skilfully enclosed. She could feel all the countless hours of care that had gone into its creation, and the fineness of it made her gasp. She barely noticed how hard it was raining. 'Carwyn, it's incredible.'

'I felt bad that you never got a ring, see, and I still couldn't afford—'

'I love it. This is better than a ring.' She looked at him and he was beaming with an endearing mixture of pride and relief. 'You'll have to make a knife and fork next though. I'm starving.'

When they got home, laughing and drenched, her father had been waiting in the yard. It had been weeks since she had seen him. Maybe months. He shook Carwyn's hand stiffly and then gave Rhian an awkward, unaccustomed hug that felt so frail his hesitancy might have been from shame at his own weakness. They all stood at the door for a long time. He looked diminished – still tall, but gaunt and greying and bedraggled. Stooped by an air of melancholy, as though he had scrutinized his life's long tapestry and found there only failure and regret, and with the prospect of her own impending parenthood she had wished she could find the words to tell him he was wrong. He was a good man. He was courageous, stoic, loyal. He had done his best against adversity, and she was proud of him. Rhian was herself, in many ways, a lasting testament to his success, a patchwork of his virtues and his shortcomings.

But in the end, they managed only polite small talk: Had they seen the plans for this new Channel Tunnel? She noticed how sunken his cheeks looked. Would Wales ever win another Five Nations? When he stirred his tea the skin on his big hands was thin as parchment paper. Had they heard the news of the nuclear accident in the Soviet Union? For the first time he appeared to her truly mortal, truly vulnerable, and she felt a strange pang of protectiveness towards him, as though she were now the parent. It was the last time she would ever see him. Afterwards, she realized he, too, must have wanted to say more, but could not bring himself to tell her – he'd been diagnosed with cancer, keeping it a secret to the very end.

'86 was the year of Chernobyl. A catastrophe, of course, but it had felt at the time like that particular sort of catastrophe that happens far away and to other people. Vaguely frightening vocabulary on the evening news that came laden with apocalyptic connotations: meltdown, radiation, fallout. Diagrams she did not understand. But all unreal and comfortingly distant, so that when she went into the fields each day she found them lush and green with April showers, and the sky still blue above the mountains, and life in her peaceful corner of the world still going on unaltered. Not little Wales's problem. 'We look after our own,' people said, as if it were a point of pride. She could see now the wrong-headedness of that philosophy – like standing on the top deck of a ship and thinking that the water flooding in below was none of your concern so long as your own feet were dry.

The months passed quickly, marked at first by mourning and her father's funeral arrangements, then by frantic preparations for the baby, then by endless, all-pervading rain. Rhian learned to knit with idle-handed urgency, producing such a quantity of tiny socks and cardigans that the child might go a year or more without wearing the same thing twice. Her bump was showing unmistakably now. Carwyn turned his nain and taid's old room into a nursery. He first painted a series of ducks on the wall, but found the mallard browns and greens and yellows bled together into swampy faecal shades. Years later they would laugh about what he referred to as the 'Shit Ducks'. How strange, she thought, that joy and tragedy could coexist as such near neighbours.

Disaster settled on them slyly in the guise of upland weather, insolently ordinary. A covering of cloud that seemed never to lift as spring rains turned to drenching summer showers. Their work had gone on as it had to, in spite of her growing, kicking passenger: running year-lambs to the barn for shearing in a deluge so intense that she and Carwyn had been soaked clean through their waterproofs in seconds, and it felt as though the very air had turned to water. In May the government had banned the sale of livestock from the hill farms of north Wales – a short-term, precautionary measure, they had been at pains to stress. They struggled on. That autumn, a balding, bespectacled man with a clipboard and a radiation monitor had stood with Rhian in the drizzle, making ominous pronouncements couched in alien vocabulary: becquerels per kilogram, half-life, radiocaesium. He scanned each sheep, and Carwyn marked all those that did not pass with daubs of sickly orange paint. Rhian stood with them, now six months along, enormous and uncomfortable. 'Is there any risk to us?' she could remember asking, gesturing to her gravidity, and in reply the man had fumbled with his damp and blowing paperwork and offered up an unpersuasive smile and told her he was sure that there was not.

But still, despite all reassurances, the next two months had taken on a grim, nightmarish quality. Events from those days blurred and sharpened in her mind by turns, at times retreating in a fog and at others blaring forth with perfect clarity at the most unexpected moments. Carwyn joking one day about glowing sheep, the next in tears at the kitchen table. There had been doctor's visits where the GP, too, insisted there was absolutely no danger to the baby from what he called the Chernobyl incident. Her dreams became almost prophetic: lambs born skinless, or with seven legs, or one cyclopic eye; her womb a nest of insects ready to come boiling forth; a tree bearing miraculous varieties of fruit that, once picked, shrivelled and turned rotten. Herself in the role of Rhiannon in the Mabinogion, her lips smeared with dog's blood by the careless nursemaids who had lost her baby and accused her of devouring the child. She felt she had been seeded with some distant opposite of birth – a death, unseen and yet inexorable, growing in her very cells.

A few weeks shy of her due date, she felt the kicking stop. A nauseous, dizzying absence first thing on waking, like noticing her own heart missing a beat – a sensation that should have been there but unaccountably was not.

'She's gone,' she'd said flatly to Carwyn as he dressed beside her, not really believing it, but as though by speaking the worst aloud she might somehow divert its course. This was not the first time one of them had panicked over what would turn out to be trifling things: a terrifying gush of blood the doctor told them was an implantation bleed; a pain that lasted hours before emerging as a resonating belch; a sudden churning in her uterus so violent that she was convinced the baby was in imminent distress.

But now, like all those other times, Carwyn had been there. He looked concerned when she explained, the colour draining slightly from his cheeks, but said, 'It's fine, del. She's probably just sleeping.' He sat down on the bed and stroked her hair and laid a hand on her stomach. 'I know it's frightening, but you're good at this. You're doing well. Think how many times you've done it with the sheep.'

She laughed at that, but the laugh felt forced and mirthless. There came with it a horrible, irrational urgency. The sense of no longer being alone in her own body persisted, but it had curdled now to something loathsome. She shook her head. 'We need to go,' she said. 'Please.'

They drove to the hospital in the red of morning. The fastest she had ever known Carwyn to drive, but still agonizingly slow, the passing drystone walls and roadside bushes monstrous in their sickly headlights. At first, the doctors and nurses had been reassuring. Nine times out of ten, they said, there would be nothing wrong. But then had come the Pinard stethoscope – she caught the frown – and then the ultrasound, and then the news that she had known would come. The rest she sealed off in the deepest reaches of her memory. And sometimes it was restless, like the dragons entombed under Dinas Emrys, sending floods and tremors, but now for the most part it was mercifully still.

She freed herself from those macabre recollections with viscous slowness, like one extricating their boots from a sucking mire. A walk. A walk in the fresh air would do her good. Down the street of grey slate shops and past the plywood stalls of a small Christmas market set up in the car park of the Royal Oak, thinking of nothing but the smell of pine and mince pies and mulled wine that drifted between the discordant strains of Kirsty MacColl and the Pogues. Then back across the Pont-y-Pair where a throng of selfie-taking tourists leaned across the mossy parapet to frame the river tumbling blackly in the cataracts below. And from there on up the boardwalk winding through the woods along the water's edge until she was alone. She would go back to Carwyn. In a sense she'd known it from the start. It was inevitable, somehow. Irresistible, though she had tried. They were not made *for* each other so much as they were made *of* each other – their memories and experiences intertwined for decades like the knots of their love-spoon until they were tangled inextricably. Whatever was afflicting Carwyn, they would face it together as they always had, and overcome it as they always did. 'It's not too late to just get out,' a quiet voice inside her cautioned. 'You can still ask for help, or find another place to stay, or spend another night here while you think it through.' She did not heed it, though. By noon, her bag was packed and she was waiting for a taxi that would take her back into the cold, forbidding mountains.

X

Onnen

PASSAGEWAY

They were the last. The frail and old had been the first to go, carried off by sickness in a single winter, and they had offered up their flesh to the birds and their bones to the mountain. The young departed one by one: some for the estuary where the logboats of copper traders left to ply their wares on distant coasts, the others seeking out a gentler life down in the lowlands, planting grains. Their sod huts fell to ruin. Within a few more seasons they would be no more than vague shapes on the hillside – their monuments, their ancestors, their god, all left to languish there, forgotten.

The man sat threading beads of tin and amber and bright-yellow seashells on a necklace – bartered dearly for his last two sheep – knowing already that Hwaspa would chide him for so frivolous a trade. They asked a heavy price, these newcomers. Their ways were strange and surely would not long endure. He had heard they planted their dead in the ground where the sun's warmth would never touch them, and even in his sorry circumstance he pitied them for such a dark and lonely fate.

A biting wind gusted across the scarp, and from outside he heard a roof collapse with a soft splintering of wood. How desolate the place seemed now, devoid of songs and laughter. When he was young there had been fires in every hearth. An uncle or an aunt or a wise grandmother in every doorway, and everywhere a multitude of cousins full of games and mischief. He missed them all, even those who had been unkind to him. They were his people in a world of strangers.

His hands were not as nimble as they used to be, his eyesight not as sharp, so he came out into the fading winter light to tie the necklace knot and hold the beads up to the sun. He hoped the gift would please her, though she was not one for trinkets. What they prized most was each other's company. A light dusting of windblown snow had settled over everything, its chill sharp even through the grass that lined his deerskin shoes. He hobbled down towards the trees, where crows eyed him as if they knew he was the last that they would carry to the sky, and in the glade the mound was waiting. Bristling with crooked wooden totems, circled with its ring of stones. In midwinter, the sun would shine into its passageway and impregnate the earth with spring. He wondered how many more years remained, now nobody was left to help their birth.

Reverently, he crouched into the sacred darkness, feeling his way down a narrow cleft of damp and dripping stone, and when his eyes adjusted he was in a chamber high enough that he could stand. Down here, the God dwelt. Carved on the walls were bears and bulls and many-antlered deer, and serpentines and spirals, and the ochre prints of hands of hundreds who had come before him. And finally, in nooks and alcoves full to bursting, were the bones. There was his mother's pelvis, decked with wilted flowers, and his father's clavicle tied with a bowstring. Here was the thighbone of his grandfather whose lap had been so comfortable a place to fall asleep. There was the jawbone of his aunt who had so often made him laugh. His friends, his enemies, his forebears, all were here. With rough but gentle hands he placed the necklace around Hwaspa's skull, and afterwards he closed his eyes and spoke to her while he knelt in the deepening cold to wait for the world's ending.

The first thing Rhian noticed, coming home that Christmas week, was how a sense of desolation had consumed the place. The farmyard felt dead or dormant. Even that word – *home*, that vague comforter that covered such a multitude of sins – fitted awkwardly, as though a vital but intangible ingredient had gone. She stepped out of her taxi in the yard under a sky of shifting overcast that seemed unable to decide on what the weather ought to be: one moment drizzle, then the next a spell of wan and wintry sun, shortly obscured by threatening clouds dark-bellied with unfallen snow. With the driver paid and thanked, she hurried inside, and the house enveloped her.

She felt the way she had at ten, when she'd gone swimming at the little beach in Porthdinllaen. The sea was millpond calm and glittering with pristine sunlight from a cloudless sky, and as she waded first up to her knees and then to where the water's coldness took her breath and then beyond the depth where she could feel the sand between her toes, it had seemed nothing in that picture-postcard world could ever be unsafe. She had swum out past the slipway of the lifeboat station, close enough to shore that she still heard her father's snoring. Then along the gorse-clad headland, where the children's laughter from the beach grew faint and seals lay basking on the rocks, so that in her imagination she was changing from the former to the latter.

She could not recall exactly when the tide had taken hold of her. Only that the cliffs began to seem a little smaller, the land a little further off, her strokes a little less effective in propelling her the way she wished to go, and when she looked towards the sweep of coast she felt a sudden lurching shock at how far out she was. The way she liked to remember it, she had not panicked. Her father's warnings had come back to her, and she had rolled onto her back and floated, looking up into the empty sky, awaiting rescue. They told her on the boat that she had not been out there long – not more than half an hour, owing to the thankful nearness of the lifeboat station – but both then and now the wait had felt interminable. Her fear had not been drowning, for it seemed she could have floated there for days until she fetched up on some far, exotic shore. It was instead the sense of dark, unfathomable depths that shelved away into the blue abyss beneath her. The dread that something might at any moment brush against her foot. She felt exactly that way now as she stepped back into the empty house, and the thought made her shudder, imagining unseen leviathans beneath her while she bobbed oblivious upon that awful millpond sea.

Carwyn was not there to greet her, though she did not need to wonder where he was nor go to seek him out, for she could hear the distant ringing of his pickaxe. Its rhythm had a frenzied, violent quality. In the living room, she found a nest of sheets and pillows, stained and curdled-smelling, where it appeared he had been sleeping. Out of habit, she whistled for Eira, and for a second she believed she heard the tap of little claws run down the hall. Whatever it had been, though, did not come into the room but only scurried past inside the wall and disappeared up through the chimneybreast. She fed the feeble fire in the wood-burner, but it refused to take more strongly, and it felt to her as though the house had fallen sickly in her absence. Even the bleating of the ewes sounded an octave off. A close but not quite passing imitation. She poured herself a cup of tea and sat down at the table to await him.

An hour passed with only the slow ticking of the hallway clock for company, the tea going cold and bitter in her hands. At dark, she heard the door unlatch. Then the soft tread of muddy boots on flagstones. She allowed herself a moment of hope, getting up hesitantly from her chair to greet him (maybe even take him in her arms) when he came through the door, and she would tell him how she'd missed him while she was away, and how she'd come to realize she needed to be here. But when he came into the room, she could scarcely believe this was her Carwyn.

He was daubed in black mud to his elbows, and it streaked the rest of him like war paint, but beneath it he was ashen. There were filthy sticking plasters on his fingertips. On one, the fingernail was missing altogether, as if he had been grubbing at the frozen earth with his bare hands. His cheeks were sunken and she wondered wildly if he might have lost some teeth, and his eyes stared grimly from deep caverns ringed with sleeplessness. He stank. Not only of dirt and sweat and sour breath, but of a vegetal putrescence that seemed to well up from deep within him. She could smell it from ten feet across the room as he stood in the doorway, and when he did not come in to embrace her but only offered a stiff greeting, she felt ashamed of her relief.

'How've you been?' he asked, his voice little more than a croak. He seemed disappointed to have found her there.

'All right. And you?'

He nodded. 'I'm almost in. It's hollow – there must be some kind of passageway. I can hear it when I lay my ear against the stone, like the sea in a shell. Like something's moving down there.' This stood, apparently, in place of how he was. He and his mound were now inseparable.

'You've been sleeping in the lounge, have you?'

A quick glance through the door to where his makeshift bedding lay, as if he needed confirmation. 'Warmer.'

'Oh?'

There must have been more disbelief in her expression than she had intended, because he continued, 'I just don't sleep well up there any more. There's noises. Dripping. Creaks.' And then, seemingly unaware of his own pungent fragrance, 'And it smells. I've looked up in the attic but there's nothing there. A rat or something in the walls, I think. The other day I found a cluster of them dried up in the chimney with their tails all tied together. *Tied*, mind, not tangled. Like they'd meant to do it.' His eyes glazed and he swayed unsteadily but caught himself. 'How long have you been gone? I've lost track of the time.' He swayed again.

Rhian stood and took a step towards him. 'Carwyn, in the morning I'm phoning the doctor. I'll drag you there kicking and screaming if I have to, but I haven't come back here to sit and watch while you just waste away in front of me.'

It looked for a moment as though he would argue, or insist that he was fine, but her sudden firmness must have caught him off guard. 'I suppose it wouldn't hurt to check. We'll give Dr Watkin a ring, see what he thinks.' The words came out a rasping, papery whisper.

'All right,' she nodded. She did not think it necessary to remind him that Dr Watkin had retired thirty years ago. What mattered was that he agreed.

The next morning, once the sheep were fed and watered and the hens' bedding had been renewed, it was already late when Rhian tried to call the surgery. Though Carwyn had insisted on sleeping downstairs again, he had at least showered, brushed his teeth and combed his hair, and now seemed closer to his old self than the muddy, reeking stranger who had greeted her the night before. Several times she'd heard him cry out in his sleep, but afterwards he told her he could no longer recall the details of his nightmares. Only that they were persistent and terrible. His months of toil had sculpted him into a being of pure bone and sinew, lean and strong in that way of old men, a xylophone ribcage with hardly an ounce of fat or muscle to be seen. There were numerous small growths on his skin which had not been there before. She would make a note to mention these to the doctor, but otherwise his condition appeared improved. Even his tattered hands looked better. A hearty breakfast was in order, but when she cracked the eggs that had been freshly laid last night, the first was black and rotten, and the second bloody, and the third contained a wretchedly misshapen embryo, so she threw the rest away lest they hold yet worse omens. They each ate a slice of buttered toast instead.

Carwyn chewed quietly, reticent. Between them there passed only the vaguest attempts at small talk. She could sense again his coiled-spring restlessness to be about his task, and when his plate was clean she almost felt a reflex to dismiss him as one might a child to go outside and play.

There was a pocket-sized address book on the table by the phone, the once-gold lettering rubbed off its cover, and its pages yellowing and brittle. All their contacts in the world contained therein. Leafing through it, Rhian was dismayed to see how many names had been crossed out, how few remained, and of those almost all were long-ago acquaintances, or businesses, or gone without a forwarding address. *Croeso i Feddygfa Llanberis,* the recorded voice intoned. *Welcome to Llanberis Surgery. I glywed yr opsiynau yn Gymraeg, pwyswch un, or to hear the options in English, press two.* A sequence of button presses. Then a long stretch of jarringly upbeat music, punctuated occasionally by a different recorded voice offering apologies that the receptionists were all currently busy helping other patients, but would answer her call as soon as possible.

No doctor could fit Carwyn in until a week on Wednesday. They were contending with the usual Christmas backlog, the receptionist explained, and a particularly bad outbreak of flu had filled the diary. 'Is it an emergency? Any chest pains? Breathing difficulty? One-sided weakness?' Rhian told them that she did not think it was (what constituted an emergency was relative, she thought, but by that narrow definition this did not).

When that was done, she set about taking an inventory of their winter stores. The weather was already bad, but she felt sure that it was getting worse. It was years since they had been snowed in for more than a few days, but she had known firsthand how close complacency could lead them to disaster. In 2010, the freeze had lasted through most of December. After the first two weeks, Carwyn had rationed out their food, sometimes forgoing meals to make sure Rhian had enough to eat, and when Tom Roberts chugged his tractor up the snow-bound lane with fresh supplies – a Christmas hamper, she recalled – they were down to their last two tins of Heinz tomato soup. There had been a winter in the nineties when they were beset by blizzards so intense they were left practically buried in the cottage: snowdrifts almost to the eaves; the cold so deep and bitter that the water in their borehole froze and they had melted icicles to drink and cook and wash. They had broken up the nursery furniture for firewood.

That year had been a hard-learned lesson. A reserve of food to last a week or two was simply not enough, especially now the seasons were becoming more capricious and erratic. She remembered her dreams from those days. Donner Party images: eating the grey, glutinous paste boiled out of cowhides; mice caught and devoured whole; the bloated carcasses of starved oxen dug from banks of snow. And grimmer meats by far, of course. She wondered, could it really come to that in little modern-day north Wales, no more than twenty miles from a McDonald's? And all her instincts told her that for her and Carwyn, up here in their isolation, yes, it could, with frightening ease.

It comforted her, then, to take stock of what they had laid in for the coming weeks. She stood out in the long barn, counting and re-counting, and with each repetition she felt reassured. There was a meditative aspect to it. Enough, enough. She ran her hand along the edge of the top shelf, careful to avoid the traps among the items there. Things had moved on since the days of Manawydan, guarding his wheatfields against a plague of ravenous, enchanted mice. There were catering-sized bags of pasta, flour, sugar, rice, stowed safely in deep plastic boxes. Baking powder, washing powder, packets of dried fruit and nuts.

Toilet rolls high out of reach where they would not be nibbled. On the shelf below were jars and tins in an array of shapes and sizes, and then UHT milk in green cartons by the pallet. The bottled water on the lowest shelf had already grown opaque cores of ice. Strings of onions hung down drying in the rafters. The chest freezer was full to bursting with all manner of stews and casseroles she had prepared the previous summer, and altogether there was probably enough to last a year or more beyond the ending of the world if they were frugal.

She stepped outside again into the grey of morning, where her breath went billowing before her like her tethered soul attempting to take flight, as though it sensed what was about to come. It happened without fanfare or foreboding. A tiny flake of twinkling, translucent ice came drifting down out of the cotton-batting sky to light, already melting, on her coat sleeve. A second followed, gone no sooner than it touched the ground, and then suddenly they were too numerous to count, a thousand or a million snowflakes falling prettily in deathly silence. The mountaintops were dusted white.

'It won't stick,' she said aloud, almost in prayer, and while the daylight lasted that was true. By lunchtime it had stopped, and it seemed as if that would be that; but it began again not long thereafter, heavier now, until the view from where she sat was lost beyond the swirling flurries. At nightfall, Carwyn came in, muddy and dishevelled as the day before, his brow damp and his hair and shoulders covered with a powdering of snow. 'Is it sticking?'

He shook his head, but in his face Rhian could read the words, *Not yet*.

That evening, they ate another mute, uneasy dinner, the

noises of the outside dulled by the continually falling snow so that those in the house were heightened. The ticking of the clock. The crackling of the fire. The creaks Carwyn had mentioned, as though the ground beneath was shifting ever so subtly. Things that sounded worryingly larger than rats went rustling up and down inside the walls.

'The Tylwyth Teg,' he said without preamble. 'The fairies. Is that what you're thinking of?' His voice was dour and unfamiliar, edged with something not a million miles from mockery. He gestured vaguely to the noises in the wall. 'That's not them, they're long gone. They're a folk memory of the people who were here before us. The real indigenous people of Wales. They used to be everywhere, but when *we* came – I mean us, the Neolithic farmers – they retreated to their burial mounds and barrows and stone circles until those monuments were all that was left of them.' It seemed to her this was a sentiment he had been bottling up for some time now, waiting for an opportunity to pour it forth. She leaned back in her chair, away from his indignant glee, away from his awful breath, and was relieved when he did not come closer. It would do no good to interrupt or try to reason with him. He was lost, she thought, in his lecture.

'And the newcomers, they didn't know what they were for. Only that they'd been important somehow. Sacred places. Magical. Forbidden, even. Maybe they told their children that the old people had gone into their mounds. Into Annwn. And then however many thousand years go by until we don't even remember them as people any more. They're little pixies living underground. The same thing's happening to us, Rhian. If we don't leave our mark, we'll be forgotten. Worse – erased.' To underline his point, he slid his palm across the table, sweeping several letters to the floor. She made no move to pick them up. Only held his gaze until he stalked out of the room.

The snow continued every night without relent, but thankfully each morning she awoke to find it had not stuck. Still only a dusting in the grass, for now. Christmas and New Year came and went unmarked, except by the bad dreams they brought. At first, they were no more than ugly memories that seeped up from some shut-off recess of her mind and made her wonder if the threads that held her sanity together had begun to fray. The doctor's surgery back in '86. The day her father lost her in a crowd at the Eisteddfod. Her mother's death. She woke each morning to the nagging of old scars, the way an amputee might feel an itch in a lost limb.

Then came more immaterial terrors. One night she clawed her way out of the bedsheets, gasping, certain that a cold oblivion was devouring her. She dreamed she was pursued relentlessly by shifting forms that seemed always an inch from catching her, like Gwion Bach the servant boy in his flight from the witch Ceridwen. When she became a hare, a vicious dog gnashed at her tail, and when she dived into the river as a fish, the dog became an otter and swam after her. The next she knew, she was a songbird and the otter now a hawk, and after that frantic escape she was a tiny morsel in a yard where hens pecked ravenously at the dirt. In the light of morning it seemed laughable, but in the dream the panic had been real, and so was the exhaustion that dogged her all day. Too old now, she thought, for such nocturnal exercises, but they were persistent. She ate the flesh of infants on a mountaintop. She wandered through the moonlit formal gardens of a country manor while a congregation of misshapen figures peered out at her from the windows. She was entombed alive.

Tonight's, though, was by far the worst, if only for its sheer lucidity and how it lingered. It was that time of twilight just a whisker shy of needing to get up to turn the light on, and without knowing how she came to be there she was standing in a vague facsimile of her bedroom, transfixed by a dark stain on the ceiling. A brownish mark, the kind that's left after a leaking roof. And the more she peered at it, the more she found that it unsettled her, as though its abstract shape hid horrors that she could not quite perceive. A passenger aboard her nightmare self, she went to fetch a ladder and a torch, and with a feeling of macabre curiosity (the body, said the lucid part of her – the body of the missing hiker), climbed up through the hatch into the attic.

Terror was, of course, the first sensation. A terror that did not feel like her own – a child's dread of cobwebs and under-bed beasties. Noises in the dark. Then, vividly, she was struck by a breath of peculiar humid warmth, like the sheep-shed in midwinter, and almost simultaneously a smell. It was an autumn scent of turned earth, wet slate, peat. Underlaid with something old and dusty that called to mind the staleness of a chapel. Other odours, potently organic – colostrum and menstrual blood and semen – filled the cloying hothouse air.

She clicked the torch on, the switch and her thumb both already slick with moisture, and its beam flickered and then steadied. What it revealed relieved her. Her fear had been unfounded, for there was nothing in the attic save its usual clutter of forgotten things. She shone the light over the stacks of sagging cardboard boxes, the empty mousetraps and the scatterings of poison bait, the crooked floorboards clothed haphazardly in wool for insulation. Everything visibly and chronically damp, so much so that blots of black mould furred every surface, with odious little mushrooms growing here and there among it all. She felt a curious sense of being underground. The source of the stain was immediately clear – the water tank was dripping, a slow drum of inky droplets. She could fix that easily enough, and she began a mental list of what she'd need to patch the leak.

She was so distracted that she almost didn't see it. In the instant she switched off the torch, the vanishing beam picked out a glimpse of something unspeakably foul, and as she fumbled for the light again she felt its ghastly, greasy presence in the darkness with her. The torch flickered back to life reluctantly. In a far corner of the attic, where the stone wall met the roof, the awful something lay. But 'lay' was the wrong word. It gestated. It *sprouted*. It grew out of the wall on stalks – a bulbous, vaguely man-shaped thing the colour of a chafer grub; but there was some grotesque foetal quality about it. The word 'homunculus' came to her mind unbidden. A pair of peeled, dead eyes regarded her reflectionlessly with a look that recalled specimens she had seen floating in jars of formaldehyde. No malice in them. Worse than that. The thing's empty stare was one of blank, detached malignance.

A groan escaped her. 'What is it?' Carwyn called up through the hatchway. 'What did you find?' and dreaming-Rhian tried to answer, 'I don't know.'

The pale, distended head rolled to face her fully, the motion squeezing out a gob of rank-smelling liquid like a rotten vegetable from its lipless mouth, its pores, and all at once she knew exactly what it was. She knew with a sense of hideous inevitability. She knew as its half-formed hand stretched towards her, the webs between its fingers taut and lacy where they had not fully finished separating into digits. It was her husband, or at least it soon would be. A perfect likeness here pupating like a bloated larva in the attic, and when it was grown it would slip down and take his place and she would never know the difference. Perhaps it was already done. How sure was she really, the dream seemed to ask, that the man with whom she shared the house was Carwyn after all, and not some sly abomination wearing Carwyn's skin?

She jolted into consciousness, tearing away the sheets despite the cold and feeling certain for a lingering instant that the thing was in the room with her – had somehow followed her out of the nightmare. In the silence, there came the quiet dripping of the water tank. The view at dawn was the one she had dreaded, framed in the small window like a gift-shop postcard: Yr Wyddfa's summit and the ridge below it brilliant white against the ash-and-ember sky. On its slopes, the snow had drifted deeper than the ancient walls. It glistened there, unblemished and pristine as the day raised it out of shadow. To her left, the valley sloped away benighted still, and she could see the lane was buried and the distant rooftops of Beddgelert blanketed as though the weather sought to shroud all evidence of man.

The house was oddly still. She felt loud and clumsy as she went about her morning tasks, the way she used to when she first had spent the night here – down the hall towards the bathroom on her tiptoes lest a creaking floorboard wake up Carwyn's nain; washing in a shallow sinkful of cold water because the hot tap would set the pipes to clanging. It used to be invigorating then, in youthful romance and adventure. This morning, she could not say what she feared to wake. From the roof there came a beating of wings, followed by a muffled whump of falling snow as something heavy settled in the branches of the oak tree. She dressed until her mismatched clothes were many layers deep, but by the time she pulled on her wool-lined snow boots beside the door and crunched into the yard, whatever had been there was gone. The twisted bough where it had perched was bare as a gnawed bone.

Carwyn's footprints led straight to the gate, and from there down into the woods. It was clear he had not stopped to tend the animals, so Rhian spent the morning making sure the sheep had hay, digging two ewes free from where they had been buried by the blizzard, and letting out the hens, who stalked defiantly into the yard with disapproval in their gimlet eyes, as though their stare alone could thaw the world. But it would not be melting soon, she thought, no matter how fervently she or they might hope. She felt it in her throbbing knuckles, in her aching knees. This was the kind of snow that settled in for weeks, and more to come. As the birds emerged, she noted just how few were left and wondered where the geese had gone. In the nesting boxes, she found two hens dead and frozen stiff, but it seemed the several others unaccounted for had simply vanished. Not a trace of fox tracks nor of feathers to suggest what had become of them.

It was hungry work out in such bitter weather, every trudging step an effort, and by midday she was ready for a bite to eat.

It occurred to her to go and ask Carwyn if he wanted to join her, but she guessed he would refuse – might even be annoyed by the intrusion. A part of her wondered if she was making excuses. The woods, the clearing, the stone circle and the mound, they frightened her for reasons she could not quite understand, and she had no desire to venture near them. Even from here, a pregnant, smothering quiet seemed to overhang the place, muffling the sounds of Carwyn's labour like the trees themselves conspired to huddle close and keep her out. Best to leave him to it. If he wanted lunch, well, he knew where the kitchen was.

She went into the long barn and took three slices of seeded bread out of the freezer – two of them to have with soup, the third with damson jam she'd made the previous September. As she was picking out a tin of leek and potato, her cold-numbed fingers knocked over a stack of cans, which toppled to the floor. 'Shit on it,' she said without much conviction. They were dented, but intact. One had rolled beneath the bottom shelf, and Rhian got down on her hands and knees to reach for it, stretching as far into the cobwebbed darkness as her ageing joints allowed.

It was unexpected, then, to feel a frayed leather band about the thickness of a watch-strap with some kind of metal tag attached that chimed against the stone floor as she grasped it. Her brow furrowed. Other objects down there, too – a bowl? A tennis ball; something soft and rubbery that squeaked; the same boot she had found a few weeks earlier, hidden much more carefully this time. When she had shoved these other things aside and dragged the strap out into view, it came gradually, almost grudgingly, as if caught on something, as if it had not wished to be revealed. 'Oh no, Carwyn,' she was whispering. 'Oh no.' The first words engraved on the round silver tag read, *Fferm*

Gwynnant. Then their own phone number, and finally, on the other side, *Eira*. The fastening was broken off. The strap itself was cut or torn. It was Eira's collar.

That afternoon was spent in nauseous pacing, turned like Branwen from a wife to prisoner in her husband's kingdom, banished within sight of her old home. A whole series of grim conjectures fell upon her all at once – things that had seemed vague and unconnected thudding into place with terrible, inexorable logic. Eira's collar, the missing man, the walking boot. And at the root of all of it was Carwyn's strange and frightening possessiveness about the mound, the stones. She caught herself biting her thumbnail – something she had not done since she was a girl – and felt the situation spiralling dangerously out of her control.

The phone book. There were few friends left in there, of course, and fewer still on whom she could rely in an emergency, but she remembered seeing one name while she had been looking up the number for the doctor. Geraint Jones from down the valley – he had always been dependable. They had not spoken since that awful day at the auction, but it would be good to talk to him. To talk to *anyone*. There was a doubting voice in her that still believed she was overreacting, and a second opinion might help silence it. And if her worst fears should be realized, at least someone outside this house would know something was wrong. She dialled, preparing in her mind the incongruously cheerful greeting she would open with: 'Helo Geraint, Rhian s'yma. Sut wyt ti?' But when she held the receiver to her ear, it was toneless and dead. The snow must have brought the line down. From the boot rack beside the front door, the carved stone head regarded her expressionlessly, and she felt sure that it had not been there when she had gone outside. She draped a raincoat over it with a convulsive shudder.

Out in the yard, the pickup stood with a six-inch covering of snow, buried nearly to its wheel arches. If she could ease it down the steep and treacherous track to the lane, she thought, it ought to make it to the village, even with the road uncleared. After all, they had bought it for just such a time as this. It was an old, expensive, inefficient beast that went through fuel the way her father used to go through pints of Double Dragon, and she could feel the polar ice caps melt a little more each time she went to do the shopping, but it was as sturdy as a tighthead prop and as sure-footed as a mountain goat, and stranded up here in the snow with no other way down, it was a godsend.

Carwyn normally left the keys in the sun visor (this was not a place for car thieves, nor was the truck worth more than its scrap value), but this afternoon she found it locked up tight. The pockets of their spare coats in the hall were empty, even the one she had used to cover the carved head. No keys on the kitchen table either. She searched the nest of musty-smelling sheets and blankets in the living room, where not so many Christmases before they had put up the tree together on a snowy day like this one. This was the spot where he had tried to lasso her with a rope of red tinsel. It had made a rather floppy, ineffective lariat, though, and they had fallen into each other's arms in fits of laughter. Over there, Eira had spent the best part of a month curled up beneath the tree, confused and delighted as she was every year by how this fragrant piece of outside was allowed to be indoors when all the sticks and branches she tried to bring in were quickly thrown back out again. There had been pine cones on the fire that made the cottage smell of pagan winter. No car keys there, though.

Upstairs, she rummaged through the wardrobe drawers, certain that there used to be a spare, but although there was a plentiful supply of sewing kits and screwdrivers and batteries and buttons, every key had disappeared. It began to dawn on her that he had taken steps to stop her leaving. A lost key here, perhaps, a disconnected phone line there. How many other small, unnoticed preparations had there been, and how long ago had they been set in motion? She sat down on the bed and tried to push the thought aside. On countless nights they'd lain here talking, propped on pillows in the warm light of the bedside lamp while rain drummed on the roof. Hard to accept the gentle, calm, devoted man who used to twine his fingers in her hair as she drifted to sleep was out there at this very moment grubbing furiously with those self-same hands in frozen, snowy earth. The room was grey and lifeless. Its familiar, homely scent had soured. She saw the house as it might be a hundred years from now – a ruined husk into whose crumbling walls a passer-by might peer through empty windows, where the rubble of the roof, long since fallen in, grew moss and mare's tail, and they would know but not truly believe that this had once been someone's home.

'Just ask him,' she said to herself. 'For God's sake, it's just Carwyn – *ask* him.' She would ask him where the keys were, and if he refused to give them to her, she would walk. Only five miles to the village. Even with the snow, it would take no more than a few hours. She threw a few essentials in a bag still half packed from her trip and judged that she could manage with only the barest minimum, but part of her wished she could take the sentimental trinkets too: a lifetime's worth of photographs, her humble jewellery, her favourite mug. The miniature love-spoon hanging from a picture nail above the bed (alongside the ornate but somewhat less traditional love-knife and -fork he'd made her as a joke). Neither time nor place for them, though. An abstract feeling of the utmost frantic urgency had overcome her, pins and needles prickling her skin as though her body could still sense the tiny atmospheric changes that her brain was too evolved to comprehend, the way the flock sometimes sought shelter from a coming downpour. It felt not unlike fleeing from a fire, where the sole permissible consideration was survival.

As she slung the bag onto her shoulders, she allowed herself a final lingering glance around the bedroom, knowing with a deep and unaccountable certainty that if she left the farm now, she would not return. Nonsense, she told herself – she would go down to get help and be back by tomorrow at the latest. Then she pulled the door to and it swung shut softly. Something in the attic groaned like black ice on a pond.

Downstairs again, she added to her pack a flask of whisky, several matches, and a box of firelighters which gave off a potent, greasy smell of kerosene that she found vaguely comforting. A moment later she was in the hallway putting on her coat and boots. The sun had already begun to set, so she also took a headtorch from its hook and hoped in any case that she could find her way downhill by simply following her feet. The torch was for what might be out there in the dark. She took a deep breath and grasped the handle of the front door, felt it sticking slightly where the frame had frozen tight around it, and stepped briskly out into the deepening snow.

What happened next might have been funny under almost any other circumstances. Had she been looking at the gate, hoping to see Carwyn returning with the car keys in his hand? Had she been looking at the sunset out beyond Moel Hebog and the ranks of snowy mountains stacked like stepping stones towards the golden sky? Had she looked briefly back over her shoulder, startled by a sudden noise behind her in the empty house? Wherever she'd been looking, it was not down at her feet. She had barely gone a step when she tripped and went sprawling in the snow, knowing before she even hit the ground that she had wrenched her ankle badly.

She lay dazed and disbelieving for what must have been a long time, waiting for her lungs to find their breath again and wondering, absurdly, if she'd reached that age when 'fall' becomes a noun. 'I've had a fall,' was all she could imagine saying, though to whom she did not know. The whisky in her bag had spilled. Her hands were scraped where they had found the gravel of the yard. Her right elbow had taken the brunt of the landing and now throbbed with numb insistence, soothed a little, at least, by the cold. She probed her hip and reckoned gratefully it was not broken. The worst of it by far was her ankle. Not broken either, she thought, wincing as she tried stiffly to flex it this way and the other, but severely sprained enough that she might need to keep her weight off it for weeks. She could have wept or laughed with equal likelihood.

There seemed a grim inevitability about it – a force of hostile destiny at work. From her feet back to the door, the snow lay rent and scattered in her wake. The object that had tripped her was half buried on the step, resting on its side so that only a part of it was visible, like the body of a prehistoric iceman thawing from a glacier. Snow clung in the contours of its carven features. One granite eye gazed to the distance with a look of empty satisfaction, and Rhian did not think to question how it came to be there. Instead, she thought about its long existence – ages beyond counting in a boulder somewhere on the mountainside until a craftsman chiselled free its present shape; then centuries spent buried in the thin earth of the bottom field while she and generations prior went about their lives unknowing; and latterly in Carwyn's workshop, where it waited patiently to play its part. All that time leading inexorably to this moment. Finally, its job was done.

She had made her way upstairs to bed when Carwyn came back from the mound. Her foot, by now, was swollen taut and livid bruises were beginning to appear around her ankle, stabbing out sick jolts of pain each time she tried to move it. He burst into the bedroom with a cry of wild-eyed triumph, this filthy, stinking scarecrow in her husband's clothes, her husband's face, and declared in a voice she barely recognized, 'I'm in! I was right. There's a passageway.' Rhian shrank away from him instinctively. His ragged hands dug in his pockets and a little hoard of objects spilled onto the bed, too many for her to catalogue even if she could understand what each one was. There were beads of quartz, a mussel shell, and sherds of pottery; a puck of rust and dirt that might have once been metal; a crescent-shaped bronze disc of crude yet striking beauty; a heavy length of iron chain; and many fragments, big and small, of burnt and butchered bones. He was grinning a mad and somehow loathsome grin, almost dancing with the joy of his discoveries, although to Rhian they did not look any different from the other little artefacts he had unearthed over the years.

THE HILL IN THE DARK GROVE

'I'm in,' he said again, 'I've broken through.' And as he uttered that pronouncement, she could see the part of him that had been Carwyn was completely gone.

At Llanystumdwy, Geraint Jones kept one eye on the weather and the other on the evening news. Nothing interesting in the latter, save for ever meaner, baser politics. He was waiting for the local bulletin that followed afterwards. Never had been one for keeping up to date, but lately he'd begun to watch it every night, out of a curious sense that something was about to happen. The horror at the auction mart back in October had unsettled him. It seemed only a token of some greater tragedy that had not yet begun in earnest.

Two years, now, he had been living in the newbuild house down by the Dwyfor Estuary. He missed the ancient cottage with its lumpy walls, and its rafters that left tiny piles of sawdust on the furniture where woodworms had been gnawing, and its nooks and crannies full to bursting with his memories. He missed the mountains, though he could still see them from his window. Still kept a small flock up there for the sake of auld lang syne. The air was different down here in the coastal flatlands. Not just saltier, but *poorer* somehow, as though turning stagnant – lacking some invigorating quality.

He went to the back door and looked across the dark swath of fields towards the silhouettes of Graig Goch and Moel Hebog and the great bulk of Yr Wyddfa just beyond them. Thin slush lay melting on the doorstep, but up there the snow would be at least a metre deep. Bass notes of electronic music carried from a neighbour's house. Car headlights passed along the street and for a moment their glare obscured his view of the mountains. He was struck by a cold premonition.

For reasons he did not completely understand, he thought of bumping into Rhian at the auction – how reduced and haggard she had seemed. How oddly cagey. In the shadow of the trauma that engulfed that day, he had not paid much mind to seeing her again, but now it came back to him with concerning clarity. She repeated herself constantly, despite saying little. Two or three times, she had paused mid-sentence as if time had stopped for her, then carried on where she left off. At one point, she seemed to forget the word for wristwatch, asking if he had a 'hand-clock' to give her the time. Something wrong up at the Gwynnant place, that was the impression he was given by her cheerful, pained insistence that things were all fine. Debt, divorce, disease? That day, there wasn't time to wonder any more than that.

They had been his friends once. A group of them inseparable despite all living miles apart and seeing one another only rarely. Reunited at the local village shows or at the auction or Young Farmers' Club. Brynmor Jenkins who had smoked a pipe since he was seventeen. Tom Roberts who had made a stir by growing vegetables instead of sheep. Dai Bad-English who could always be relied upon for mischief when he'd had a pint or ten. Glenys, his own dear late wife. And Carwyn, who had scored the winning try the day they'd beaten Rydal School, and Rhian, who had seemed the only one among them clever enough to get away, and the only one who truly wanted to stay put. A real community was what they'd been back then. They could go years without talking, then call one another up and carry on as though no time had passed. But one by one they died, or moved away, or simply lost the knack for it. You could live in the middle of the wilderness, alone, he thought, and not be isolated so long as you could depend on someone. Yet here he was down in this bustling little village, neighbours just the thickness of a wall away, and feeling utterly estranged.

Before he knew it, he was pulling on his boots. He dug the car keys from his winter jacket in the porch, and wondered if his ageing Land Rover would make it up the snow-bound mountain lanes. 'It's New Year,' he said aloud to justify this sudden madness to himself. 'A little visit – a surprise. They'll probably be glad to have a bit of company.' A hasty search among the tins and bottles in the kitchen cupboards for anything he could offer as a present came up empty, as did a dig through the deepest reaches of the wardrobe. By the time he came back downstairs, defeated, most of the enthusiasm at the thought had left him. The local weatherman was warning of another blizzard. It had been a stupid idea anyway, driving unannounced to drop in on his old friends at this hour. They had their own things going on – they didn't need him butting in. He might give them a ring tomorrow, he told himself as he dozed off in front of the television with his boots still on and his car keys still in his hand and the thumping rhythm of the neighbour's music still vibrating through the house. He felt suddenly very tired. Very tired indeed.

XI

Criafol

PURIFICATION

When the ice of ten millennia retreated, they arrived. A dozen intermingled families, clothed in furs and hides, their implements of flint and wood and bone. They came across the windblown tundra with their whole lives dragged behind them on travois and sleds, following a herd of horses up into the mountains, not yet knowing what awaited them. It had been patient in Its many centuries of solitude. When they arrived, It was already ancient.

They each perceived It differently when first they set foot in Its clearing. To some, It was a sudden radiance – a sense of joy and brightness that washed over them when they were near It. Others saw It as a colour they had never seen before. Some heard a distant music that moved them to tears, and some a perfect, blissful silence. Noses bled, fingers prickled, heads ached. None ever truly saw It, but in their campfire stories It might be glimpsed by the sick or dying – a colossal movement up among the crags, or a million tiny, winged shadows in the boughs of trees. They etched It on their precious objects, and no two depictions were alike.

They regarded It as any other aspect of the nature that surrounded them, which is to say, with frightened awe and unconditional respect. Loved It in the way their half-tame dogs loved those who fed them. Neither seeking understanding nor demanding explanation. It was to them a thing like fire or a river or the sky, and to attempt to comprehend It would be wasted effort. They recognized that there were some stones better left unturned.

In every generation there were those more heedful of Its will: the thinkers and the dreamers and the mad. It spoke to these sometimes in their own tongue, sometimes in signs, sometimes in images and urges, visions that could not be rendered into speech, and they would gather in their smoky lodges to impart Its wishes. The ones who came before the ice revered It too, in their way – festooning Its glade with the bones of bears and skins of bison and the scrimshawed antlers of great elk – but their constructions had been short-lived by a mountain's reckoning. What these newcomers offered was a chance of permanence.

For many lives they visited only infrequently, passing with the seasonal migrations of the herds. It was a place that they looked forward to, a place to meet and feast and celebrate and mourn, an anchor-point in their itinerant existence. But gradually they settled in Its shadow. They put down roots; they marked their territory and defended it with a newfound warlike ferocity; they quarried mighty stones to build for It a sacred circle. And over time, their superstitions grew to rituals, their rituals to ceremonies, and their ceremonies to traditions, until so much time passed that no one knew nor thought to question how they had begun. They wore masks hollowed from the bark of trees, the nests of wasps, the skulls of deer. They painted their skin with red ochre and bone black. They danced with wild abandon in the firelight under a waxing moon, and It watched them dance for It, and It was pleased.

It might have been February, but she was no longer sure. Things had deteriorated quickly. At first, she had tried to keep track of the date, marking off each day in her planner on the bedside table – to do so seemed a proof of sanity, evidence of progress towards some inevitable resolution. But time had ceased to obey any logic she could parse. Hours dragged on interminably, but when she looked at the clock only minutes had passed; then she would open her diary and find a week was missing from her recollection. Some mornings she could swear a second sunrise followed closely on the heels of the first, or that the sun had travelled backwards from where she had seen it last. Days passed in a fog. Nights in shallow sleep haunted by nightmares and delirium. Tiny voices like the wings of beetles chittered in the rafters. Shadows tall and gaunt as trees went striding past the window at the corner of her eye but left no tracks upon the snow-white fields. A god dwelt on the mountain, crowned with rings of jagged stone.

The snow still lay thick on the ground, as deep in places as the long barn's eaves, and every time the midday sun grew warmer and a thaw seemed imminent, a night of howling blizzards followed so that by the morning all was blanketed afresh. For all Rhian could tell, the greed and apathy of man had tipped the world into an age where spring would never come. The phone line was still down. The lane remained uncleared and trafficless. There were only Carwyn's daily footprints and the smoke of distant chimneys and the trails of passing aeroplanes to speak of anyone yet living in this frozen land but her.

Her ankle was a little better, though – still badly bruised and swollen and unable to bear weight, but steadily improving – a fact from which she drew some hope. Not just because it meant she could soon make good her escape, but also because it assured her that she had not slipped into an endlessly repeating purgatory. Contrary to all appearances, time was still passing. The healing of her ankle was a testament to that. For a walking stick, she used Carwyn's taid's crook, adorned with metal badges from the places he had travelled up and down the country, and this too served as a reminder of a Wales beyond these snow-drowned peaks and valleys.

In daylight hours, while Carwyn was off ferreting among the crumbled relics of the dead, Rhian had the house all to herself. She had become adept at getting up and down the stairs and hobbling to the barn for food, although she spent as little time out of bed as she could. The supplies in the winter pantry never seemed to diminish beyond what she took. She did not want to wonder what Carwyn was eating. The fire in the hearth was just enough to keep the little cottage liveable, especially with the insulating layer of snow on the roof, but it was not the cold she was afraid of. After dark, she locked the bedroom door and propped a chair under the handle, placing on the seat a tin can and a jar both filled with cutlery whose rattling would wake her if he tried to creep in while she slept. She kept a hammer underneath her pillow, with a loop strung from its handle she could slip around her wrist. That advice had been her father's. A knife could wound but might not quickly incapacitate and was as prone to cut its wielder as its target if it slipped. A hammer, on the other hand, could fell a charging bull. She tried hard not to picture the poor pulped man at the auction, nor how she might bring herself to cave in her lifelong companion's skull. He was different now.

It seemed that he, too, was awaiting something, though what it might be she could not guess nor dare conjecture. Perhaps he simply waited for the spring, the thaw, as she did. His digging ceased. Instead, he now embarked on some grand and unfathomable project of construction, departing every morning through the snow with tools, or bales of straw, or pots and cans of marking fluid and returning empty-handed as though he had squirrelled them away. He stood out in the yard each dawn to gauge with his thumb where the sun rose in the creases of the landscape. He was tireless. Or rather, he appeared to tire visibly, growing gaunter and more tattered, but he did not slow. All the previous day, Rhian had heard him sawing, punctuated by the crash of falling trees, and in the evening the grey sky was lit with an almighty pyre of branches where he had begun to clear a V-shaped opening into the circle's hollow. When he trudged into the yard again, his hands were stained with paint.

There was no use in asking what his purpose was, for in the rare few moments when their paths crossed, he had fallen largely mute. She worried constantly about the flock with nobody to tend them. But her questions were ignored or met with grunts or shrugs. Seldom did he even look at her directly, and when he did, she was left with the disquieting sense that he was gauging her the way he did the progress of the sun, weighing her as they had used to weigh the year-lambs to be sent for auction. Not hungrily – somehow that would have been less unpleasant. At least hunger would have been an understandable emotion. Instead, there was a calculating quality about his gaze that made her skin crawl. It was as if he was assessing when she would be ready, not for slaughter, but for market.

She woke at a bleak hour of moonless night, where perfect snowflakes drifted past the windowpanes like stars shaken loose from the firmament. The generator must have died, for the clock face was blank, and the bedside lamp she kept alight was dark, and the air beyond her blankets was so cold she could have cracked it with a spoon. The house lay under a vast and brittle silence. Her dreams had been of melting, and she was roused out of them by a desperate need to urinate – to brave the walk along the hallway to the bathroom. Quick and quiet, so as not to wake him. The first night barricaded in her room, she'd used a chamber pot, and when she got up in the morning it was frozen solid, so that idea was abandoned. She had never felt so elderly.

At the bedroom door, she stopped and listened, leaning on her crutch and waiting for her eyes to find the outlines of familiar shapes. Not a sound in the house, save her own nervous breathing. Carefully, she moved the chair from underneath the door-handle and waited, edged the door ajar, waited again, then stepped out onto the landing. The hallway tapered dimly to her left. Before she turned along it though, her gaze was drawn into the yawning shadows at the bottom of the stairs. There was the faintest exhalation of a draught. Carwyn was down there somewhere, and she was struck by the image of him saucer-eyed and owl-like in the darkness, lying wakeful as she listened for him, listening back. She hurried to the bathroom, wincing at how loud her limping steps were on the floorboards, leaving the door open to permit a vantage back along the hall. Then quickly back towards the bedroom.

She sensed him more than saw him. A fox-den scent of sweat and earth and carrion came faintly up out of the stairwell. It carried something of the grave about it, something old and dankly subterranean. He was standing just beyond the foot of the stairs, a shadow among other shadows, and had she been reliant on her eyes alone she might have been unable to discern him there. It was her instincts – primal ones recalling times not long enough ago when humans had been prey – that felt his presence. The fine hairs on her nape stood up. Her heart gave an ectopic flutter. When she held her breath, she fancied she could hear his steady exhalations like those of one still in deepest slumber.

'Carwyn?' she managed in a whisper. 'What's the matter?' No answer came, except the sighing of the wind under the eaves. The figure at the bottom of the stairs remained unmoving. 'Carwyn,' she hissed again, not daring to give voice to any louder utterance, but once again this garnered no response beyond, perhaps, the slightest shifting. His silhouette gave the impression of a withered nakedness. They stood thus for a span of minutes, until finally Rhian eased open the bedroom door and, without turning, slipped inside.

She told herself he must have been sleepwalking. That was why he had not heard her. But she knew, somehow, that this was not the case, for she had felt again his cunning stranger's gaze upon her all the while, and sensed his coiled-spring readiness, and she was sure the only thing that held him back was that he judged the time was not yet right. She propped the chair back firmly underneath the handle. Placed the jars and cans of cutlery back on the seat. For the interminable hours from then until she heard him crunch out through the snow at dawn, she sat upright in bed clutching the hammer. When daylight came, she dozed in thin and haunted sleep.

It was gone midday when she was finally able to force herself out of bed. She felt exhausted and ill, beset by the beginnings of some trembling sickness that made her heart race and her hands unsteady, her body insubstantial as though a stiff breeze might scatter her like chaff. The snow-reflected sun glared through the window to assail her eyes. In the mirror, she found an old woman, older even than she felt – grey of hair and hollow of eye and papery of skin. A fairy-tale gwrach embittered that her ripe age had not brought the promised compensation of great wisdom.

But she was not yet beaten. On the contrary, she found this loss of hope emboldening. There was to be no easy resolution: the snow had not melted, and the phone lines had not been repaired, and Carwyn had not snapped out of his strange bewitchment. No help had come, nor would it. The way out would have to be charted by herself alone, and she was ready now to grasp at any chance with all her failing strength. To die in the attempt no longer seemed the greater risk.

She was reminded of grim headlines about lonely, unloved people chanced upon by passers-by – their gardens overgrown, their letterboxes stuffed with post, and milk turned sour and lumpy on their doorstep – dead for months or years. A mummified husk sitting in an armchair like a pharaoh in the age of television, attended by the relics of their sad existence while the world outside, in easy reach, went on indifferent to their passing as it had been to their solitude. That, she decided, would be the worst of fates. To waste away awaiting rescue that would come too late, if it came at all.

No, she would fight. The coda of her tale would be that she had battled tooth and claw and kept on going to the bitterest end. A sad ending to what had, on reflection, been a mostly happy time on earth, though every story, she decided, ended sadly if you followed it right to the finish. Bold Pryderi was slain in a squabble over stolen pigs. Culhwch and Olwen's fabled love grew stale once there were no more giants to forbid it. Owain Glyndŵr fled, defeated. What a poor successor she made to those legendary forebears. She thought of all the times she'd fretted over things that were inconsequential: her eleven-plus exam results and whether she would miss her train and how much weight she put on that one Christmas. But after all, was that not what life was about – the small things every bit as much as the big ones? What did it matter if she died today and left no grand and glorious legacy when she was gone? Her life had mattered to her, and it mattered to the people to whom she mattered in turn. That was her monument. She did not need it told in myth or built in stone.

Her ankle had again improved. She tested her weight on it cautiously, grimaced slightly but bore it, then went back and forth the length of the landing without the aid of the walking stick. Not yet, she thought, but in another couple of days it should be strong enough to make the gruelling hike down to the village. All she needed was to hang on until then. That seemed an eminently reasonable goal.

* * *

That evening, though, no sooner than the sun began to set, he came for her. A fearsome gale roared down from high atop Yr Wyddfa, making the cottage groan and shudder, rattling the doors and windows in their frames as though a thousand unseen hands were clamouring to get inside. Somewhere far across the mountain, the Gwynnants' sheep were bellowing. Rhian had already been in bed, reading the story of Lleu by the light of several candles and a battery lamp while snow in an unending flurry swirled out in the tempest, when she heard a gentle tapping at the door. It might have only been the wind. She glanced up briefly to check that her barricade was still secure before returning to her book, but when hardly a second had gone by it came again. Tap, tap, tap. Another gust struck the house, and she heard something outside give way with a rotten, splintered rending and fly off into the night.

'Carwyn?'

The soft reply came in a voice that could have almost been his own. 'It's me, my cariad.'

She felt a sudden surge of hope that made her sit up and throw back the covers. Her heart was pounding so hard she could hear its thudding in the bedsprings. 'What's wrong?' she called.

There was a long, uncertain pause. The door-handle turned slightly this way and that and then fell still. Falteringly, he said, 'My hands. I need you to look at my hands. I think—' His words trailed off or were lost in the thunderous noise.

Rhian got out of bed and pulled her coat on over all the layers she was already wearing. She slipped the hammer up her sleeve, head downwards, then limped over to the door. Was this a trick? If so, she would be ready. She eased the chair aside and edged open the door, keeping her weight behind it on her good leg lest he try to barge his way into the room, but he did not. A narrow slit of candlelight fell on him where he stood in darkness on the landing. He was attired in the tatters of the clothes he'd worn for weeks, at some midpoint between naked and dressed, and to these he had newly added brightly coloured ribbons from her sewing tin so that he now resembled a bedraggled Mari Lwyd come knocking. There was time to wonder how he managed to survive so lightly garbed out in the cold, and then she saw his hands.

His fingers were badly frostbitten, in places blistered and in others withered black from nail to knuckle where he held them up before his chest. The tip of his nose, too, was scabbed and reddening, and his lips were one great mass of cold sores. There was ice in his hair, his eyelashes, his beard. She gasped and reached to take his hands reflexively, but he drew them away. He said, 'We need to go, Rhian. It's time.'

'Go now?' she asked. 'In this?' The gale still howled outside, and it felt as if the house might be shaken apart. He nodded gravely. Finally, he had seen sense. Her reservations lingered, but her mind raced to devise a plan for them – the lane down to the village would be treacherous, of course. They'd have to take it at a crawl, both injured as they were. From there, it was all reasonable roads as far as the emergency department at Ysbyty Gwynedd. She made a mental note to pack an extra jerrycan of fuel, and blankets, and a shovel just in case. Doable, she told herself, it's doable. She followed him downstairs in darkness, leaning on the banister and pausing on each step until they reached the bottom, where she sat to lace her boots. 'Have you got the car keys? I hope it'll start. We'll need to dig it out.'

Carwyn towered over her. 'Not the car,' he said. 'We're going to the circle first. I need to show you something there before we go.' There was a slyness in his voice that made her look up at him, and then a sickening and sudden clarity – all of this, right down to his frostbitten fingers, was an act.

She stood and took a step or two back up the stairs and knew she would never outrun him. Nor did she think that she could best him in a fight, for despite his emaciation he looked fearfully lithe and quick. To buy a moment more to think, she took a deep, deliberate breath and said, 'You're not my Carwyn.' This was met with a quizzical expression. A bemused but indulgent rictus grin of rotten teeth. 'If you're Carwyn, prove it. What were your mam and dad's names?' He scoffed and then held out a blackened hand to her. 'Just humour me,' she said carefully. 'You know how I love stories.' She climbed another step away. He matched the move without a pause.

'Mam was Nerys. Dad was Huw. What are you on about? We need to go.'

But she persisted. That had been too easy. The thing under the mound would surely know about the farm and all those who had ever lived there. 'All right then. Where did we first meet?'

'At Gelert's grave,' he answered without hesitation, an edge of impatience creeping into his voice. 'You were in the tree. You told me the story of the prince and the dog and how it was a load of made-up nonsense.' Again, he held out a hand, and again it went untaken. 'Come on, now, we'll reminisce about old times when we get down there.'

That was better, but she still was not convinced. She was suddenly aware that this impostor might have watched them all their lives and seen their every move. There was no question she could think of asking that would prove beyond doubt this was Carwyn. What if it knew everything about him? How could a farmer's wife outsmart a god?

And with that, at once, she had it. 'What about our first kiss, where was that?'

The thing in Carwyn's skin gave her a look of dumb incomprehension, as though she was asking the rams to calculate the root of pi. 'Here,' he offered, 'in the barn.' His voice was cracking slightly.

'Try again,' she said. She came down a step so she could look him in the eye and see if she discerned there any vestige of the man she loved. He seemed to radiate a feverish heat. 'Come on. If you were Carwyn, you would know.' The memory came back fiercely to her of that night in the church, another place of sacred stones built for another deity in man's futile attempts to bargain for eternal life. She was no Christian, but she now believed those stones and the intent behind them had a curious power. 'You couldn't watch us in there, could you?'

His mask of husbandly indulgence peeled away then, one side of its haggard face falling, one eyelid drooping, leaving in its place a look of cold, inhuman cruelty. 'You've gone mad, woman! You've lost your bloody marbles!' He lunged for her with Carwyn's ruined hands, catching her around the neck and by the wrist with startling strength.

They struggled for what must have only been a moment, lengthened by its awfulness. His full uncanny weight bore down upon her, dragging her down from the stair, and she gave ground so as not to lose her footing until soon they fought amongst the scattered coats and wellies in the hallway. Up close, his breath was like an abattoir, a knacker's yard. It stank of bile and carcasses and sundry rot that could not be digested, save, perhaps, by flies or buzzards. She kicked at his shins. Her free hand clawed uselessly at his face. Distantly, she heard her own choked pleas, but he only gripped her tighter still and dashed her head against the wall, and her skull rang like the inside of a bell, and she saw a flaring galaxy of stars behind her eyes and thought her knees would buckle.

In unthinking desperation, she let slip the hammer from her sleeve and swung it blindly down upon him. It connected only glancingly in the tight space, striking somewhere near his temple and gouging a strip of skin and hair from one side of his scalp. The rubber-coated handle jarred out of her fingers. Defenceless now, she braced herself against his answering blows.

None came, though. The hammer had apparently caught him off guard, and as it bounced from Rhian's hand he lunged for it reflexively, loosening his grip. It was enough, but barely. She shoved him as hard as she could, and he reeled, staggered back, and overbalanced. Nearly falling with him, she tore herself free and stumbled for the door, where his furious bellowing pursued her out into the snow.

Nothing in her long decades of mountain life could have prepared her for the storm into which she emerged. A brutal wind threw wide the door and buffeted her as she crossed the yard. It had been loud inside the house, but out here it was deafening. The cold was sudden and vicious. Gusts struck her from everywhere with an untrammelled fury that made even breathing difficult. It might have been dusk, though there was no way of telling for sure, for the snow flew in such merciless intensity that she could see no further than her outstretched fingertips and it could have been noon or night with equal likelihood. Not delicate and dainty flakes but scouring shards of ice that pelted her like birdshot. The world was grey and indistinct. Ahead, the buried shape of the pickup loomed suddenly out of the squall, and she paused briefly in its meagre shelter before pressing on, knowing he could not be far behind her.

She followed the rough stone wall of the long barn until she came to Carwyn's workshop, where her blunt hands fumbled with the loop of baling twine that held the door, and slipped in, shivering. The tin roof sang a dire, unearthly music in the gale. Hurriedly, she cast about for anything she might use as a weapon should he find her here: the shelves laden with dusty biscuit tins of artefacts fished from the stream since Carwyn's childhood; spanners and wrenches and pliers, all too small to do much harm; coils of extension cable, fishing rods, and a great variety of partial things forgotten mid repair. Her vision blurred momentarily and then swam back into focus. Above the roaring of the wind, with a voice like slate and scree, a voice that seemed to echo from some crevice in the very rocks, she heard him calling for her.

The gas wand stood propped in a corner behind the armchair, its stubby bottle of propane sitting potent at the hose's end. There was just long enough for her to turn the valve and hear the hiss of gas, to aim the barrel vaguely at the door, to click and click again the stiff ignition switch. A frantic pause where nothing happened. Then many things at once with unanticipated suddenness.

He was halfway across the threshold when the propane

wand ignited. A flurry of snow burst in with him as though he and the storm were inseparable. He held the hammer in his upraised hand, and blood from the wound in his scalp had sheeted one side of his face. In an instant, his expression changed. There was a whoosh of gas and then a jet of clear blue flame that hit him at about chest height and flared outwards in a spreading ring of incandescent orange, lighting tiny fires at the tips of his ribbons and the tatters of his clothes, but it did not, as she'd imagined, set him full ablaze. The snow on him evaporated into steam. A nauseating reek of burning hair struck her, and he let out an agonized, unearthly yowl that made her let go of the trigger. Then he retreated into the blizzard, leaving the door flapping open where he'd stood.

Rhian fell into the armchair, breathing hard. The shock had numbed her, left her feeling sluggish and exhausted. For a long time, it seemed as if it would be the easiest thing in the world to sit there and wait to die in the cold – perhaps even to wake and find that all of this had been a cruel nightmare. The back of her head throbbed. Her ankle, too.

For what might have been a moment or an hour she drifted in and out of shivering delirium. Beyond the wall, the few remaining chickens fluttered in their roost, and she imagined they were not quite chickens any more – their feathers iridescent as a hummingbird's, their combs and wattles grown to intricate, repugnant shapes. The eggs they laid might swim with writhing shadows if she held them to the light. The sheep out on the mountainside were bleating dire songs in otherworldly cadences. They felt disturbingly like an attempt at speech. From out of the howling dark, there came the jingling of bells, the chattering of teeth, and when she woke she was confronted by the gaily ribboned horse skull of a Mari Lwyd regarding her with alabaster eyes, whose white shroud did not conceal a man but a meandering neck of bones that stretched away impossibly into the night. She heard the groaning of the corrugated roof. She felt the paralysing cold. How curious it was, she thought, to die in this chair she had owned near all her life without ever suspecting it would be the last she'd ever sit in. She wondered if she would have looked at it differently for all those years if she had known.

But by and by, the instinct to survive returned, and with a conscious effort she was able to get stiffly to her feet and brave again the merciless snow. She was, she reasoned dimly, shaped by her cynefin – by her homeland, her environment, her past – for this specific purpose. She and Carwyn and the generations that preceded them had carved their lives here in this place of hostile beauty by their sheer tenacity. To go on was the only thing she knew. Back to the house was not an option – even in her incoherent state, that much was obvious. The thing that was not Carwyn, or perhaps worse things than that, would find her there eventually. She did not have the faintest clue where she would go, but in that moment destination seemed irrelevant. 'Where are we running to?' Carwyn had asked her once, and she had answered, 'Just away.'

Downhill she went, in meagre moonlight through the blizzard, a dark speck dwarfed against the monumental land. She had stopped to retrieve Carwyn's shotgun from the tool-shed, and for a time his tracks ran parallel to hers, first walking and then crawling, and finally slithering along the ground until their paths diverged and they were lost in the whiteout. He had headed for the circle, she assumed. The snow was knee-deep and the going slow and difficult. Bereft of landmarks, she could only feel her way, letting the slope of the land guide her and hoping that at some point she would strike the lane. Occasionally, she would come to a drift that marked the course of a stone wall. She crossed mysterious expanses of hardpack and tussocks broader than the cottage and the yard combined, and had to quash the thought that these were footprints. There seemed too many fields. Once, a narrow cleft swept bare by the wind where the gale rushed down across a stile, and she could find no reference in her mind to any place she could recall.

Above the roaring of the storm, it seemed the mountain was alive with other sounds. Somewhere a ewe was calling for its lamb. Then distant drumbeats, gone no sooner than she paused to listen. She trudged across a blind expanse of open field, putting up her hood and gathering her coat more tightly at the collar to keep out the driving snow, and through this muffling she thought she heard the crying of a baby in the lulls between the fiercest gusts. The ground beneath her shook and stilled – a sound of such dreadful immensity that it was felt as much as heard. Not far ahead a gatepost loomed out of the stinging flurries, and here again she stopped to catch her breath and rub the snowflakes from her eyes, and the air tasted sweetly of caramel and nitroglycerine, underlaid with something decaying and foul. Then, when the wind changed, ashes. A friendly voice shouted her name. No time to ponder on these faint hallucinations that she told herself were just the last-ditch firings of her failing brain, distractions from her stubborn course. Downhill, downhill. The lane was close. She knew it in her bones.

Another field bereft of landmarks, following a brand-new

fence line where a latticework of rime ice formed a ghostly echo of the wire squares. There were no fences like this on their land – just drystone walls – and so she took its presence as a sign that she was going in the right direction, whichever that might be. She could have sworn, out in the dark, a tacked horse went by at full gallop. There came again a deep, resounding rumble like a roll of thunder, but from underneath the earth and not the sky. The howling of the wind sounded briefly like a choir of ululating voices raised in savage triumph. She limped on, ignoring them. It seemed the empty mountainside was teeming with wanderers lost as she was, as though a great river of time was passing through a narrow gorge, but though she felt them dimly all around her, she saw not another soul.

If her sense of direction held, she gauged the circle to be uphill now, far to her right, the house perhaps a quarter of a mile behind her, and the lane ahead. The cold was slowing her. Not just her pace but every process of her body, right down to her thoughts. The urge to simply curl up where she was grew more insistent, but out here it was just one of a great multitude of voices speaking over one another in a gabbling cacophony. Or just the wind. It took some effort, too, to keep her gaze averted from a gargantuan silhouette that seemed to shadow her descent, shapeless and incalculably vast and looming always at the very corner of her eye.

A half-remembered fragment of the *Llyfr Taliesin* came to her, and she spoke it aloud in place of rosary or incantation. 'I have been in a multitude of shapes,' she began with some uncertainty, the exact words and order of the ancient poem not quite solid in her mind, 'before I took this form.' The shrieking of the gale intensified as if to drown out her small voice, but she continued

THE HILL IN THE DARK GROVE

undeterred. 'I have been a narrow, gleaming sword. I have been a teardrop in the air.' A flurry of snow pelted her. She wiped it from her eyes. 'I have been the light of a lantern. I have been the radiance of stars. I have been a bridge across the mouths of threescore rivers.' Louder now, more confident that even if the words were not correct, they were the ones she meant. 'I have been a path, an eagle, a coracle on the sea. I have been a droplet in a downpour. I have been a string in a harp and spray in water.' There it was again – a momentary glimpse of something nauseatingly colossal, outlined briefly where the snowflakes fell on it, then gone as if it had been no more than a distant mountain. 'I was a spark in a fire. I was a post in a palisade.' These last words she belted out at the top of her lungs, defying anyone or anything to silence her. 'I am not one who does not sing,' she shouted at the falling sky. 'I have sung since I was small!'

And with each word, and with each hard-won downward step, she grew more confident. She was not only the Rhian she was now, but all the Rhians she had ever been at every moment of her story. She was eighteen, spending her first winter up here at the farm, enveloped by the warmth of a new family who welcomed her as if she was their own. She was thirty-six, venturing out to break the ice on all the troughs, and when she got back to the house it would be bright with Christmas decorations and the smell of mulled wine and the company of the man she loved, who loved her back with boyish wonder and unshakeable fidelity. Fifty, celebrating New Year's Eve surrounded by her friends. Sixty-two and driving up the snowy lane after a long weekend at Aberystwyth, with Eira's tail thumping the back seat, glad to be home again.

And she was Carwyn – her Carwyn, the *real* Carwyn – with

her all those times and all the times between, unshakeably and inextricably. So much a part of her that even now, in spite of everything, she found herself unable to conceive of any life she might have lived without him. She was Carwyn now for both of them.

And she was all the atoms of the universe before they coalesced into this current shape, and everything they would be after she was gone. This latest iteration, elderly and dying, was just one of countless others that were every bit as real. She understood, now, that there was no reason to allow the present more significance than it deserved. Time was laid bare for the illusion that it was. An awful year, even if it was the last one, did not overrule the rest. Whatever happened next, there was no need to be afraid, no need to leave a mark when she was gone. She had lived. Not always perfectly, but well enough.

When finally the blizzard started to subside, she found herself at an old iron gate that led into a copse of trees. It was full and starless dark, the moon a pale luminescence in a bank of clouds, and the snow-capped peaks a ragged and unbroken silhouette that towered all around her. A part of her had known, somehow, that she would fetch up here. Beyond the woods, it waited, as it always had. The snow had tried to bury it the way the earth had done, so that the dark and leaning stones stood clothed in white, their sharpness blunted, and the mound in its grove lay blanketed between them. There was a passageway cut in its face, tall as a man but slender such that one would have to enter sideways. Nearer, she went, and nearer. She let the shotgun fall into the snow and grasped instead the tiny love-spoon in the pocket of her coat. From somewhere deep within the chamber, she could see the flickering glow of firelight.

XII

Gwern

THE LAMBS IN THE SNOWDRIFT

The hall of Cynddylan is dark tonight, as the poem goes. It was the bailiffs who first noticed they were gone. They drove up when the roads were clear again and found the place deserted but oddly intact, as though abandoned in great haste: the front door ajar, boots in the porch, a pile of dishes in the frozen sink. The bed upstairs unmade, and downstairs a nest of sheets and pillows. The clocks all stopped at different times and gathering dust. The pickup truck out in the yard with three flat tyres. For an hour, they waited in their van, not wishing to spend longer than they needed to inside the house and hoping that the occupants would soon return. There was an eeriness about the place, reminding Ritchie of the story of a lighthouse in the Flannan Isles where all three keepers seemed to vanish overnight, and for some reason a strange image came to him of the old couple roosting in the hayloft or the chimney or beneath the floorboards. Hibernating like a pair of snakes. Ridiculous as the thought was, it made him shudder. They left the necessary papers with the pile of others on the kitchen table and were glad to be away from there in daylight.

A few days later, the police stopped by. They, too, found nothing untoward besides the obvious abandonment. A thorough search revealed no signs of foul play, nor a trace of where the couple might have gone (although the scorch marks on the door of the outbuilding were a puzzler, and bloody hell, that stone head gave them both the creeps). The stacks of bills and letters were their biggest clue. Of course, they went through all the usual missing persons motions, but deep down they hoped the poor old dears had made good their escape.

Next came a team of representatives sent by the bank – a young solicitor and a surveyor, someone from the council with a van to cart away the first few bits of furniture. Then a sharp-suited estate agent with a set of brilliant-white teeth and a spray-on tan in a shade of orange that nobody in north Wales ought to be at this time of year. They took measurements. They prodded and tutted and noted things on phones and tablets. An awful smell of something nesting in the attic – they would need to get the fumigators in – but structurally it all seemed sound. Period properties like this were built to last.

The Gwynnant farm's been standing empty for a few years now (some might reasonably call it derelict), with a forlorn *For Sale* sign down beside the lane. Eventually, there will be buyers. Not locals, mind – few of the young round here could ever dream of such a house. No, someone from the city with enough spare cash to sink into the lengthy renovation that it sorely needs. It'll make a lovely second home, the estate agent says. Period features, stunning views, fantastic outdoor space. A wealth of history right on the doorstep. The listing makes no mention of what's in the bottom field, past the old, rusted iron gate and through the woods. Landslips have likely buried it again by now. The ferns will have grown back, and anything still standing above ground would look completely unremarkable to all but the most imaginative of eyes. An overgrown stone circle – one of hundreds in this ancient country.

Nobody knows exactly what became of the old couple to whom it had once belonged. Run off to escape their debts, is the consensus locally. There's no one left to miss them much, for they were self-reliant sorts, paranoid and insular and protective of their privacy (the weathered signs with their grim warnings are a testament to that). Occasionally, you might hear wilder rumours of dark goings-on up there, and some claim to have seen lights moving across the mountainside in howling storms, but in this age of rationality they're given short shrift. Mostly it's not spoken of at all.

In their absence, little else has changed. The old ladies of Llandudno take their tea at Tiffany's Café while gulls wheel high above the restless sea. Perhaps one more among the former, but they're used to strangers in this town. In Bangor, students hurry to their lectures after one too many drinks the night before. Office workers with umbrellas squeeze aboard the train. Crows perch in the ruined keep of Dolwyddelan Castle, croaking indignation at the motorbikes that roar along the icy road below, and coaches pull up at the Penderyn Distillery where their passengers can smell the rich and heady mash before they even leave their seats. Downriver from the dam that drowned the valley of Tryweryn, boatloads of white-water rafters brave the swollen rapids, unaware, perhaps, what lies beneath the artificial lake. 'Cofiwch', people say – remember – but remembering is a forgotten art. Life, in short, goes on with scant regard for two more farmers lost.

The Gwynnants' flock is doing well, I'm pleased to say. A little scrawnier, perhaps, and dirtier; a little wilder and more wiry of wool, but still surviving. This year they lost a few more lambs when the late snow came, but there are enough to see them through. They are a stubborn, hardy breed, hefted to those high pastures for a thousand years. They know their way instinctively, by sight, by sound, by scent. And I believe the Something underneath the mountain has been watching over them in Its peculiar way. Perhaps when someone buys that tumbledown old house, they'll start to feel It watching them as well.

Diolchiadau

Sincere thanks to my brilliant editor, Sophie Jonathan, and to her lovely colleagues at Picador, whose insight and kindness elevated the book to something better than I thought it could be. Thanks also to my wonderful agent, Louise Buckley at HSLA, who saw the potential in Rhian and Carwyn's story and who continues to help me navigate the scary world of being an author. To everyone else involved in the publishing process, too – I really appreciate all your hard work and enthusiasm.

Thanks, of course, to my amazing wife Leonie, who was my editor before I ever thought I'd have a real one, and without whose constant love and support and wisdom this book (like so many other things in my life) would never have happened. Although the writing was done by me, she has laboured with me over every scene and paragraph to get it right. The book is hers as much as it's mine.

To my mam, for reading me books that I was too young for until I was too old to be read to, and who has probably read this book more times than everyone else combined (including me). To my dad, who used to tell me and my sister stories to make us laugh, but always takes my writing seriously. To my stepdad, Ade, who loves the mountains, and who told me I would never get a girlfriend because I liked to sit on the floor. Thanks to my sister, Rachel, who has always been there for me, and to my nieces Amelie, who listens to all my stories, even the boring ones, and Willow, for being a great baby. Thanks to Nanna Jean and Granda John and Bampa Ray and Granny Betty. All these people are in this book in one way or another.

Many thanks as well to all my friends – here in the UK and across the Channel and across the Pond. Particularly Daff, who helped correct my rusty Welsh. Also to Dave and the rest of my colleagues at Llandudno Pier (except Barry) for helping me stay relatively sane throughout this process.

For Rhian's paraphrasing of Taliesin's 'Cad Goddeu', I'm very grateful for the excellent translations by W. F. Skene, J. Gwenogvryn Evans, Patrick K. Ford and Marged Haycock. During the research stage, I watched many of Dr Gwilym Morus-Baird's fascinating videos and strongly recommend his Celtic Source YouTube channel to all who are interested in Welsh mythology. Thanks too to Jimmy 'The Welsh Viking' Johnson, who also has a brilliant YouTube channel and who helped proofread the Welsh parts. Any factual or linguistic errors that remain are my own.

Lastly, my deepest gratitude to anyone who picked up the book and read this far. Diolch yn fawr iawn. I hope you liked it.

About the Author

Liam Higginson was born and raised in rural north Wales and lives in Llandudno with his wife. *The Hill in the Dark Grove* is his debut novel.